The Burning Sun

William J. Benning

BENNING

THE BURNING SUN

THE BURNING SUN
Book II of the First Admiral Series

Copyright © 2012 by William J. Benning
Edited by Tara Williamson
Cover Copyright © 2012 by Andrae Harrison
ISBN-13: 978-1623750244

First Edition

Visit our website: www.mquills.com

BENNING

THE BURNING SUN

Prologue

<u>Planet Earth - 3.5 Billion Earth Years Ago</u>

Slowly, Inguz the Lame raised his head from the cool liquid of the stream. His instincts tingling, he sensed that something was wrong. What he had to do now was work out if it was some kind of threat to him. His three eyes darting anxiously, he scrutinised the yellow and pale green landscape for any sign of possible danger. Slowly, he scanned the bank opposite taking note of the patches of pale brown scrub in the dry, yellow dusty soil against the light green sky.

Rising to his full height, Inguz opened the four-leaved fleshy covering that hid his all-in-one nose and mouth orifice to sniff the air for any clues as to what was troubling him. Scanning the terrain behind him, Inguz could see or smell nothing out of the ordinary. Yet, the feeling of unease could not be shaken from the back of his mind. There was something wrong; he just could not pinpoint it. Grasping the stone-headed club that he had fashioned with animal sinew from a fallen branch and a heavy rock, he switched his gaze to the shimmering horizon and still found nothing out of the ordinary.

Nervously, he squatted back down to the stream and scooped some of the clear liquid into the cup of the four-fingered hand of his wasted left arm. Still alert, Inguz opened his facial orifice and allowed the refreshing liquid to run over his split tongue and down his parched throat. When he had been little more than an infant, his mother had rolled onto her baby son as she had slept. It was the accidental damage that she had caused that night that had condemned her son to a life of exile from the tribe. Despite having been driven from the tribe, for fifteen summers Inguz the Lame had survived all of the dangers that his world had thrown at him; but he would not survive this one.

Out in the depths of space, the great Burning Circle, the Sun, had produced a massive solar flare. The super-heated plasma had seared across the emptiness of space devouring the second planet in the solar system before approaching the yellow and green marble of the young Earth. It was the massive disruption to the magnetic field that Inguz had sensed, but had been unable to comprehend. The other animals in the scrub-land, however, far more attuned to magnetic fluctuations, instinctively realised the danger and began to stampede.

Having let the cool liquid quench the back of his throat and run down into his stomach, Inguz heard the first stirrings of the great flight. The faint rumble of the ground was confirmed by the growing cloud of pale yellow dust that slowly blossomed on the horizon. Inguz knew the signs and started to run towards his shelter; a cleft in the rocks close to the stream. But, Inguz was not destined to reach that sanctuary. As he ran, Inguz felt panic well up in his chest as the horizon changed from its normal pale green to the harsh vivid yellow of fire that dashed inexorably towards him. The distant crash of charging animals was replaced by the shrill howling shriek of something far more deadly. A great wall of flame moved with amazing speed consuming everything in its path. As the panicking Inguz ran as fast as he could for his shelter, he became aware of other beings around him.

Predators and Jumping Creatures ran side-by-side, away from the screaming barrier of fire. Species mingled in their blind panic to escape the approaching cataclysm.

Running for his life, Inguz, in sheer terror, ignored the sharp-toothed predator that sped past him; seeking the hoped-for sanctuary of the rocks. As the noise grew louder and louder, all Inguz could do was scream to relieve the pressure on his bleeding eardrums. Looking over his shoulder as he ran, Inguz saw the wall of flame was catching up with him far quicker than he could run for shelter. As he stared at it, filling the entire horizon, Inguz knew in his heart that he would not survive. However, the instinct for life, and animal fear, drove Inguz and all the other fleeing animals onwards. Behind him, the mass of fire consumed the surface of the planet like a great rolling curtain, vaporising all living creatures and surface material.

With the last of his strength, Inguz drove himself onwards, discarding the stone-headed club to lighten his burden. But, it was all to no avail. With the heat from the great fire searing his flesh, Inguz stumbled. He landed on his back and began to dodge the panicked animals that trampled blindly past him. Trying to rise to his feet, Inguz saw the wall of flame bearing down upon him. The heat was intense, and Inguz had no time to feel the flesh being burned away from his bones before they too were vaporised.

Two minutes later, the super-heated plasma had devoured the entire planet surface and was still consuming the atmosphere. When everything had been destroyed the great fire was extinguished, leaving the young planet Earth as nothing more than a charred cinder floating in space. All life on the planet had been snuffed out except for a few handfuls of microscopic bacteria buried deep in the charred and molten ground.

Life on Earth would have to start all over again.

THE BURNING SUN

Chapter 1

The Terran System – Earth Year 1986

In a blinding flash of brilliant, white light, the Black Rose slipped smoothly out of the Thionic Web from behind the red planet called Mars. Having emerged from the Web, well clear of the gravitational pull of the planet, Billy Caudwell initiated the stealth mode on his personal shuttle in case of a freakishly accidental discovery by the tracking and monitoring equipment that scrutinised Planet Earth's nearest neighbour in space. There were still those on Earth who waited and hoped for the appearance of 'little green men' and Billy Caudwell was in no hurry to fulfil their wishes.

Convinced that the Black Rose was invisible to all forms of terrestrial detection equipment, Billy set course for Planet Earth, the northwestern quadrant of the continent of Europe and a rendezvous with another stealthed spacecraft. With coordinates set, he let out a long sigh of relief and sat back on the solitary chair behind the central Control Pillar in an otherwise empty cabin and savoured the peace, quiet and solitude of the journey. It would take the two massive Thrust Engines of the Black Rose only two and a half minutes, at half-power, to drive the shuttle to Earth; but, it was still two and a half precious minutes of paradise for the pilot.

After a long duty shift of almost twelve hours as Supreme Military Commander of the Universal Alliance Fleet aboard the flagship, the Star-Cruiser Aquarius, Billy was exhausted. He was starting to feel the pressure of the responsibilities that the burgeoning Alliance, he had formed less than a year before, placed upon him with a constant clamour for his time and attention. At the start, the fourteen-year-old schoolboy had thought that it would be a marvellous adventure with space travel, fighting aliens and commanding battle fleets. A year later, the fifteen-year-old Billy had discovered a very different reality; the biggest headache and drain on his time was the tedium of day-to-day administration.

The myriad files, reports, budgetary constraints and projections weighed heavily on the teenage First Admiral. They were, however, a necessary evil with which Billy Caudwell knew he had to wrestle until the politicians got their act together and started to make the civil administrative functions of the Alliance work effectively. Until an Assembly of civilian representatives had been convened, there could be no legislature, no executive arm, no Supreme Council; and no President of the Alliance could be elected to carry the burden of civil governance. Until that day dawned, Billy Caudwell would have to operate as the *de facto* Head of

State, working in cooperation with the dozens of planetary and system governments that made up the fast-growing but still fledgling Alliance.

The blueprint for civilian government already existed. The last leader of the Garmaurians, Teg Maggor, had laid down the structure of the Alliance before his death from the virus that had wiped out the whole Garmaurian species. There was even a draft Constitution that almost fifty intelligent species had signed up to on their admission to the Alliance. But, it still required an Assembly of representatives to ratify this document. Officially and legally the Universal Alliance did not exist as a civilian body. It was purely a military institution at this point in time. That, however, did not stop governments and systems from seeking admission to this very powerful military club.

From the former Garmaurian city on the planet Gardarus, now being called New Thexxia, the fledgling Alliance sprang outwards in all directions requiring greater and greater military resources to defend and police the rapidly expanding frontiers. To date, the Universal Alliance military consisted of only three fully-constituted Fleets plus a further two Fleets that were still works-in-progress. The warships were drawn from the huge gas nebula that hid the Garmaurian battle ships after their self-destructive civil war, and were crewed by a growing myriad of species that had to be integrated into the Alliance military infrastructure. It was a massive headache for Billy Caudwell; and the headache was getting bigger by the day.

Still, as he approached the big blue marble of Earth, Billy still had time to pause and reflect on the sheer beauty of his home world from space. One day, he considered; when the human population was ready, he would be proud to sponsor Earth and Humankind into the Universal Alliance. But, not yet, he mused. They were not ready for the culture shock that would strike when they discovered that they were not alone in the universe. The human belief that they were the only intelligent species in existence was still too strongly embedded in the leaders and governments of the planet.

If only they knew. Billy smiled to himself, setting the controls of the Black Rose to hold her in orbital position. The human race existed as an intelligent species only because of the genetic manipulation experiments carried out on their primitive ancestors by the Garmaurians some forty thousand generations before. And, ironically, after all of the work and experimentation, the Garmaurians had finally rejected humans as a viable and useful species for their colonial adventures. They had then turned Earth into a dump-planet for their other failed genetic projects. That was

8

going to come as quite an eye-opener to the dominant species on planet Earth; and, one very tough sell for whoever had to tell them.

It was a beautiful clear, summer night in northern Europe; the dark brown continental outline was clear and precise against the deep blue of the oceans. The major cities and population centres were clearly visible from the electric lighting that made them look like hundreds of stars in the sky. As the Black Rose drifted into position, the great shining orb of the Sun burst around the edge of the planet and cast a huge yellow-white halo into the depths of the darkness of space. The sunburst caused Billy to catch his breath and marvel at the sheer magnificence and power of the yellow dwarf star that allowed life to exist on his home world.

Unfortunately, Billy did not have a lot of time for solar sightseeing. He had to get back to his mundane life as a schoolboy on the planet that stretched out below him.

With the Black Rose safely established in orbit, Billy sat forward in the single chair of the shuttle's Command Cabin and activated the signal button on the central Control Pillar that stood out from the floor. A stealthed Ranger Patrol vessel would receive the signal and know that the recent arrival was not hostile and would maintain its vigil over Billy Caudwell's home planet. A few moments later, the Black Rose's teleporter pad activated with a blinding flash to herald the arrival of another recipient of the signal. When the dazzling flash had subsided, Billy watched calmly as an identical copy of himself stepped away from the mechanism.

"Good evening, sir," the Billy look-alike, wearing denim jeans and a blue sweatshirt, announced his arrival from the planet's surface.

"Good evening, Jed," Billy replied completely unfazed by the appearance of his exact double, "have I been a good boy today?" he asked as the twin altered his appearance, by deactivating the shielding on his Personal Environment Suit, and reverted to his true form in an Alliance pale blue uniform overall.

Jedithram Prust, known to Billy simply as Jed, was a Thexxian who served in the Alliance Fleet as a Supply Technician. Shorter than the average adult human and possessing the olive skin of his species, Jed had the striking pink eyes and a single nostril planted firmly in the middle of his face. Watching the alien manifest in his own form, it still amazed Billy that all intelligent life in the universe followed the upright humanoid shape imposed upon them by millennia of Garmaurian genetic manipulation.

"Yes, sir," Jed replied as Billy handed him a clear glass-like data-sphere from a recess in the Control Column.

It took a simple thought from Jed to activate the thousands of microscopic machines that swarmed to the data-sphere and began to download the memories and experiences of the 'Billy Caudwell' role that Jed played on Earth, directly from his memory cortex.

"I'm very pleased to hear it, Jed," Billy smiled watching as the nano-bots crowded around the contact point of the data-sphere; which began to glow a pale red.

As part of his mission to act as Billy's double, Jed had been ordered not to draw attention to himself. Billy Caudwell did not want Earth governments becoming aware of his double life and his access to the most advanced technology in the universe. There would always be unscrupulous people who would try to use his family as leverage to gain control of that technology. And, that was a situation that Billy Caudwell was determined to avoid.

After a few moments the data-sphere on Jed's sleeve returned to its usual clear appearance. The memories of the last twelve hours had been successfully transferred.

"There you go, sir," Jed announced handing the clear sphere to the human.

"Here we go again," Billy replied, taking the sphere and holding it against his own left sleeve, just above the large, single, gold star that indicated his rank.

With his own simple thought-command, Billy activated the microscopic machines in his own Personal Environment Suit to download the data from the sphere into his own memory. It took a few moments for the tiny machines to congregate at his sleeve, but when they had gathered and formed a connection to his brain via the PES, Billy felt a sudden and firm jolt. The sphere flashed red for a few moments as Billy tensed up; the memories flowing directly to his cerebral cortices.

When it was over, Billy gasped, blinked his eyes rapidly several times and shook his head. Sighing heavily, Billy put the data-sphere back into the recess and wiped his face with his hands as the memory cortices integrated the data into his own recollections. The last thing he needed was to be found out because he had "forgotten" something important.

"You all right, sir?" Jed asked, as he always did, when Billy was gathering his new thoughts and memories.

"Yes; thanks, Jed," Billy replied as the memory images flashed through his mind.

It had been a good day for Jed/Billy down on planet Earth. Nothing untoward had happened. He hadn't been in or caused any trouble that day. But, it did appear that his parents had argued again. They seemed to be constantly arguing and irritated with each other and that frustrated Billy. He had given them both the Mind Profiles of successful Garmaurians. They had no money worries now, so they shouldn't be arguing, Billy conjectured. They should be happy and enjoying life; but all they seemed to do was fight and bicker. Billy Caudwell just did not seem to be able to comprehend why his plan was going so wrong.

"What were you doing before you left?" Billy asked sending a thought command to his PES to initiate the jeans and sweatshirt image.

"Algebra homework in your room," Jed replied nervously as the First Admiral's blue PES began to morph into the required configuration, "your father has been in the loft since he got home from work; and your mother is in the kitchen writing," he reported.

"Algebra," Billy groaned, "oh, thanks a bunch," Billy shook his head in dismay.

He hated Algebra. Despite the fact that his mathematical knowledge was in the region of two centuries ahead of anyone on Earth, he still detested the subject, which had been his least favourite before the failed abduction that had made him First Admiral.

"Fairly easy, sir," Jed reported with a mischievous smile, "Simultaneous equations; should take you no more than a couple of minutes."

"Yeah, great," Billy replied, "So, what are your plans for tonight then, Jed?" he checked that the image being projected by his PES was correct.

"Back to the Officer Texts, sir," Jed said matter-of-factly, "and catch-up on some sleep," he added.

Jedithram Prust was quite happy to use his down time to study to become a Supply Officer and further promotions. He was young and ambitious and knew that the fledgling Alliance would soon expand presenting him with greater opportunities.

"Are you comfortable on the Ranger? I always thought they were cramped and untidy ships," Billy asked.

"No problems, sir," Jed replied, "I've got my own cabin and the crew pretty much leave me alone."

"OKAY, then, I'll try not to disturb you," Billy promised, "but keep a watch on the Emergency Command Frequency in case I've got to come back in a hurry."

"Yes, sir," Jed replied, knowing only too well that if some crisis arose then he would be back down on Earth in the First Admiral's place in rapid order.

Satisfied that the image was perfect, Billy stepped over to the teleporter and activated it through a thought command in his PES.

"Don't do anything I wouldn't," Billy smiled, with a cheeky wink.

Then, he disappeared in a blinding flash.

Chapter 2

The Imperial Palace, Bardan

Lullina, the Grand Empress of the Bardomil, stared in shock and incredulity at the object on the small, circular, legless table hovering before her.

"It's...a rock!" Lullina said icily, her voice echoing around the cavernous Throne Room, to the two yellow-clad figures prostrate on the floor before her.

"If it pleases Your Imperial Gloriousness," one of the prostrate figures raised his head, smiling nervously to explain just exactly what this "rock" was.

"This had better be good," Empress Lullina replied haughtily still staring at the object.

Sammut Claggit, of the Xanath species, tried to rise to his feet only to be brutally shoved back down by one of the two black uniformed Imperial Bodyguards who hovered menacingly over him and his young assistant, Bem. Raising himself up onto his elbows, Claggit realised that this was going to be a tougher sell than he had first imagined. Looking up at the Bardomil Empress, sitting on the green and white onyx throne, Claggit shuddered inwardly. She was a beautiful creature to look at, tall, slim, elegant and graceful. Her pale peach gown seemed to shimmer at her slightest movement creating a swirling pattern of various shades in the gossamer-fine material. Her face was almost angelic with the high angular forehead; created by binding her head when she was just an infant, to achieve that haughty superior expression. The golden skull cap, wreathed with the jewelled coronet, set off her pale grey facial features perfectly; even those sinister completely jet black eyes that stared malevolently at anyone who incurred her displeasure.

That displeasure was something that Sammut Claggit did not wish to incur. Claggit was well aware that the Bardomil Empress was completely insane and the comparison to the infamous Tarselian Ground Frog was more than apt. The males of the species, during the mating season, would indiscriminately eject small, highly venomous spines from their skin to eliminate their rivals. In the frenzy of the mating season, all reason and sanity completely vanished from the male frog with their deadly spines killing anything and everything that got in the way. The Empress could be just as unreasonable in one of her towering rages, and equally lethal.

"If it pleases Your Radiance," Claggit began once again, "please do not be fooled by the appearance of the weapon before you..."

"This...rock...is a weapon, Master Claggit!?" the Empress sneered, "do we have to hit our enemies over the head with it?" she barbed.

"No, Your Graciousness," Claggit smiled weakly, "this is, in fact, the perfect stealth weapon...if I may be allowed to demonstrate?"

"Proceed," the Empress waved languidly to allow the Xanath to stand up.

"Thank you, Your Radiant Magnificence," Claggit began, nervously eyeing the Bodyguard; who drew back, and rose to his full height of just over one metre, "if I may approach the...rock?"

Like most Xanath, Sammut Claggit was short in stature, but possessed a mind and intellect far greater than most in the universe. His lank greying hair hung down in long ringlets around a sharp, pale blue, angular face that was marred by a deep, livid, red scar that ran from his forehead down to his chin.

"Yes, yes...get on with it!" the Empress sighed with an edge of irritation in her voice.

"If you will observe, Your Serenity..." Claggit began, nervously approaching the rock, and touched its surface.

Instantly, the rock façade melted away to reveal a silver metallic sphere the size of a soccer ball.

"No! No! No!" Claggit cringed, his hands raised high above his head as two dozen Bardomil weapons were charged, ready to fire, at the sudden transformation of the object.

"Well, well, Master Claggit, you might just have something of interest there for Parlour Trick Magicians," the Empress said slowly, moving to the edge of the throne, her attention suddenly taken.

"Thank you, Your Greatness," Claggit replied, nervously glancing at the dozens of weapons still pointed at him, "this is a small, self-contained Lissian Pulse Emitter," he continued.

Nervously, Claggit stretched out his hand towards the sphere, whilst still watching the Bodyguards, and pressed the side of the object. Rapidly, the sphere broke down into four leaves on a shallow dish base, showing an array of circuit boards and mechanical moving parts.

"A Lissian Pulse Emitter, Master Claggit?" The Empress queried, "What does that do, exactly?"

"Well, Your Perfectness, under normal circumstances," Claggit began, "absolutely nothing, but in close proximity to highly conductive super-heated plasma it creates what is called magnetic reconnection."

"Which is, Master Claggit?" the Empress began to lose the thread of the description.

"Well, Your Fabulousness, in simple terms, if you were to put it close to, say, for example, a yellow dwarf star, it would cause a super-charged extremely powerful solar flare. May I demonstrate?" Claggit asked.

"By all means," the Empress conceded starting to become bored again.

"My assistant, Bem," Claggit motioned for the other prostrate figure to rise up, "has created a visual representation of the weapon in action, for your edification."

"Do get on with it Claggit," the Empress snapped, "our Imperial patience is wearing thin," she warned, the novelty of this new distraction beginning to wear off.

Bem, the assistant, nervously stood up. He reached just over one metre in height. He was several decades younger than Claggit, and fresh faced for a Xanath. His hair, darker than Claggit's, was neatly shorn to expose long pendulous ear lobes. Nervously, Bem set down a small cube on the floor behind the hovering table and activated it. After a few moments of grainy static, a three-dimensional image of a solar system cleared to a crystal sharpness. At the centre a large yellow dwarf star burned, surrounded by eight planets. The sixth of the eight planets was the most striking, with a spectacular ring system around it.

"Your Brilliance has asked me to design a weapon that would eliminate all life-forms on the third planet in this solar system," Claggit began, the image focussing closely on a blue and brown planet with white clouds, "this planet, here, I believe it is called Terra or Earth," he paused for effect pointing to the large image.

"I would humbly submit," Claggit continued as the image pulled out to show the whole solar system again, "that we send the Lissian Emitter," the image showed a silver object approaching the yellow dwarf on the opposite side of the Sun from the Earth, "and bring it into a safe orbit around the star in direct opposition to the planet itself," the image changed to an overhead shot of the spinning planets with the moving silver object being hidden from the Earth's line of sight by the star.

"Yes...go on?" the Empress said, her interest piqued again as she leaned forward in her throne.

"At a time of Your Majesty's choosing, the Emitter would send forth a highly concentrated pulse of Lissian radiation that would excite and destabilise the solar plasma creating a massive super-charged solar flare," Claggit continued, with a graceful bow, as the image returned to a profile view of the system and a huge yellow mass shot forth from the surface of the Sun towards the Earth image.

THE BURNING SUN

Rapidly, the yellow mass overwhelmed the first two planets in the system before slowing down. The image then cut back to the Earth close up as the yellow mass engulfed the blue planet.

"The super-charged flare would take around two Terran hours to reach its target, but would effectively be unstoppable. All life on the third planet would be vapourised in exactly three minutes and fifteen seconds as the solar flare material, trapped by the Terran atmosphere and gravity, swept around the planet until the increasing heat finally burnt away the entire atmosphere," Claggit intoned matter-of-factly at the simulated annihilation of a life-bearing planet, "The flare material would then continue to engulf the fourth, red planet, before running out of energy, leaving the Terran planet sterilised with no hope of life ever being re-established", the image showed the planet Mars being swamped by the yellow mass before the image cut out.

For a moment, the entire Throne Room fell into a hushed awe. Claggit and Bem eyed each other nervously as the Empress stood up and walked slowly towards them.

"Master Claggit, we salute you," the Empress smiled, approaching the opened silver sphere.

"Thank you, Your Phenomenal-ness," Claggit replied as both of the Xanath backed anxiously away from the slowly advancing Empress.

"And, how do we get it past the Alliance Scanners?" the Empress asked.

"We have disguised it as a simple space rock, Your Generosity; the Alliance Scanners will simply detect a lump of floating material with a high-metallic composition," Claggit bowed low and slapped Bem on the side; to copy him, as the Empress began to slowly circle the table, "and, it can assume a liquid state to meld with passing objects as well as change colour to further blend in. In fact, it would be completely undetectable unless you were looking for this specific piece of equipment."

"Very clever, Master Claggit," the Empress praised with her best insincere smile, "we are pleased with your work."

"Thank you, Your Marvellous-ness; we are happy to have been of service to you," Claggit smiled nervously bobbing yet another bow.

"We hereby decree and command," the Empress began formally, "that you take your device to our scientists and show them how it operates. You will then be taken to the Imperial Treasury and handsomely rewarded before being returned in great honour to your home planet of Xanart."

"You are most generous, Your Terrific-ness, most generous indeed; thank you, thank you," Claggit stammered, with relief. He grabbed the

Emitter and closed it down whilst Bem grabbed the floating table and display cube.

"We thank you for your efforts Master Claggit and assistant Bem," the Empress smiled as the two Xanath were led away bowing, scraping, thanking and praising.

"Sudrus," the Empress beckoned the Captain of Bodyguards when the Xanath were out of ear-shot, "when they've showed us how it works, take them to the Treasury and then kill them," she turned, striding toward her Onyx Throne.

"Majesty," the tall Bodyguard, uniformed in black, saluted, bowed and was about to back away when the Empress turned to him again.

"But, don't let them bleed all over the Imperial Jewels, Captain Sudrus; their Xanath blood is very corrosive," the Empress added and dismissed the Bodyguard.

Returning to her Onyx Throne, she sat down again, gracefully.

"Those things are a nightmare to keep clean in the best of circumstances," she sighed despairingly.

THE BURNING SUN

Chapter 3

Planet Earth

"Emma!" the familiar voice of Billy Caudwell called out through the hubbub of the school corridor.

It was ten-thirty, the end of second period, and the corridor was jammed with the shuffling feet of hundreds of students making their weary ways to whatever delights awaited them in third period. Teachers called out above the general mayhem to round up tardy students to their classes or to keep the corridors and passageways moving freely. Through the press of book-clutching uniformed bodies, Billy Caudwell forced his way breathlessly forward to speak to the tall, blonde, blue-eyed girl who was the object of his attention.

With her back to the struggling, sweating Billy Caudwell, Emma Wallace winced. Too late, she thought, he's seen me, so I can't pretend I didn't hear him and walk away; though that would have been her preferred option. The friend she had been walking along the corridor with smiled, nudged Emma on the arm, and walked onwards to her next lesson, her books clutched tightly to her chest.

"Billy!" Emma Wallace turned and smiled nervously as the sweating and out of breath fifteen year old schoolboy finally managed to work his way to her through the crowd, "how are you?"

"God, this place just gets worse!" Billy gasped breathlessly as the other students jostled and pushed their way past him to their own next lessons.

He had dashed along three similar corridors to catch up with the beautiful blonde girl he had become enamoured of in the last few months. His second period in history was to be followed by a third period in Mister Laughlin's German Class, which was two flights up, and another two corridors along. So, to speak to Emma, he had to move quickly to avoid the dreaded detention that was the sanction for lateness to classes.

Oh God, he's all horrible and sweaty, Emma thought as Billy gasped for breath amidst the press of bodies.

Billy Caudwell, despite being a year younger than Emma, had really only appeared amongst her circle of "friends" since the beginning of that year. She used the term "friend" loosely as she was aware that Billy Caudwell probably harboured some romantic intent towards her. She had always had that instinct of knowing when young men were attracted to her, and she was quite prepared to utilise the knowledge to her advantage. They were male, and, hence, were only after one thing; therefore, she considered, it was entirely acceptable to make use of that attraction for her own benefit. Billy Caudwell, however, did not really rate in Emma Wallace's estimation of potential boyfriend material. Billy was nice, kind and sensitive. He was also kind of cute in a little-boy-lost sort of way that some other girls found quite appealing. But, handsome and exciting, he was not.

In the Emma Wallace ranking system of boyfriend material, Billy Caudwell was a "probably not".

But, like a few other boys she had assigned into the "probably not" category, Billy Caudwell had his uses.

He was always a good listener when she was troubled and could always be relied upon to cheer her up. He was good at maths and history; and an aspiring fashion designer, such as Emma Wallace, had to have good grades at several subjects to get into one of the prestigious Art Colleges in Glasgow or London. The end-of-term exams were due in a couple of months and she was weak in maths; so she would have to rely on Billy's expertise to get her through. These were the important pre-Qualification exams. If she made a mess of the actual final exam, then she could fall back on the pre-Qualification as the basis of an appeal.

So, gritting her teeth in a weak smile, Emma Wallace tried her best not to show her distaste for the perspiring, red-haired boy who had stopped her in the corridor.

"What are you up to then, Billy?" she smiled her best attempt at friendliness, hoping that she wasn't going to smell that dreadful sweaty odour.

"Just wanted to ask you about the school dance next week," Billy gasped nervously, his pale, freckled face red-flushed from exertion.

Oh God, he's going to ask me out, she shuddered mentally. Emma had hoped that the dreaded "let's-just-be-good-friends" conversation would be able to wait until after the pre-Qualification exams. But, now it appeared that that particular occasion was drawing closer than she had anticipated.

"What about the school dance?" she replied slightly on edge.

"Well, if you're not going with anyone," Billy swallowed nervously, "would you like to go with me?"

Well, there it is, Emma thought, the worm has finally developed enough backbone to ask me out.

"Well, I don't really know," Emma tried to hedge her options.

The school dance was only a week away, and suddenly she realised that to date, no one had actually asked her to go. The dance had not been high on her list of priorities, until now. But, it just wouldn't do for a popular and attractive young woman with fashion design ambitions to turn up without an escort. After all, she wasn't one of those geeky, bookish girls that fainted with expectation whenever a boy spoke to them.

"Well, if you're not going with anyone," Billy Caudwell pressed his argument, his sweaty face visibly shaking with anxiety.

"Yeah, okay, alright, Billy," Emma replied interrupting his proposal a little more sharply than she had intended.

Oh God, did I sound a bit desperate there, she considered. I hope he didn't think I was actually keen to go with him. It's just he's going to have to do for the moment, Emma thought, I'll push some of the better looking, older, hunky guys to ask me out later on. At least one of them might have a car, and hopefully the ability to keep his hands to himself, she shuddered.

"Oh, fine, great," Billy Caudwell smiled broadly his previously concerned face now wrinkling with relief, "I'll meet you Thursday night then," he added.

"Yeah, looking forward to it," she smiled with as much faux-sincerity as she could muster.

"Sorry, but I'm off to Mister Laughlin's for German," Billy smiled and began to walk away briskly.

Five steps later, he half-turned to flash a broad beaming smile at Emma and lost his footing. Recovering from the half stumble, Billy Caudwell blushed, turning bright red, and smiled sheepishly while waving feebly before turning away to dash to his next class.

What have I done? Emma Wallace thought to herself, clutching her books closer to her chest. Her next class, English, was only a few steps away. The large brown sliding door was as inviting to her as the fiery pit of Hades. Still, she had to attend; fashion designers had to have good grades in English. With the sun streaming brightly and warmly through the large arched windows of the corridor, Emma Wallace trudged leaden-footed to her next class.

Well, at least she now had a fallback position for the school dance, she considered. He wasn't ideal, but it was better than the shameful embarrassment of arriving all dressed up and no one to dance with. There were a lot worse than Billy Caudwell at the school who might have asked her to the dance. He wasn't that bad looking and was better than nothing at all, she consoled herself; besides, it would be easy enough to ditch him when they got there.

But, red hair?

Uuurgh!

BENNING

Chapter 4

The Artreaus System

The Bardomil Empress was not happy. As a creature who had grown used to immediate obedience, any delay in fulfilling her wishes was a cause of major irritation and anger. Silently, she stalked around the specially prepared Battle Command Centre aboard the flagship of the Bardomil Imperial Sixth Fleet. With her beautiful angelic-like face twisted in a rictus of annoyance and frustration, she stomped heavily amongst the terrified senior Officers who stood at attention in a semi-circle in front of her elevated throne.

"Incompetent fools!" she bellowed as her immaculate dark green dress swished and swirled around her in response to every small movement, "Why are we still waiting!?"

"M...M...Ma...Majesty," the terrified Fleet Commander began to explain.

"M...M...Ma...Majesty," the Empress sneeringly mocked the frightened senior military Officer, "We have been here for nearly four hours waiting for you imbeciles to test this weapon. How much longer!?" she raged, shoving her angelic, hate-twisted, face close to the Fleet Commander's.

"Majesty," the Fleet Commander swallowed nervously; hoping that he wouldn't pass out from terror, "we have to wait for the planet to align correctly to make best use of the weapon's potential," he stammered.

"That's not good enough," she shrieked, as if her temper tantrum could somehow speed the orbit of the doomed planet, "How much longer must we wait for your stupidity to make any progress!?"

"The planet should be in optimal position in twenty-three minutes, Majesty," the Captain of the Imperial Bodyguards, Sudrus, reported from one of the consoles close to the Empress.

For a moment, the Empress paused, her face changing from a mask of hate to one of placid calm and gentleness in the blink of an eye.

"There, Gentlemen," she addressed the terrorised Officers sweetly, "that is how to do things efficiently; thank you, Captain Sudrus," she smiled.

Turning with balletic grace, the Empress tiptoed daintily up the three steps to her specially positioned throne, and sat down.

"You are dismissed, Gentlemen," she smiled relieving them with a regal wave of her pale grey hand.

THE BURNING SUN

Having been sent away, the senior Officers scattered rapidly in all directions like chickens in a coop that had been disturbed by a hungry fox, relieved to be out of her icy and deadly glare.

Sitting comfortably on the throne, the Empress pushed a button on the Control Panel built into the right armrest. Immediately, four, two-dimensional, screens were projected from the floor of the Battle Command Centre. The screens formed a huge semi-circle that seemed to engulf the front of the Imperial throne. Each ten metre high screen, though curved, did not distort its image allowing the Empress a full panoramic view of the scenario that was unfolding before her.

The first screen showed the disposition of the Bardomil Imperial Sixth Fleet. The Sixth Fleet was not an active front line combat formation, but was purely for ceremonial and security purposes. It was, in effect, her own private protection and display formation. The flagship of the Sixth Fleet, her own personal Imperial yacht, was the three-decked Imperial Fighter-Carrier named "Taurai". The Taurai had never carried, let alone launched in anger, one of the feared single-seat Harpoon fighters that had terrorised hundreds of galaxies. Nor had it played host to any of the Flying Devil gunships that struck dread and fear into an enemy's heart. The Taurai was a pleasure craft designed and utilised for the transportation of the Bardomil Imperial Court and Retinue. The decks and hangars had been stripped of the paraphernalia of warfare, which had been replaced by luxurious quarters and staterooms plus various entertainment facilities and the communications equipment from which to issue orders and instructions to the sprawling Bardomil Empire.

The Taurai was, however, protected in-formation by eight further Imperial Fighter-Carriers, which bore an over-full complement of Harpoon fighters and Flying Devils. In their tight triangular formation, the Imperial Fighter-Carriers were screened by swarms of the large, heavily armed M-Cruisers. The long cylindrical body of the M-Cruiser with its bent gull-wings was as menacing and sinister as it was impressive. Through the serried ranks of Imperial Fighter-Carriers and M-Cruisers, the Harpoons and Flying Devils darted and weaved, maintaining their vigil for any possible threat to the Head of State and absolute ruler. In neighbouring solar systems, other Bardomil Imperial Fleets would be maintaining a security cordon to protect their Empress. The full panoply of the Bardomil war machine was now on show around what was normally considered to be a backwater system in a remote galaxy of the Empire.

The second screen showed the purpose of the visit for this huge array of Bardomil military strength. The image was of a large beautiful golden planet called "Collizon". The planet of Collizon had no significant strategic value, nor any valuable mineral or natural resources. Its vast deep emerald green oceans supported a flimsy ecosystem with a meagre scattering of indigenous species. The dark yellow and pale brown continental landmasses reflected from the clear cloudless skies to give the planet the shining golden hue that made it instantly identifiable amongst the fourteen other drably coloured planets of the system. The top species were a few hundred thousand humanoid-type people called the Manuch. The Manuch lived by subsistence farming in their small, scattered tribal groups and presented no military threat to the Bardomil Empire. Collizon was not a hotbed of rebellion against the Empress. It did not shelter any of the numerous rebels or enemies of the Empire. It did, however, possess one vital characteristic. Collizon was a life-bearing planet with an atmosphere primarily composed of Nitrogen and Oxygen that circled a yellow dwarf star at a distance of just over one hundred and fifty million kilometres.

The third screen displayed the yellow dwarf star that sat at the heart of the fifteen planet system and which was being orbited by the emitter weapon developed by the now deceased Sammut Claggit. The weapon itself was too small to be seen by the naked eye as it circled the star, however, a hollow red square was superimposed upon the solar image to indicate the object's position. The faint box tracked the weapon as it quietly and smoothly crossed the face of the star before disappearing behind the great burning orb.

The final screen displayed a schematic image of the fifteen planet solar system from a perspective located above the planets. It indicated their orbits relative to each other and the yellow dwarf at the heart of the system. When the Lissian Emitter Weapon was activated this screen would show the destructive path of the super-charged plasma as it seared across the solar system destroying the planets in its relentless path. The sixth planet; Collizon, was highlighted in pale blue, in contrast to the other drab brown planetary images.

The tension in the Battle Command Centre rose dramatically as the appointed hour for the test firing of the Emitter Weapon approached. The Battle Centre personnel, under the implacable scrutiny of the Empress, hurried about their duties, hoping that on this of all days they would not make even the tiniest mistake. In the Imperial presence, even the smallest of errors could land someone in an execution chamber or on the very short trip out of an airlock into the emptiness of space.

Lullina watched intently as the last few moments of the countdown were intoned by a frightened Technician who drew heavy breaths to hide her fear. But, when the count reached "zero", nothing seemed to happen.

THE BURNING SUN

The Empress scrutinised the third screen image for any changes, no matter how insignificant, whilst Technicians and scientists scrambled and sweated profusely over their calculations and projections. Long seconds that felt like decades drew out in the deathly silence of the Battle Command Centre as the scientists tried to work out what had happened. The Fleet Commander, ultimately responsible for the deployment of the weapon, shuffled anxiously at his Battle Station.

The quiet buzz of communications traffic broke the almost painful silence of the Battle Centre as orders, requests reports and speculations flowed through the networks. All through the Taurai, silent wishes arose; if there's been an error, please let it be someone else's fault. The Empress, growing ever more agitated, shifted on her throne, her face changing from the benign and peaceful angelic half smile to the more animated and treacherous scowl that indicated her displeasure.

"Gentlemen, why are we wait..." the Empress began from her aerie-like Imperial throne.

She never got to finish the question as the third screen before her flickered several times and the image of the yellow dwarf star began to change colour. Moving from a bright yellow to a slightly more orange-yellow tone, the magnetic polarity of the star was altered just sufficiently to destabilise and magnify the huge nuclear reactions deep within its core.

A moment later, a huge burst of super-heated plasma spewed out from the top left-hand quarter of the celestial body and began to snake and slither away towards the planets of the system.

The collective sigh of relief in the Battle Command Centre was masked by a loud celebratory cheer while the personnel watched as more and more super-heated plasma was ejected from the yellow dwarf. The Empress, her face shining with delight, sat back on her throne and marvelled at the sheer volume of material being sent forth from this one tiny star.

Snake-like, sinuous tendrils of intense plasma were speeding away from the yellow dwarf out into the emptiness of space. If the scientists were correct, the planet of Collizon would follow its normal orbital path and spin directly into the path of the advancing fiery nightmare.

Meanwhile, on Collizon, the plant and animal life had no idea that in two hours time, they would be seared out of existence, and went about their day to day business oblivious to the horror that was heading towards them. The Empress clapped her Imperial hands excitedly and watched; her black eyes shining with delight, as the stream of charged plasma burst forth seemingly without end.

BENNING

After two minutes of constant eruption, the yellow dwarf was finally exhausted. The violent plasma eruption stuttered to a halt as the last deadly spume was sent hurtling into the void of space. And, with the last lurching outburst of plasma, the Battle Command Centre put up one last cheer as the Empress smiled with satisfaction and reclined onto her throne once more. On the fourth screen before her, she saw the first streaks of yellow plasma bursting away from the yellow dwarf out into the Artreaus solar system. In two hours she would be able to see just how powerful this new weapon was and how much devastation it would wreak upon her enemies.

And, as she marvelled at the new sadistic power the late and unlamented Sammut Claggit had bestowed upon her, an idea had already formed in her mind.

She was going to have to be careful how she handled the deployment of this new weapon. She would have to make sure that the next solar flare disaster looked like a naturally occurring phenomenon for which the Bardomil Empire would attract no blame.

She was going to have her revenge against Billy Caudwell and his upstart Universal Alliance.

THE BURNING SUN

Chapter 5

<u>Planet Earth</u>

Elizabeth Caudwell was an angry, confused and frightened woman. She was used to being angry about the myriad of problems that life had always thrown at her. But, what she was not used to were the violent temper tantrums that seemed to appear at less than a moment's notice from the depths of her mind. This kind of violent outspoken reaction was totally out of character for Elizabeth, and it worried her.

It had been just over a year since her first book "My Lost Little Angel" had stormed to the top of the book-reader's sales charts in the English speaking world. Her honest, heart breaking, and yet, heart warming reaction to the loss of her stillborn infant daughter had connected with the public in a way that had astounded even her publisher, Mr George Teddington of Teddington International Publications. Over twenty million copies of "Little Angel" had been sold in the space of that single year, making Elizabeth an extremely wealthy woman. According to Mr Teddington, sales were likely to hold up, if not improve further in the next year as the book was translated into a host of European and world languages. If Elizabeth could produce a second book, perhaps a sequel, then sales could potentially be astronomical.

But, the great success of her first book had appeared to come at a price for Elizabeth. Something was going very badly wrong with her family life.

She couldn't understand how, or when, exactly, it had started, but suddenly, she felt very unhappy and violently angry with her life. She had been married to John Caudwell for almost sixteen years. At times, they had struggled to make ends meet, and there had always been arguments; usually about money. But, now they had lots of money. They had more money than they had ever dreamed they would have. The Caudwell family now wanted for nothing, but still she and John argued. They would argue about the most trivial of things, and some of the arguments could get quite fiery. She knew she had a temper; it came with the red hair, her mother had told her, but she had never known herself to be so vicious and personal in her attacks.

Elizabeth was not a tall woman, nor did she consider herself strikingly beautiful; her nose was too sharp and her mouth was not quite straight. However, her mane of fiery red hair and bright blue eyes had set her apart from all of the other girls in the small former mining town where she had grown up.

BENNING

It had been in the old Miner's Social Club that Elizabeth Mackintosh had met John Caudwell. He wasn't a strikingly handsome man, but still, she found herself strangely drawn to him with his shock of bright blond hair and soulful blue eyes. The relationship had been going well with John Caudwell, until the day she found out she was pregnant. She knew how it had happened, and cursed herself for her drunken stupidity. It had been her birthday, and John had managed to "borrow" a large expensive car that he was working on at the garage where he had just completed his motor mechanic's apprenticeship. It had chrome bumpers, huge fins at the back, and very, very comfortable seats. The alcohol had flowed freely that night at the celebration.

The drive home had taken a long detour round some of the quieter country lanes of the area. Elizabeth had not objected to the stop in a quiet lay-by. Maybe it was the occasion or maybe the alcohol had had too great an effect, but Elizabeth soon found herself on the long luxurious leather back seat of the car making love. In those moments of passion, all reason had been abandoned, as had all sense of responsibility. It was four weeks later that she discovered that she was pregnant. In those days, the early 1970's, single motherhood or termination would have been severely frowned upon in her hometown. The smiles of the townsfolk may have been open and welcoming, but their minds were firmly closed; none more so than Elizabeth's strictly traditional and conservative mother's. A wedding was hastily arranged by both Elizabeth and John's quietly angered parents, before the baby bump would show under her long flowing ivory dress. So, with some degree of resignation and finality she had paraded down the aisle, her older sister in tow as her Matron of Honour.

At twenty-three years of age, Elizabeth had found herself to be a pregnant married woman. John had left the garage where he worked and joined the local Police; which was a better paid and more secure job than a journeyman mechanic. With a child on the way, paternal responsibility meant that he had to forego his love of motor vehicles and subsume his life to that of his wife and child. When Elizabeth went into labour, it had been the harshest winter in living memory. Still, somehow, with a couple metres of snow on the roads, John had managed to drive the large powerful police car to the County's main hospital.

When Billy was born, Elizabeth could not have been more proud, and she quickly settled into the routine of marriage and motherhood. Yet, the guilt of an unexpected pregnancy gnawed at her mind. John had never said anything, and, perhaps, she was imagining it, but she was convinced that he resented her for trapping him into a marriage and life he did not particularly want. John tinkered with old motor vehicles in his off-duty moments, and made a valiant attempt to grow vegetables to supplement his police salary, but still she sensed that he was far from happy.

At first, he appeared to be the doting new father, but as Billy grew older she began to notice just how hard he was on their son's failings and weaknesses. She considered that young boys needed a firm hand from their fathers to keep them in line and out of trouble. They needed to know what was right and what was wrong. And, John certainly had a very strong sense of right and wrong. There were very few grey areas in the world of John Caudwell. She could look at the boys of Billy's age in the local community and see the ones who would be troublemakers and jail-fodder in the future. She did not want Billy to go off the rails like them, and turned a blind eye to her husband's severity.

But, it was John's inconsistency that troubled her. Billy seemed to be one of those children who could do no right but for doing wrong. When he came home from school with a poor report, John would be scolding him for being stupid and lazy. When Billy came home with good grades, he was scolded for that most British of failings; being too clever by half. It was a situation that Billy seemed never to be able to win. Yet, John had often told her how proud he was of their young son. He just didn't seem to know how to tell the one person who needed to hear it most. And, that was Billy himself.

Still, as Billy grew older, he worked hard at school, got good grades and stayed out of trouble as best he could. Certainly, he got into some scrapes, but then so did most boys, and it was never anything really serious like stealing or being in a gang. But, she noticed that slowly young Billy was slipping deeper and deeper into his own shell. He became quiet and shy as an older boy, quite the opposite of the energetic, carefree, robust and sporty child he had been. Well, to each to their own, she had though, maybe, he's just matured beyond his years.

It was a denial-based strategy that Elizabeth was happy to maintain to hold her marriage together. But, with the stillbirth of her daughter and the news that she would not have any more children, she began to dote further on Billy. The loss of one child had made her especially protective of the one that had survived. When John's inconsistent treatment of Billy led to a scolding, she would side with Billy and comfort him as much as possible. Thus, she was drawn into the difficult contradiction of ignoring her husband's inconsistency whilst trying to convince Billy that everything was fine. It was a strategy that caused anger and resentment within her; at her husband's unfairness, and also at herself for not standing up to him. It was a pressure cooker waiting to explode.

BENNING

With the success of her first book, "My Lost Little Angel", everything seemed to change for Elizabeth Caudwell; it seemed almost immediately. The first twenty thousand pound advance from George Teddington was quickly followed by other royalty cheques. With the first, Elizabeth had wanted to go on a huge spending spree, but John had been much more levelheaded. Her new accountant had supported her husband's stance arguing about investing for Billy's future; buying property, Stocks, Shares and Bonds, things she really didn't understand anything about. John had suggested that she take a few thousand and spoil herself. That had been like a red rag to a bull for Elizabeth, and she had exploded in anger and rage.

She had said something about not needing him to tell her what to do with her money. A stunned and shocked John had walked away confused and bewildered. Up until that moment in time, there had only ever been one bank account into which both incomes were paid, and all expenditures monitored. There hadn't been very much of it, but it had been "their" money. It was John, Elizabeth and Billy Caudwell versus the rest of the world in John's mind. It had always been a struggle to make ends meet, but they had always struggled together. And, to be honest, he had been the major contributor to the family funds. Elizabeth's job, working in a department store, paid less than a third of what John earned in the plastics factory.

Feeling guilty at her outburst, she had tried to bribe her way back into his affections with small, but well-chosen gifts. Not sure how to respond to the person he once thought he knew, he smiled politely, and uncomfortably accepted them. No more was said of the outburst for several months. In that time more and more money flowed into their bank account. Then, one day John disappeared up into the loft and started to work on something. He didn't appear for dinner that evening, and the following morning Elizabeth found him fast asleep on the living room sofa. After snatching a hasty breakfast he returned back the loft, and had to be summoned to go to his shift at work. Then, when he returned home, he ate a quick sandwich and disappeared back to the loft again.

Billy did not seem to be overly concerned about his father's strange behaviour, and Elizabeth herself had spent many hours obsessively creating her second book.

John's new routine became quickly established; go to work, come home, eat, shower, then up into his loft. He was quickly becoming a stranger to his family in his own home; and Elizabeth, far from being concerned, began to focus on her next literary project and worrying about Billy. Billy was still a little too quiet and lacking in self-confidence for her liking. Elizabeth then decided that it was, perhaps, best for him to be sent to a select private school. There, she reasoned, they would know how to build up his confidence and develop his considerable intellect. She believed that the problem with Billy was not that he was stupid; he got really good grades at school. He was just shy and not very self-confident; and part of her knew that she had to get Billy away from John.

John dropping a bottle of milk had been the prelude to the most recent irrational verbal assault. During the verbal explosion she had called him a "Thermag" which was Garmaurian for a lazy, idle wastrel. Of course, John had understood her, and replied with "Gamrut" which meant arrogant and opinionated. Thankfully, it had struck neither of them that they had insulted each other in an alien language, nor that both of them had understood what the other had meant.

It was only a stupid pint of milk, Elizabeth had realized, a few pennies, what was that to her when she had hundreds of thousands of pounds in the bank?

But, yet she had exploded, once again, as if he had dropped and smashed some priceless family heirloom. The red mist had descended in front of her eyes and she had let fly with all the insults she could muster. She had called him names that she would bitterly regret afterwards, shocked at how deep her anger and rage really was. Once again, he had replied in kind and had stormed off to his loft to work on whatever he was up to in there. Again, she was left alone with the brutally oppressive silence. So much had been said in anger, and, yet, she had so much more still to say.

It never used to be like this, she thought. It hadn't been like this when they had next to nothing. Sure, they had argued; there had always been arguments, but they had never been about trivialities like a broken milk bottle. They had argued about important things like buying new furniture or a better cooker. Something was going badly wrong with the marriage, and Elizabeth could not understand what it was. Even worse than that, she had no idea what to do about it.

But, more importantly, there was Billy. What was happening to Billy? His grades were the highest in the school over almost all subjects, and if he did like to be alone; developing a sense of identity and self-reliance, then that was something to be encouraged. Maybe, she was just being overly anxious about Billy, she considered.

She would just have to get used to the idea that, perhaps, Billy was growing up; and that she could stop fussing over him like an old hen.

BENNING

Chapter 6

The Star-Cruiser Aquarius

Chief of Staff Marrhus Lokkrien sat alone in the peace and tranquillity of his Private Quarters contemplating yet another thorny issue. This time it was a personnel issue. A fourth Alliance Fleet was about to be commissioned into service, and it needed a commander. Normally, it was not the responsibility of the Chief of Staff to select a Fleet Commander, a Second Admiral. However, Marrhus Lokkrien liked to keep himself occupied even with more trivial matters than his job really required. He liked to keep busy. It kept his mind from straying back to the family he had been compelled to abandon on his home planet of Bardan when he had joined the young Alliance.

It had been almost a year since his defection and almost eighteen months since he had last seen his wife and two sons. He missed them all desperately. To them, he would be considered dead. One of the so-called Glorious Fallen; faithfully recorded in the ledgers of the Bardomil Imperial Fleet. He would be a hero, a dead hero, who sacrificed his life for the honour and glory of the empire rather than surrender. Fleet Commander Sarvin, his old commanding Officer, would be blamed for the disaster that had lost the Empire nine Imperial Fighter Carriers, but the supposedly-dead Lokkrien would be held up as a shining example of courage and dedication to duty.

Yet now, he was feeling neither honourable nor heroic. He just missed his children. He missed them so badly at times that it made every bone, muscle and sinew in his body ache. There were times he would lay down at night and think that perhaps death was better than this living agony of emptiness. He was an exile with no family, and certainly no friends in the Universal Alliance. The Alliance was still, technically, at war with the Bardomil Empire. As the only Bardomil working for the Alliance Fleet, he was a figure of mistrust and suspicion. Amongst those Fleet personnel from species who had suffered under Bardomil cruelty and tyranny, he was a figure of hatred and loathing. Amongst others he was an enemy in their own uniform. Marrhus Lokkrien was alone, horribly and frighteningly alone. He hated the loneliness and spent every waking hour working, rather than face the terror of his own company.

Only the thought that someday soon Billy Caudwell and the Alliance Fleet would sweep away the Empress kept the hope alive that, one day, he would see his family again. For now, he had to lie low. If the Bardomil Government even suspected that he was still alive, then all of his family would be summarily executed. He had to remain anonymous, silent and hidden to protect his family. In Fleet communications he was simply a code name: Enigma. He had to avoid combat situations or any possible activities that would expose his true identity or leave him vulnerable to capture. He hated it. He was a Bardomil, brought up to fight and to be in the thick of the action. And, there was plenty of action out there on the Alliance's rapidly expanding frontiers for him to be involved in. Instead, he knuckled down and worked the facts and figures, made the decisions and helped the burgeoning Alliance as best he could with his expertise and experience.

As he worked through the Performance Folios of the potential Second Admiral candidates, the faint buzz of an alarm indicated that someone was standing on the pressure pad beyond the door and requesting admission to his Quarters. Looking at his desk-monitor, Lokkrien saw the unmistakable figure of Senior Intelligence Officer Karap Sownus shuffling nervously beyond the grey opaque force-shielding that formed the door of his Private Quarters. Checking the Time-Keeper on the monitor Lokkrien realised that the short, squat Thexxian Intelligence Officer's duty shift would have ended several hours previously.

It also surprised Lokkrien that any Thexxian, a species hunted almost to extinction by the Bardomil, would be even contemplating speaking to him in an off-duty capacity. But, Lokkrien considered, Sownus was very different to the vast majority of Thexxians who, daily, went through the motions and saluted him with unspoken hatred and loathing in their eyes. Sownus was a professional, always formally correct, always matter of fact and always guarded with his opinions. He said very little, but when he did speak people paid attention.

"Come!" Lokkrien intoned passing his hand over the small white plate built into his desk that operated the door mechanism.

An instant later, the opaque force-shielding became transparent; exposing Officer Sownus and clearing to allow him entry.

"I hope I'm not disturbing you, sir?" the unusually nervous Sownus piped up as he entered the room.

As soon as he cleared the doorway, the force-shielding automatically reinstated itself.

"Officer Sownus, come in, this is most unexpected. What can I do for you at this late hour?" Lokkrien dropped into the politely formal routines of senior Officer to subordinate; but, he was unable to hide the edge of surprise and curiosity in his voice.

"I know, I'm sorry, sir; but, I thought you might want to see this," Sownus replied waddling forward towards Lokkrien's work desk.

BENNING

Having spent his early years as part of the Thexxian Exodus, fleeing from the Bardomil, the lack of proper nutrition had caused the bones of his lower legs to bow outwards. As he had grown to adulthood, the weakness in his lower legs had caused problems when he walked. This left Sownus with a strange almost waddling gait that for some was a source of mirth and amusement. Marrhus Lokkrien, however, was not one of those cruel and mocking individuals. Lokkrien knew a good, competent and efficient Intelligence Officer when he saw one. And, Karap Sownus was one of the best he had ever known.

"What is it, Officer Sownus?" the puzzled and confused Lokkrien asked his eyes drawn to the pink folio file in Sownus' hand.

"It's a low-level intercept from a local civilian broadcast on Bardan," Sownus began, "fairly routine stuff, very little intelligence value, but I thought it might interest you, sir."

"Why should it interest me, Officer Sownus?" Lokkrien asked, even more perplexed.

"Well, sir," the now anxious Sownus stammered, "it's about your eldest son, Gryeth, winning some kind of award," he held the folio over with a slight tremble in his hand, "there's no audio on it, I'm afraid, our lip-readers are still transcribing what they can from the images."

Stunned to silence, Lokkrien reached out his now shaking hand and took the folio sheet from the nervous Thexxian. Then, Lokkrien, still unable to believe what was happening, carefully set the folio on a larger plate built into his desk. A moment later, the mechanism automatically activated and a three-dimensional image sprang to life above the pink folio.

It was a surprisingly clear image for a civilian broadcast. The image opened with several rows of brown-uniformed young adult Bardomil males standing to attention in a large open courtyard that might have been a school or a military academy. A group of adult Bardomil males in slightly darker brown uniforms approached the parade of younger males. Then the shot cut to a head and shoulders close-up of a young Bardomil male who bore a striking resemblance to Marrhus Lokkrien.

When the young male's face appeared, Lokkrien let out a gasp of recognition and covered his mouth to choke back a sob. The image was unmistakably that of his eldest son, Gryeth. And, for a brief moment he felt a surge of paternal pride amongst the pain, anguish and loneliness.

Completely transfixed by the image, Lokkrien watched as one of the older Bardomil placed a medal, on a brown and blue ribbon, around his son's neck. He immediately recognised the diamond-shaped silver medal as a Vigilance Medal. Young Bardomil males only received such awards if they had successfully completed the military training element of their education to an exceptionally high standard. The award would mean that Gryeth Lokkrien would automatically qualify for Officer Cadet Training when he completed his schooling in two years time. Lokkrien himself had won such an award almost thirty years before. And, those proud memories flooded back into his mind, as he watched his son step smartly back and raise his right fist to shoulder level to salute the adult Officer.

The image then cut to a shot of an adult Bardomil female. Again, Lokkrien gasped. It was his wife, Senza, the proud mother watching her son receive his award. To Lokkrien she looked more beautiful than that first moment he had set eyes on her and fallen head over heels in love. The proud mother, Lokkrien wryly noticed, was wearing blue, not the traditional mourning red of the Bardomil widow. For a moment his heart sank down to his boot soles as he realised that to her he was dead. He had been listed as dead for many months now. But, life did go on, even for the widows of Imperial Fleet heroes on Bardan. As if to emphasise the point, an image of Lokkrien's own stern face, surrounded by a red ribbon, appeared to emphasise the award-winners illustrious connections to a fallen hero of the Empire. The fallen hero image was replaced by the broad beaming smile of his son as he was mobbed and congratulated by his class mates before the image finally faded.

For several seconds, Marrhus Lokkrien sat in a deafening silence. A swirling cocktail of emotions swept through his body as he tried to comprehend what he had just witnessed, and fought, in vain, to make some sense of it. Only the uncomfortable shuffling of Karap Sownus drew him back to his present reality. Looking at the anxious and now embarrassed Intelligence Officer, Lokkrien spoke softly. With his eyes glistening as he fought back the tears and struggled to hold his composure, he dropped back into his formal mode.

"Thank you for this, Officer Sownus" Lokkrien said, his voice barely above a whisper in the heavily charged silence, "I'll review it, and send you any relevant Intelligence details," he added almost as an after-thought.

"Yes, sir, anything you can tell us would be much appreciated," Sownus replied keeping up the professional pretence of the situation, and waddled slowly back to the door.

"Officer Sownus?" Lokkrien said with greater composure as the Thexxian reached the door.

"Sir?" the Thexxian responded and half-turned.

"Thank you," Lokkrien said with genuine sincerity.

"Good night, sir," Sownus replied, acknowledging that unspoken understanding that now existed between the two senior Officers.

BENNING

Both Sownus and Lokkrien would never speak of it, even in private, but a bond was being formed between the two of them. It was not quite friendship, but it was beyond the normal boundaries of duty and professional respect. Billy Caudwell would have called it common human decency. Lokkrien, the grieving husband and father, and Sownus, the orphan who had lost his mother and father at an early age, had found a degree of common ground.

"Good night, Officer Sownus," Lokkrien replied softly and operated the door mechanism.

When Karap Sownus had passed through into the corridor beyond, the opaque force-shielding returned Lokkrien to his thoughts. The most urgent of which was that the Alliance had to subdue the Bardomil Empire within the next three years. Gryeth had two more years of schooling, and then a year in Officer Training. After that, he would be commissioned to the Imperial Fleet and quite possibly sent to fight against the Universal Alliance. The very thought of his eldest son facing the Alliance's superior military technology and Billy Caudwell's strategic genius made Lokkrien shudder. He now had to double and re-double his efforts to bring down the Empress before he was forced to make the choice between his son and his loyalty the Alliance.

Activating the mechanism on the folio player, Marrhus Lokkrien re-played the images for the first of many dozens of times on that long night. He sat quietly, the tears streaming down his pale grey face, as he tried not to contemplate the horror of facing his own son in battle.

Silently, he prayed that Billy Caudwell would defeat the Empire before the nightmare of that particular day dawned.

THE BURNING SUN

Chapter 7

The Artreaus System

Two hours after the ignition of the emitter weapon, the Bardomil Empress waited patiently on her throne for the final act of the celestial drama that had unfolded before her. Slowly, and gradually, the yellow image of the advancing super-heated plasma had crept across the field of view on the fourth monitor.

For those two hours, the Bardomil Empress had sat quietly, eagerly anticipating the coming destruction and devastation. The tension and sense of dread and terror in the Battle Command Centre had, however, shown no discernible sign of decreasing. The faint murmur of communications traffic struggled to become distinct over the brutal hush of fear and intimidation. The crushing silence of the Battle Command Centre was broken only twice by the girlish shrieks of delight and dainty applause of the Empress as the super-heated plasma engulfed the second and fourth planets of the system. Both of these worlds were uninhabited, and now uninhabitable, but the Empress squealed like an overjoyed schoolgirl as the searing hot plasma scorched the already scarred and overheated surfaces of the two planets into a fiery oblivion.

With the fourth planet still being seared by the tail end of the super-hearted plasma flow, the Empress sat back on her throne with an air of malicious expectation. The next planet to orbit into the path of the plasma stream was Collizon. The peaceful, life-bearing planet was spinning slowly around to that side of the yellow dwarf star, filling the Bardomil Empress with a feeling of morbid delight and excitement.

It was all going exactly to plan, the Empress pondered as she watched the plasma stream edge closer to the orbit of Collizon. Just as the Xanart had predicted, the stream of super-heated plasma was able to emerge from the yellow dwarf star and cover the required distance to the intended target. It was a shame to have to kill Claggit and his assistant; they might have been of some limited value in future weapons development. But, the theoretical basis for the emitter weapon was now known to the Bardomil scientific community, which meant that bigger and more powerful weapons could be developed. And, more importantly, they could be developed without the risk of betrayal by aliens whose loyalty to the Empress was, at best, questionable. There would be no security leaks from the Imperial Ordnance Laboratories about this new emitter weapon.

The one remaining question was now whether the plasma stream would still have enough destructive power to wipe out everything on the inhabited planet. The scientists with their computer models and complex calculations had assured the Empress that there would be sufficient strength in the plasma flow to engulf Collizon three times over. The proof of the pudding, as the Empress well knew, would be in its eating. Computer models had been wrong before and costly mistakes had been made. But, this was one project the Empress was determined to see work. The scientists, like the senior military Officers were huddled at their stations hoping for a good outcome to the test. When the consequence of failure was a short trip out of an airlock, checking, double-checking and even beyond triple-checking became a way of life.

Silently, her black-orb eyes shining with anticipation, the Empress sat on the edge of the large throne. Scanning the four curved screens in front of her, she counted down the minutes and seconds until the super-heated plasma impacted with the atmosphere and surface of the planet. When it finally struck Collizon, the Empress stood up, her beautiful angelic face twisted in a snarl of evil delight. Fixing her gaze on the second screen, the Empress saw the live-action images of the destruction of a planet with millions of living creatures on it.

The first snaking tendrils of plasma swept in from the solar eruption and, for a few moments, it looked like the planet's magnetic field was going to protect the vulnerable world from the scorching horror. But, to the delight of the Empress there was just too great a volume of super-heated matter. The initial fingers, deflected away by the magnetic field, flared up like huge white hot waves crashing against the seashore as they surged out into space. With her fists clenching and her face growing into a mask of anxiety, the Empress watched as the following waves of plasma overwhelmed the magnetic field and were drawn down by the planets gravity, through the atmosphere to the defenceless surface.

Within moments, the deep emerald green oceans began to boil and evaporate causing a huge billow of white steam to radiate away from the first impact site. Fractions of a second later, the following waves of super-heated plasma scattered the ocean steam as it began to lick voraciously at the golden land masses of the planet. The great waves of searing death splashed onto the surface of the planet, and within a few seconds were sending out a front of surging plasma that rapidly spread away from the impact that covered almost half of the northern continent. Like a puddle of white hot liquid being forced outwards by more liquid being poured into it, the plasma wave began to sweep around the planet.

On the planet surface, the humanoid Manuch and all of the other living creatures in the path of the scorching onslaught spent their final moments in abject terror before succumbing to the mercifully short sting of instantaneous incineration. From her throne, safe aboard the Taurai, the Empress watched in vicious delight as the great fiery puddle spread even further across the golden surface of the planet. The doomed planet, set on its course billions of years before, spun slowly and languidly into its own destruction.

Within a few more seconds the wave-fronts collided; a beautiful yellow rippling effect showed that shock waves were surging through the ever-spreading lakes. They quickly poured over the northern and southern polar caps and disappeared to devour the obscured side of the planet. The Empress, meanwhile, sat in awe of the devastation being wreaked on the unprotected planet as the wave-fronts splashed toward the eastern and western horizons devouring everything in their path.

On the planet surface, nothing survived as a huge wall of surging fire swept across the landscape incinerating everything that stood in its way. The lush vegetation ignited for a few brief moments before the great roaring and shrieking wave of destruction swept over grasslands and forests with the same indiscriminate ferocity. Rivers boiled and evaporated in an instant as the fleeing animals screamed and made their final futile attempts to outrun the terror that pursued them to a horrible destruction. Rocks and soil on the surface melted under the intense heat; fusing for a few brief seconds into a beautiful golden glassy substance that was incinerated with the passing wave-fronts that would finally leave black charred carbon in their wake.

Aboard the Taurai, the Empress watched the lake of fire that now engulfed the hemisphere of the planet that she could see. Greater splashes of plasma were now hammering into the inferno that pushed the wave-fronts onwards on the blind side of the planet until they finally met. The end of all life on Collizon was marked with a huge rippling shock wave that swirled and eddied over the entire yellow scorching surface of the now dead world. For a few more seconds, the planet of Collizon looked like a huge shimmering yellow pearl hanging in the darkness of space. To someone not aware of what had just happened, it looked just like a newborn star as more waves of super-heated plasma hammered downwards.

The final agony of Collizon finally came when the atmosphere disintegrated. The following waves of plasma seemed to flow over the shimmering yellow pearl that had once been a living breathing thriving planet like a river over a rock. As the great stream of super-heated plasma swept over the planet, the intense heat finally broke down the gravitational field. With nothing to hold the burning plasma onto the surface of the planet, the fiery lakes that had incinerated Collizon were dragged back out into space leaving a scorched, bright-red glowing cinder.

With tears of delight in her black-orb eyes, the Empress daintily clapped her hands and marvelled at the power to destroy that she now commanded. It was beautiful and magnificent she praised the weapon that had wrought annihilation to an entire world. The weapon worked, she now knew, and it had the power to destroy Billy Caudwell's home planet. Sitting back on her throne, exhausted by the exhilaration of the demonstration, she began to outline in her mind the orders that would finally avenge the defeat suffered at Caudwell's hands. She had seen Collizon annihilated, planet Earth would go the same way very, very soon.

For the Bardomil Empress, that day couldn't come soon enough.

THE BURNING SUN

Chapter 8

Planet Earth

Jedithram Prust moved briskly along the corridor from first period Economics to second period History. Once again, the corridor thronged with the chattering press of students who were savouring the few minutes of liberty before submitting themselves to the classroom discipline required for their ongoing learning. The noise and bustle of the corridor was punctuated by excited shrieks and screams as well as the shouts and calls of horseplay and the flash of books being thrown around. Once more, overheated teachers attempted to impose some form of order onto the melee of young adult humanity that surged past the brown wooden sliding doors on the brightly lit corridor.

Smiling broadly, Jed was enjoying his mission to Earth. It had been almost a year since Senior Intelligence Officer Karap Sownus had approached him with the offer to double as First Admiral Caudwell. In that year, Jed had grown to enjoy his days and nights amongst the First Admiral's species. His orders had been straightforward and easy to carry out. Do not draw attention to yourself, do not get into trouble and defend yourself only as a last resort. Being invisible in a school of nearly one thousand students was easy. Staying out of trouble was a little less simple, but with the First Admiral's reputation, having brought down arch-bully Tim Reilly, there was no need for any form of violence or self-defence. So much so, that Jed had stopped using the force-shielding on his Personal Environment Suit for protection; it was now used simply to project the Billy Caudwell school uniform image.

"Move along there! Come on! Move it on!" an angry sounding male teacher called out above the scrimmage of jostling students as Jed turned left into the Staff Corridor.

The Staff Corridor, flanked by the various departmental staff rooms, was an adjoining corridor that linked the old Victorian-built school to the new modern tower block. It was one of those travesties of planning that had located the venerable History Department in the newest part of the school. The Staff Corridor was usually quiet and almost deserted as the two access points to the tower block from the old school were on the first floor above Jed.

Still smiling, Jed walked briskly along the Staff Corridor only vaguely aware of the group of older boys that had gathered by the stairwell close to the connecting door. It was a common enough sight in that part of school; the Monitors Common Room for the Sixth Formers, nominally charged with school discipline, was also located in the Staff Corridor. The group of half a dozen or so boys were laughing and joking as Jed approached them and made his way to the connecting door and his History lesson.

Suddenly, a leg shot out; the foot leaning against the wall opposite, blocking his progress along the corridor.

"Hello, hello, who do we have here then?" a voice called out from amongst the group.

"Come on, guys; I gotta get to mister McCrindle's," Jed smiled.

"I gotta get to mister McCrindle's," the voice mocked in a falsetto tone as its owner emerged from the depths of the group.

Michael Thomas Stewart, known as Micky, had just turned eighteen and was new to the school. By some strange quirk of fate, Micky had become a Monitor, having been appointed by the Rector. At just under two metres, Micky was tall with a powerful athletic physique. As a newcomer, Micky was an unknown quantity amongst the school body, but he seemed to be popular, especially amongst the girls; and he was quick-witted with a ready smile to share a joke.

"Seriously, I'll be in trouble if I'm late," Jed smiled.

Horseplay was part and parcel of any school's culture. At this school it was always intended to be fun and with no malice involved. With that mindset, Jed did not notice the other boys in the group beginning to form a circle around him.

"You're already in trouble for trespassing, Caudwell," Micky smiled wickedly.

"Come on, guys," Jed began and suddenly felt a powerful tug at his arm as his shoulder bag was snatched away from him.

"Oi!" Jed called, turning to see the smiling face of one of the boys holding his bag.

"Over here, Jimmy," a voice behind Jed called; and the bag was flung just over his head, to the caller.

"Hey, you may not have classes to go to but I have," Jed protested resigning himself to a game of chase and catch for his own books.

"Over here, Pete," another voice called and the bag sailed through the air once more.

Turning quickly and reaching up, Jed found he was only just a little too short to catch the bag.

"To me, Mike," another voice called out as the bag arced upwards once more.

Turning quickly again, Jed suddenly felt like his head had exploded as he was flung violently forwards onto his face. Stunned and dizzied, Jed then felt a vicious stabbing pain in his ribs as a well aimed kick was delivered to his torso. Being flung onto his back, Jed saw Micky with a heavy lump of wood in his hands.

"Hold him!" the hollow and distant sounding voice of Micky demanded as powerful hands dragged him to his feet pinioning his arms behind his back.

A split second later, Micky stepped forward and rammed the end of the piece of wood into Jed's stomach, doubling him over in a world of agony. No sooner had the impact of the wood registered in Jed's abdomen than Micky swung the lump of wood upwards to connect with Jed's face. For a few seconds, the world of Jedithram Prust disappeared into a loud BANG followed by darkness as he hung limply between the two boys who held him. As he came to, still unable to stand up, Jed started to curse his carelessness and with an effort of will instituted full force-shielding on his Personal Environment Suit before any more damage could be done.

"Listen closely, Caudwell," Micky Stewart hissed in Jed's ear, "they tell me that you're the tough nut round here, but as far as I'm concerned you're a loser; d'ya hear me?"

Unable to respond, Jed just stared blankly at his assailant.

"That's right, loser, you're finished," Micky continued, "this school's mine now, and as for taking Emma Wallace to the dance? Forget it, loser. I'm gonna take her away from you just because I can, comprendo? So, just remember who's in charge around here, loser."

Aching badly from the attack, Jed said nothing and felt himself being dropped to the ground. Lying on his side, Jed sent a thought-command to the microscopic machines in his Personal Environment Suit for medical assistance. A few seconds later, the pain from his beating was gone as tiny machines stimulated his brain to produce large doses of painkilling chemicals. The machines also began to produce the phoronic radiation that would start the healing process for his damaged muscles and tendons before he could teleport up to the Ranger and proper medical attention.

Staggering to his feet, Jed picked up his bag and began to lurch his way to the next lesson. The pain relief and the image of the PES would get him through that lesson. The First Admiral would pick up the incident at the next shift change, but Jedithram Prust vowed that any payback was going to be delivered by him.

"I thought you said this Caudwell was a tough nut?" the arrogant voice of Micky Stewart echoed in the distance.

BENNING

Chapter 9

<u>The Imperial Palace, Bardan</u>

Empress Lullina sat back on her onyx and white throne and yawned. Shifting her weight from one side of the throne to the other she felt the tedium of the situation even more acutely in her aching legs and buttocks than she did in her mind. Arranged in a loose semi-circle before her, the Military Advisory Council went through the motions of reporting the current status of the Empire to the bored, yawning Empress.

Required by ancient Bardomil law, the Military Advisory Council had no real authority or influence over the absolute power of Lullina, but she kept the tradition going mainly as a convenient means of keeping watch over the most powerful aristocratic families in the Empire who filled the ranks of its senior Officers. In days gone by, more than one Bardomil ruler had fallen foul of the leading military aristocratic families; many were related to the Empress, and as such were potential distant claimants to the throne. In reality, they were simply conduits for her orders to the vast Bardomil Imperial Armed Forces.

"...and finally, Your Imperial Majesty, may I present Junior Fleet Officer Batarrien?" the elderly General who spoke for the Council indicated.

"Proceed!" Lullina said with a formal stiffness, inwardly rejoicing that the current routine ordeal was almost over.

With a beckoning wave to one of the anterooms, the harsh sound of uniform boots on polished floor shattered the ominous silence of the meeting.

"Majesty, an honour," the voice of a young adult male sounded respectfully around the Throne Room.

"Yes," Lullina said languidly, and then noticed the young Officer, "and what do you have to present to us, Junior Fleet Officer?" she suddenly brightened up.

Always with a ready eye for a handsome young Officer, Lullina noticed the pleasing features and handsome physique of the young male before her, and sat forward on her throne.

"Majesty," the young Officer bowed and began nervously, "I have just completed a cultural, political and demographical survey of this so-called Universal Alliance, and I believe I may have discovered a military weakness that we can exploit."

"A weakness," Lullina smiled, "how interesting; do tell us more, Officer Batarrien."

"Majesty," he bowed once again, "I have taken the liberty of looking further into the composition of member species within this upstart Alliance; this is an area where our own Intelligence Services are remiss. I have also looked at the species within Alliance territory that are not Alliance members, and, hence, not considered to be a threat to the Empire,"

"How exciting," Lullina praised, "do continue," she waved her hand daintily to indicate for the handsome Officer to proceed.

"Majesty," he began again, "there is a group of five solar systems within the Nezadir galaxy that have no affiliation to the Universal Alliance. They are strategically located between the two main power blocs of the Alliance; the Thexxian..."

"Do not mention that name in my presence!" Lullina snapped, her mood changing in an instant.

"Majesty, a thousand pardons, but I merely wish to demonstrate a weakness that could well lead to the destruction of that, shall we say, troublesome, species," Batarrien bowed once more.

"Really?" Lullina suddenly smiled sweetly to the young Officer, "please tell us," she simpered.

"If I may, Your Majesty," Batarrien activated a huge holographic Display Screen that projected from equipment hidden in the Throne Room's high ceiling, "the current territorial extent of the Universal Alliance,"

On the huge screen, two large intersecting blobs, one blue and one red, indicating a schematic of the Universal Alliance as viewed from above.

"To Your Majesty's left, centred around the planet of Gardarus, we have THAT species expanding out towards the unclaimed territories beyond our frontier," he indicated, "to the right, we have the bloc centred around the planets of Colos, Therallian and Skrax that are pushing out towards the Ganthoran frontiers and those unclaimed territories."

"Yes, that's all very nice, but we are well aware of the Alliance's geography," Lullina started to lose interest even in the handsome young Officer.

"But with Your Majesty's permission, the Alliance is not a unified body within that territory. There are systems and species that have refused to join the Alliance or are uninhabited or are considered too primitive for membership, and are, thus, undefended," the young Officer activated the screen once more where patches of black appeared within the red and blue, "if I could draw Your Majesty's attention to this section."

The image zoomed down to five black areas, bordered by white, at the edge of the red sector that formed a ragged path from one side of the very edge of the red bloc to the other. The Empress, a very strategically aware creature, like most of those on her Military Advisory Council, stared open-mouthed at what appeared to be a fatal weakness in the Alliance's territorial possession.

"What are these systems, Officer?" the Empress watched the screen intently scrutinising the details and a plan forming in her mind.

"Erm, they are Praxos, Terra, Sidionas," Batarrien began to list the systems.

"Terra!?" the Empress interrupted, "did you say Terra!? Earth!?" she suddenly challenged, leaping up from her throne.

"Yes, Majesty, the second system," the confused Batarrien highlighted the second black shape in yellow, "is the Terran system; it has a yellow dwarf star and one inhabited planet called Terra or Earth."

"Majesty, if we could..." the General who spoke for the Council interjected excitedly.

"Yes, General, if we could," the Empress smiled, "Officer Batarrien, if we could drive a wedge between the two Alliance blocs, what would the effect be on our enemies?"

"Majesty," Batarrien began, "politically, the Alliance is still quite fragile. There is no centralised political control apparatus. Other than the military, this Alliance exists only as some abstract concept. If we can split the two blocs, those species such as the Hraxxon, the Ceradors and the Kalthans would abandon the Alliance and sue for peace with us. Withdrawing those species from the Alliance Fleet would seriously weaken their combat power. Many other species would question the wisdom of joining in the first place leaving the rump of this Alliance divided and, militarily, much weakened."

"Your Majesty, if we could only..." the General interrupted again, his eyes gleaming with excitement.

"Calm yourself, my dear, gallant, loyal, General Tetherrien," the Empress soothed her old war horse, "Fate has presented us with an opportunity to smite our enemies and bring glory and conquest to our Imperial forces, but we must lay our plans carefully if we are to succeed."

"Majesty, I live to serve," the elderly General bowed lowly, almost bursting into tears.

"Officer Batarrien, you have done well; we shall speak again later," Lullina promised, "Councillors, go back to your commands, prepare for battle and await instructions. We must meet with our Imperial Strategic Staff," she dismissed them all.

When the Council had gone, Lullina looked once more at the ragged pathway through the Thexxian territories and wondered why none of her planners had spotted this weakness. Perhaps, it was time for another purge of the intelligence services, she considered, and then dismissed the idea. What had originally been a retribution strike against Caudwell's home planet was now taking on a much greater significance.

One question still niggled at the back of Lullina's mind. Would Caudwell defend his home planet or the Alliance frontier? If Caudwell was a weak sentimental human, then the Alliance would fall, the loss of the Imperial Fleet Carriers would be avenged and the hated Thexxians finally exterminated.

It was far too good a chance to pass up, she considered.

BENNING

Chapter 10

The Star-Cruiser Aquarius

Intelligence Technician (Junior Grade) Marilla Thapes drew in one last anxious breath and sighed heavily. Steeling herself, she stepped forward onto the pressure plate that would announce her presence to Senior Intelligence Officer Karap Sownus.

Clutching three red Intelligence folios in her right hand she wondered, for the dozenth time in the last hour, whether she was making a mistake or not. However, having stood on the red fifteen centimetre square pressure plate, she realised there was no turning back now.

"Yes!?" came the familiar soft and reassuring reply from within his Private Office; the opaque grey force-shielding of the door cleared, allowing Marilla to enter.

"Sorry to bother you, sir...if you're busy I can..." Marilla began nervously.

"No, not at all, Marilla," Sownus beckoned her into his work space.

"I'm sorry to trouble you, sir, but there's something bothering me about some data I've viewed," Marilla drew a deep breath and approached the huge, harshly-lit work desk that was strewn with reports and data folios.

"What's on your mind, Marilla?" Sownus said in his usual matter-of-fact way.

Marilla Thapes, as one of the Intelligence Technicians aboard the Aquarius had an access to her senior Officer that very few Junior Grade, or JG, Technicians in other fields enjoyed. Karap Sownus actively encouraged this degree of access to his office, and greater informality, since he believed strict adherence to ranks and structures acted as a barrier to the communication that was so vital to this section.

"You might think this is pretty stupid, sir..." Marilla began stopping at the colossal desk; the three red folios in her clammy, sweaty hand suddenly felt very heavy.

"There's no such thing as stupid in Intelligence, Marilla; possibly wrong, but never stupid," Sownus began with a gentle smile, "take a seat and tell me what you think you've got."

Long experience had taught Karap Sownus never to ignore the suspicions of any of his Officers or Technicians. Even the craziest and most outlandish Intelligence Assessments could hold some vital nugget of truth or information. So, dismissing concerns out of hand was not part of

46

Sownus' normal response. From the side of the huge desk, a large black rectangle emerged and folded out into a high-backed chair.

"Thank you, sir," Marilla smiled awkwardly and set the folios on the desktop.

At just under one metre fifty, Marilla had to activate the adjustment control lever on the side of the seat to allow her to clamber onto the comfortable chair. As a Thexxian, like Sownus himself, Marilla Thapes had pale olive skin with straight dark hair. Where Sownus kept his hair regulation short, Marilla kept her hair long, as was tradition in her family. And, where Sownus wore the two-piece tunic and trousers uniform that allowed him to conceal his bowed legs, Marilla was happier in the figure-hugging one-piece overall.

"Well, sir," Marilla began, "I was scanning some of the data from the Bardomil Desk, and I think there's a possible development that you should be aware of."

Like most Intelligence organisations, the Universal Alliance divided its operations into what were called 'Desks'. There were currently twelve desks under the supervision of Karap Sownus, the Bardomil Desk being the largest in terms of people and resources. The Bardomil, as a hostile species, bore closer watching than the others. Some Desks were smaller, with only one Technician to monitor activities. And, some of these one-person Desks could cover whole sectors with hundreds of planets within them. It all depended on the level of threat that each species or area presented. The Bardomil Desk currently occupied almost one fifth of the capacity of Karap Sownus' department, with hundreds of Officers and Technicians, monitoring, sifting and analysing the data from a myriad of gathering sources. But, they all had the same objective; they were looking for patterns and clues to try to predict any possible threats and dangers from the Bardomil.

"Okay, what have you got, Marilla?" Sownus asked sitting back in his own comfortable chair.

"Well, it started with the report on the Bardomil Empress' sightseeing tour of that big solar flare in the Artreaus System, sir," Marilla opened, "quite a big flare from the yellow dwarf at the system's heart, it scorched three planets of the system."

"Go on," Sownus indicated to the nervous Technician.

As Senior Intelligence Officer, Sownus monitored the activities of the Bardomil Empress and knew that sightseeing and celestial fireworks were not part of her normal routine.

"Analysis was kind of stumped by that one, and put it down tentatively to one of her various vicious amusements," Marilla continued, "but, then I thought, sir, what causes large solar flares?"

"Magnetic anomalies within the star," Sownus answered correctly, "go on," he added, a strand of thought developing in his head.

"Then, I remembered a broadcast report from the planet Xanart," Marilla continued, an edge of excitement in her voice as she scooped out the first folio from the pile, "if you could, sir," she asked Sownus to put the folio on the reader.

Karap Sownus dropped the red folio onto the plate and watched the three-dimensional image of an elderly male Xanath, with long dark ringlets develop above the surface of his desk.

"This is Sammut Claggit, sir," Marilla announced, "Claggit and his assistant Marrut Bem were, according to planetary sources, killed in a hunting accident several weeks ago, which is rather strange as Science Master Claggit had a weak heart, was a herbivore and had a major aversion to blood sports."

"You suspect that he was killed?" Sownus asked.

"Yes, sir; furthermore, Sammut Claggit was a respected authority on magnetic and gravitational fields. In fact, it was last reported that he was researching magnetic field manipulation to alter planetary magnetospheres to make them suitable for habitation."

"Well, well," Sownus said with an edge of growing surprise and certainty in his voice, "our late friend Sammut Claggit was into magnetic field manipulation, was he?"

"Yes, sir," Marilla answered growing more confident in her theory, "and his last known location was on Bardan working for the Imperial Academy of Sciences, Peace and Friendship,"

"That well-known weapons development facility close to the Imperial Palace," Sownus smiled wryly.

"The very same, sir," Marilla smiled at the shared irony.

"So, you are speculating that the Bardomil have developed some kind of weapon?" Sownus asked.

"It is one possible interpretation," Marilla replied, "I contacted Long Range Scanners, and they sent me over the analysis from the Explorer-class Scientific Survey Ship, Vasco da Gama, which was scanning the Artreaus system's area at the time," she indicated the second folio on the desk.

"And, it indicated?" Sownus questioned half-knowing the response before it came.

"The Vasco da Gama data indicates that it is unlikely the solar flare was natural in origin," Marilla began, "it was a quick-burn eruption outside the regular cyclical pattern of activity for that particular star, and it was a yellow dwarf, so it's too young and small as a star to produce enough material to burn planets in the system under normal conditions."

"So, our sightseeing friend, the Bardomil Empress, just happened to be passing when the Artreaus sun decided to magically become active with an unfeasibly large solar flare?" Sownus pushed the speculation onwards.

"A bit of a coincidence, sir," Marilla replied, "and, the Vasco da Gama data showed a massive interruption in the Artreaus sun's magnetic field prior to the eruption of the flare,"

"That would not be a natural phenomenon would it?" Sownus asked speculatively, seeing where the conversation was leading.

"Not by any stretch of the imagination, sir," Marilla confirmed.

"Very well, I'll bite, Marilla," Sownus sighed wearily not liking the conclusion one little bit, "what do you suggest we do next?"

"Well, sir, with your permission, I could contact the Fleet Engineers Corps and speak to the people in Theoretical Weapons," Marilla suggested relieved that her theory was being taken seriously.

"That's a good idea, have a word with the 'Funnies' about it, see if such a thing is even feasible," Sownus indicated the nickname of the Theoretical Weapons Developers who produced weapon solutions for some of the most unusual situations.

"Could I also have a look at some of the more sensitive data from the Bardomil Desk and the long-range data?" Marilla asked rising from her chair.

"Hmm, are we being just a little bit ambitious here Technician Thapes?" Sownus smiled, being aware that her Security Clearance was only a few steps above basic level.

"Sorry, sir, if I've over-stepped my..." Marilla replied swallowing heavily, her growing confidence now shaken.

"No, Marilla, not at all, I'm temporarily raising your Clearance level to bronze, that should give you access to the Sensitive-level data on the Bardomil Desk," Sownus said, "you've earned this opportunity; if you do well, we can think about moving you up the board."

"Yes, sir, thank you, sir," Marilla Thapes beamed broadly.

In the Security structure of the Intelligence Department, bronze clearance was only three steps down from the Ultra-Sensitive level clearance that carried a Diamond-icon on their Security file. She had gained a significant temporary promotion, and was determined to do her absolute best with the project.

"Your new clearance should be active by the start of your next shift," Sownus added, "now, take your findings to Officer Drang. She will be your supervisor on this and coordinate any resources you need to clarify what is going on here. But, you report your findings to me, am I clear?"

"Yes, sir," Marilla barked, the broad beaming smile still plastered all over her olive face.

"Good," Sownus said, "now, go and get some rest and be ready to hit the deck running first thing."

"Sir," Marilla replied and gathered up her folios before stepping briskly to the door.

"And, Marilla?" Sownus halted her just before the door.

"Sir?" she half-turned expecting more instructions.

"That's a good piece of work, Technician," Sownus praised.

"Thank you, sir," Marilla's smile got even broader as she stepped through the door and walked breezily along the corridor to her own quarters.

Back in Sownus' office, the Senior Intelligence Officer now had a new nightmare to add to the growing pile of potential threats to the Alliance. Moving to his dimly-lit relaxation couch, Sownus scanned the folios left by Marilla Thapes and began asking himself the questions that First Admiral Caudwell would ask him. Is it feasible? Where would they target such a weapon? How would they deliver it to the intended target?

But, as he thought, he found the answers elusive.

Chapter 11

Planet Earth

"Emma, Billy, would you like some tea!?" Gillian Wallace called brightly from the foot of the stairs.

It had been a whole ten minutes since she had last offered them some refreshment. The constant procession of young men into the Wallace household had made Gillian Wallace cautious of just what has likely to be happening in her daughter's bedroom. The liberally-minded parent understood that Emma needed her freedom to meet young men, but the mother in her wasn't quite ready to let go of her 'little Emma' just yet.

"No thanks mum!" the voice of Emma Wallace replied from behind the solid rampart of her closed bedroom door.

"Some lemonade or juice!?" her mother persisted.

"No! Thanks mum!" Emma responded wearily.

"I think we should take a break," Billy Caudwell suggested as he stood up from the cramped little table in the corner of Emma Wallace's room.

It had been a long and exhausting two hours since he had arrived at the Wallace's house to help Emma with her maths revision. Burying his face in his hands and wiping his eyes, Billy had to admit that in terms of mathematics, Emma Wallace was not the brightest candle on the tree. But, he had promised to help her through the pre-Qualification exams, and help her he would; even if it did take over half an hour for her to grasp the most fundamental concepts of equations.

Yet, strangely, Billy felt calm and at peace as he gently guided the struggling girl through the finer points of algebra; where x and y took on new meanings, but still retained some semblance of constancy and familiarity. Rather like his own life, Billy considered, as he tried to integrate a life on Earth with that of the First Admiral of the Universal Alliance Fleet. But, the worries of the rapidly expanding Alliance were far from the thoughts of Billy Caudwell this night.

"Yeah, my head hurts," Emma said, "but, you're really helping me here," she flashed the dazzling but wholly insincere smile.

"It just takes a bit of time and practice," Billy modestly deflected the praise as he stared at a poster of four well-dressed young men who appeared to be wearing more make up than his appearance conscious grandmother usually did.

"My dad would go mental if I ever turned up looking like that," Billy smiled indicating the poster.

"I think they're quite cool," Emma replied from the table "I suppose you're a classical music man?" she questioned.

"No, not really," Billy countered, "My dad's into Italian Opera and when he has a drink he thinks he's Enrico Caruso."

"Who's that then?" Emma asked.

"A famous Italian tenor, died years ago," Billy said absent-mindedly looking at another poster.

"I'm more kind of machine music, Human League, Soft Cell and Gary Newman, that sort of stuff," Billy continued, being careful not to mention the Thexxian musicians in a band called "Splarge" that he found particularly enjoyable.

"My mum says that Gary Newman needs a good dinner or two," Emma smiled mischievously.

"She might be right," Billy grinned, and had to agree; the memory of the very pale and very thin lead singer/composer flashing through his mind, "he is a bit on the skinny side."

"Hey, you want to listen to some Duran Duran?" Emma enthused rising from her seat behind the table.

"Yeah, sure," Billy replied as brightly as he could manage, not all that excited about listening to a singer who seemed to sound like he was constantly in pain.

"I think they're brilliant," Emma chirped happily as she trotted over to her clock/radio/cassette player that doubled as an alarm to get her out of bed in the mornings.

"I liked their early stuff better," Billy commented, "a real good old-fashioned gutsy rock and roll band, then they kind of went all Spandau Ballet didn't they?"

"You're in very real danger of becoming a square, Billy Caudwell," Emma chided as she dug through the collection of cassettes scattered on her bedside table.

"Well, just shoot me now," Billy said absent-mindedly as he watched the tall blonde girl, her face set in determined purpose, as she sought out the desired tape.

God, she is just so lovely, Billy thought to himself watching the object of his affections. Yet, in the back of his mind, the part of his consciousness that was the now-dead Garmaurian First Admiral, Teg Skarral Portan, warned him not to get too close. A Supreme Military Commander really did not need any emotional distraction from an unstable relationship. It was going to be difficult enough to keep the secret of his double life from his family without the added complication of romantic entanglements. But, God, she was just so lovely, he thought.

"Billy?" Emma broke into his daydreaming, "you were far away there," she said.

"Yeah, sorry, it's just..." Billy began and leaned forward to kiss Emma.

Seeing the movement, Emma twisted her face away and pushed hurriedly past Billy as the music from the cassette player cut in.

"What's the matter?" a confused Billy asked, as Emma stepped over to the study table.

"It's just...it's just," she flustered, trying to find an excuse that would placate Billy without exposing her true intentions of keeping him on as a free disposable Math tutor to be cast aside when finished with but without giving the impression of leading him on.

"Don't you like me...?" Billy asked his heart slowly sinking.

"Yes, yes I do," Emma flustered again, holding back the infamous 'but-not-in-that-kind-of-way' sting in the tail, "it's just that you caught me by surprise that's all,"

"You do!? Well, surely you guessed that I really liked you?" Billy smiled, his confidence growing, as Emma sat down to her books once again.

"Well, yes, I suppose I did; I just didn't think you'd want do anything about it before the dance," she said coyly, trying to keep it as ambiguous as possible.

Sitting at the table, Emma silently cursed herself. The defence of 'you-must-have-misread-the-signs' had bitten the dust. She now had to find an alternative exit strategy to extricate herself from the predicament.

"But, we can do something about it now?" Billy questioned joining her at the table.

"Look, can we focus on the maths, here?" Emma countered trying to work her way of the maze, "I just need some time to take it all in...it's just so sudden."

"I'm sorry if I've upset you, Emma," Billy said sensing something was not quite right.

"No," Emma responded shakily, gently taking hold of Billy's wrist "I just didn't expect...so soon...look, we should leave this until Thursday and the dance; then we can start going out together properly. I really want to understand these equations, and I can't if my mind's..." she chose her words carefully.

"Yeah, sure," Billy smiled, his heart leaping, and took up his pen to set Emma some problems for what they had been working on.

BENNING

"Thanks, Billy," Emma smiled gently squeezing his wrist, relieved to have bought herself some more time to get out of this increasingly awkward situation.

Oh dear; this is going to get very messy, Emma Wallace thought to herself.

Chapter 12

<u>The Nezadir Galaxy, Bardomil-Alliance Frontier</u>

"What are they up to Scanners?" the Ship Commander of the Universal Alliance Ranger Class patrol vessel, Clements, asked hunching over the Scanner monitor.

"I don't know, ma'am," the Scanner Technician, a young Cerador named Tharrum replied, "I've never seen this kind of activity before."

"They're up to something," the Ship Commander, a Thexxian named Gallus Takkrienen muttered softly, "I can feel it in my bones."

On the Scanner screen, a single Bardomil M-Cruiser with the bent gull-wings was loitering just within its own side of the frontier. Beside the M-Cruiser, four Flying Devil gunships seemed to be providing a security screen. The Flying Devil was a simple saucer design with two horn-like projections to the rear of the vessel, which produced the electro-magnetic drive. The drive sparked angrily, as the vessel moved, giving it the appearance of a flaming Devil. A dozen Harpoons, single-seat fighters shaped like a curved arrow-head that were the mainstay of the Bardomil Imperial Fleet, scampered and swooped through the small formation providing picket duty amongst the host of tumbling space rocks.

"What are they up to?" Gallus muttered in frustration as she watched the Harpoons blast at the slowly tumbling and rolling rocks with their laser weapons, "I'd entertain any speculation," she added to the hawk-like Scanner Technician.

For some unknown reason, the M-Cruiser had to be stationery in the area and the Harpoons and Flying Devils had to protect it from the flying rocks.

"I'd be happy to share it if I had one, ma'am," the equally puzzled Technician replied.

"It just doesn't feel right, Tharrum," Gallus sighed, "notify the Magellan to keep an eye on this little gathering."

"Aye, ma'am," Tharrum replied and ordered to signal the Explorer-class Scientific Survey ship, Magellan, which was in the area.

The more sensitive and accurate scanners of the Magellan could capture and relay a far superior quality of data than the Ranger-class patrol ship.

Built originally by the Garmaurians for covert surveillance, the Ranger was nearly obsolete by their standards. The inability of any species to discover the Ranger had meant that the design had changed very little in several centuries. More suited to policing, the Ranger was not designed for battle. Consequently, the Ranger was poorly armed although it did have force-shielding protection and a Trion Drive for long range patrols. Two long, cylindrical, energy-hungry Thrust Engines sat on a heart-shaped super-structure that gave the Ranger its shape. But, with only one medium-yield pulsar-cannons for armament, it was badly outgunned by the M-Cruiser and the Flying Devils just over the frontier.

"Magellan reports eye-on, ma'am," Tharrum announced.

"Very well," Gallus replied, "Navigator, take us in for a closer look."

"Aye, ma'am," the Navigator, another Thexxian, replied from his console.

The Command Cabin of the Ranger was laid out in a semi-circle with three consoles to the left and two to the right of the Ship Commander's seat. To the left of the Ship Commander was the Weapons And tactical Officer or WATO, the Flight Engineer, and the Navigator; to the right, the Communications Officer and the Scanner Technician maintained their vigils.

"How close do you want to get, ma'am?" the Hubbart Navigator asked.

"Close enough to see, but don't crowd them," Gallus replied, "Just stay this side of the frontier."

"Aye, ma'am," the Navigator replied.

No sooner had the Navigator spoken than Gallus felt the Clements move away from her station.

The two massive Thrust Engines drawing energy from the proto-star reactor drove the Ranger out towards the Bardomil position. In the Command Chair, Gallus activated her own personal Display Screen. The side of the Command Chair detached itself on a long, spindly telescopic arm that pivoted into place in front of Gallus like a dinner tray. When the Screen finally whirred and clicked into place, a two dimensional image of the Bardomil contingent came into sharp focus.

The stationery M-Cruiser surrounded by the Flying Devils and the darting Harpoons still lay amongst the rocks that floated and drifted across Gallus' screen.

"Any indication of what they're doing?" Gallus asked the Scanner Technician once more.

"It looks like they are collecting rocks, ma'am," the Scanner Technician replied.

"What?" a puzzled Gallus asked.

"Just exactly as I said, ma'am," Tharrum replied, "they've just taken in a small rock through their forward air lock."

"What are they..." Gallus asked.

"Maybe they're doing some exploratory mineralogy," The WATO, another Thexxian, butted in.

"There's nothing of any value out there," the Scanner Technician answered.

"Rock being ejected, ma'am," the Scanner Technician added.

"What is going on?" a frustrated Gallus blurted once again and tried to focus her Screen image on the air lock of the M-Cruiser.

In close-up, the image was blurred and grainy, but the discernible shape of a rock was visible emerging slowly from the rectangular black aperture.

"Was that the same rock that went in?" Gallus asked, suddenly forming a thought in her mind.

"Unknown, ma'am," the Scanner Technician replied honestly, "I'm retrieving data and analysing."

"Well?" Gallus asked impatiently.

"It appears not, ma'am," the Scanner Technician answered, "the rock being ejected is smaller and a different shape than the one that was just taken aboard."

"What's so special about that rock then?" Gallus mumbled to herself.

"Nothing, ma'am," the Scanner Technician picked up on her question, "there are no metals, no precious minerals, nothing."

"There must be something," Gallus stared at the image more intently.

"We're at five thousand kilometres from the Bardomil position," the Navigator explained.

"How close are we to the frontier?" Gallus asked.

"One hundred kilometres," the Navigator answered.

"Right, nobody sneezes or we'll be at war," Gallus said sternly.

The Clements was as close to the frontier as they dared. Any nearer to Bardomil territory and there would be a major incident. The tension in the Command Cabin was high; however, the crew trusted Gallus Takkrienen. Gallus had played a lot of brinksman-ship with Bardomil vessels over the last year and seemed to know just how far to push them.

"The M-Cruiser has picked us up on their scanners," the Communications Officer announced.

"Stay calm everyone, we're on our side of the frontier, let them have a good long look," Gallus answered.

For several seconds that seemed like hours, Gallus held her anxious crew in check with her calm and confident manner as the Bardomil scanning beams swept over the Clements.

"Another rock being ejected, ma'am," the Scanner Technician added to the tension.

"The same one they just took aboard?" Gallus challenged.

"No, ma'am," the Scanner Technician responded, "it's the one they took aboard just prior."

"So, they're testing them for something?" Gallus speculated as the screen image showed a small rock tumbling and rolling slowly away from the M-Cruiser.

"Would it be worth picking one of those rocks up, ma'am?" the WATO asked speculatively.

"No," a distracted Gallus replied, "If they're rejecting these rocks, then they obviously haven't got what the Bardomil are looking for."

"The Flying Devils are changing course, ma'am," the Scanner Technician warned, "They're heading straight for us."

"Very well, keep your hair on kiddies," Gallus warned as she watched the four Flying Devils start to manoeuvre in her direction on the screen image.

Now, Gallus Takkrienen was convinced that the Bardomil were up to something very secretive and, hence, very dangerous to the Alliance.

"Challenge them, Comms," Gallus instructed.

"No response, ma'am," the Communications Officer responded.

"Well, keep trying," Gallus ordered as the Flying Devils seemed to be forming into a rough line formation that was rapidly closing on the frontier.

"Still no response, ma'am," the Communications Officer called out anxiously.

"Engineer, get the force-shielding up," Gallus ordered starting to feel anxious herself, "WATO, get the pulsar-cannon activated."

"Shielding established!" the Flight Engineer barked.

"Pulsar-cannon ready," the WATO said more calmly.

"Are they still not answering?" Gallus asked the Communications Officer.

"No, ma'am," the reply came back.

"Notify Fleet Command, that we might have an incident here," Gallus said as calmly as she could manage in front of her crew.

"Do we withdraw, ma'am?" the WATO asked.

"No," Gallus said grittily, "we stand our ground; if they cross the frontier then they start a war, not us."

"Ma'am, we can't handle four Flying Devils," the WATO explained.

"I'm well aware of that," Gallus responded as she watched the Flying Devils hurtle towards her on the screen image.

"They're getting awful close, ma'am," the Scanner Technician alarmed.

"I see them," Gallus responded her own level of anxiety rising rapidly.

"They're closing on the frontier," the Scanner Technician called out.

"Come on, come on; turn around!" Gallus urged the Bardomil Flying Devils as they approached the line on her image that indicated the frontier.

Whatever the Bardomil were up to out there it couldn't be worth starting a war over, Gallus considered. Yet, the four Flying Devils were heading straight for her position on the Alliance side of the frontier.

"They're opening fire!" the WATO yelled and Gallus saw the tell-tale tiny yellow streaks of laser fire on her screen image.

"Inform Fleet Command," Gallus began before the Clements was hit by Bardomil weapons fire, "Bardomil have opened fire upon us; repeat opened fire upon us."

The Ranger craft, although force-shielded was shaken like a rag doll in a child's hands. Crew members were flung from their consoles as the Bardomil laser bolts struck home.

"Navigator, get us out of here!" Gallus ordered as she clambered back into her Command Chair.

"Do we return fire!?" the WATO yelled as the Clements was shaken once more by the Bardomil lasers.

"Negative!" Gallus replied and resumed watching her screen.

The Navigator; having resumed his seat at his console, quickly swung the Clements around and engaged the massive Thrust Engines. As the Clements beat a hasty retreat from the action, she shook under the impact of laser fire once again.

"They're over the frontier!" the Scanner Technician yelled.

"Message from Fleet Command, return fire only as last resort," the Communications Officer shouted.

"Give me the strength to live!" Gallus muttered the old Thexxian curse at the sheer stupidity of it all.

"Clarify, 'last resort', Comms," Gallus ordered.

What did Fleet Command mean by 'last resort'? The Bardomil outnumbered her, were chasing her ship and were trying to kill her and her crew, how desperate did the situation need to be, she grumbled to herself.

"Alliance Star-Cruiser exiting Trionic Web ahead of us!" the Scanner Technician yelled as the Clements was hit once more, "it's the Vanguard!"

"That's more like it!" Gallus cheered.

She knew the Ship Commander of the Vanguard. He was another experienced Thexxian commander who had served against the Bardomil.

The Vanguard would have the Bardomil back over the frontier before they could snap their fingers, Gallus thought.

Still scampering away from the Flying Devils, Gallus considered dropping the Clements into the Trionic Web, but then considered a more aggressive course of action.

"Navigator," she called out, "let's take these heroes for a little ride shall we?" she lurched about in her Command Chair, "set course to the Vanguard, please."

"Yes, ma'am," the Navigator smiled.

Gallus was going to lead the four Flying Devils straight into the path of the approaching Vanguard. A brief course deviation later and Gallus was feeling a lot happier about the situation she now found herself in.

Switching her screen to a rear view, Gallus could see the Bardomil laser bolts rushing towards the Clements, but missing. Like fireworks, the laser shots zipped past the Clements as she dodged and weaved her way towards the bigger Alliance vessel. With each flash, Gallus' heart seemed to leap into her mouth, but she knew that with every passing second she was leading them closer to the Vanguard.

Seconds later, the rear-ward image on the screen showed dozens of the Alliance's, wedge-shaped, single-seat Eagle fighters swarming past the Clements and rushing in to attack the Flying Devils.

The four Bardomil craft had no real chance against the Eagles. The first pass from the Eagles slammed the rapid fire, low–yield pulsar-bolts into their hulls at the rate of five per second. Before their crews could even realise what was happening, two of the Flying Devils had vanished in great blossoms of red roaring flame. The two surviving Devils tried desperately to swing around, but were instantly caught in a hail of deadly white-hot pulsar-bolts. The bolts slammed into the hulls of the Flying Devils like a torrent smashing them to space dust in a few moments.

"Right, Navigator, bring her about," Gallus ordered as the last of the Flying Devils perished in a cataclysmic explosion, "and send a message to Vanguard, say 'thanks for the assist' and sign it Gallus."

Feeling the Clements swing around Gallus watched on her screen as the contingent of Eagles from the Vanguard swept on towards the frontier.

"Message from Vanguard, ma'am, 'our pleasure, do you have any more friends that want to play' and it is signed Falkus."

"Falkus Targianen, you old space pirate," Gallus laughed at the message from her old friend, "send reply 'unwelcome visitors at frontier' and give them the coordinates," Gallus ordered.

"Aye, ma'am," the Communications Officer smiled as Gallus settled back into her Command Chair.

THE BURNING SUN

"Navigator, let's go and see how rough the big boys play," Gallus smiled as she looked forward to the Vanguard hammering these Bardomil out of existence.

In the shadow of the big Star-Cruiser, the Ranger-class patrol vessel Clements sped back towards the frontier.

When Vanguard and the Clements arrived, the battle was all but over. The surviving Harpoons were already scampering away from the rampaging Eagles, whilst the solitary M-Cruiser was trying to execute a lumbering turn. It was already doomed as the faster and more agile Eagles hammered their low-yield pulsar-bolts into the Bardomil vessel's vulnerable hull. Gallus arrived just in time to witness the M-Cruiser's death throes as the Eagles strafed along its cylindrical fuselage. The low-yield bolts tore lumps of metal and debris from its hull as they sped over the doomed craft. In the final moments, an Eagle shot along the top of the fuselage causing plumes of flame and destruction to sprout up like orange and red summer flowers. When the Eagle had passed over, the M-Cruiser seemed to collapse in on itself. Both of the gull-wings fell in against the fuselage just before the whole vessel exploded.

"Gotcha!" Gallus cheered along with the rest of her crew as they watched the huge conflagration of the M-Cruiser tearing itself apart.

Having dispatched the M-Cruiser, the Vanguard slowly set off in pursuit of its own Eagles. Meanwhile, the Clements stayed behind and began to investigate the area where the Bardomil had been so interested in the rocks. After ten minutes of exhaustive scanner sweeps, Gallus Takkrienen was still no clearer as to what the Bardomil had been up to.

"Anything?" Gallus asked the Scanner Technician, not sure whether she wanted to find something out of the ordinary or not.

"Nothing, ma'am," the Scanner Technician reported bleakly, "There's nothing out there but a whole bunch of rocks."

"Whatever they were up to, I think we might have stopped them," Gallus sighed hopefully, "right Navigator, get that Trion Drive warmed up they'll want a report of this at Fleet."

A few moments later, the Clements disappeared into the Trionic Web with a blinding flash leaving the rock fields to their lonely unending orbits. When the Clements had disappeared, the emitter weapon that had only just survived the destruction of the M-Cruiser detached itself from the large rock it had been clinging to and turned metallic silver and fluid once more. Then, resuming its original rock-like structure and colour, the weapon opened four small vents in its outer body work. At some unspoken command the vents spurted fire and flames for a few moments as the small guidance and drive engines sent the small, but deadly, weapon on its long and lonely odyssey to its target.

<u>Chapter 13</u>

<u>Planet Earth</u>

John Caudwell sat in the opulently decorated lounge bar of one of the most exclusive and expensive, hotels in London. In front of him, on the elegant green marble table, stood a large glass of some cheap imported cola flooded to the point of watery tastelessness by a dozen roughly-shaped cubes of ice, and a shrivelled excuse for a slice of lemon.

The tall elegant glass was coated with a heavy mist of condensation that told John that the cola was chilled to well below room temperature. That was just fine by John, who enjoyed watching the little rivulets of moisture creep slowly down the side of the glass carving a cola-dark furrow through the white sheen. Once again, lost in his known thoughts, John wondered what on earth was happening to him. The calmness and serenity of the quiet lounge bar was quite at odds with his troubled mind. The soft subdued lighting greatly at odds with the seething cauldron of his thoughts.

Life had never been this complicated before, he considered, and took a sip of the watered-down cola. Somehow, something had changed, and in John's mind the responsibility for that change lay squarely with Elizabeth's literary success. Before the success of her book, they had managed to get along with each other. Now that she had a great deal of "her money" she had become an entirely different person. The mood swings, the temper tantrums, the fights about nothing and the rages were something that John had suspected Elizabeth was capable of. He had just never seen such a torrent of unbridled rage and anger directed at him, and he had never expected to see it from Elizabeth.

Elizabeth wanted to pack Billy off to some ridiculously expensive private school up in the Scottish Highlands; which would at least keep him out of the way of the arguments and rows. That was probably for the best, John thought. Elizabeth had coddled and cosseted the boy since the loss of their daughter, and it was about time he got sent out into the big wide world to learn how to be a man. It was a tough life out there, and John wanted to see his son toughened up to face it. He also wanted to make sure that Billy Caudwell didn't make the same mistakes that he had made in life. John, after almost sixteen years, was still not quite sure that Elizabeth's "accidental pregnancy" hadn't been a deliberate trap.

Well, whatever the truth, he had walked into that trap, and he was going to make sure that Billy worked hard at school, got good grades, went to University and had a good career. After that it was very much up to Billy himself, but John would make sure that no opportunistic female would trap his son the way he had been trapped. He hated having to do it, but it was for the boy's own good, John had convinced himself. At fifteen years old, John had been bringing girlfriends home to his parents, but at the same age, Billy was showing very little interest in the young girls at school, and that was just fine by John.

But, if truth were to be told, John was also jealous of his son. John had made many mistakes in his life. Now, Billy was likely to be able to achieve all the things that John had been denied. And, a part of John hated Billy for that. Sure, John dearly loved his son, and he was so proud of what Billy had achieved, but a part of him also hated and resented the young boy who would have the opportunities in life that he himself had squandered or had been denied by circumstances.

It was something that annoyed and angered John, because he did feel guilty for resenting his own son. His duty as a father was to support and encourage his son, and John did the best he could. John would sacrifice, sweat, slave, bleed and die, if necessary, for his only son. But, he had no idea how to speak to the boy. Having never really been close to his own father, John didn't exactly know how to communicate with his son. As a result, the boy was far closer to his paternal grandfather than he was to his father. John remembered that he too had been closer to his grandfather than he had been to his father. Again, this was something that John resented deep down. It seemed to be the curse of the Caudwell males never to have close relationships with their fathers.

He knew he was hard on young Billy at times, and that sometimes he didn't get it right. Sometimes the anger of his own failures crept through, and he lashed out verbally at young Billy. But, it was a hard cruel world out there, and Billy needed to be equipped to handle it. Life wasn't fair and Billy had to understand that. A part of John actually believed that the inconsistencies would make Billy a stronger person. The other part of him knew that he was pretending to himself, and made him feel accordingly guilty and ashamed. That was one of the drawbacks of being a father, you just couldn't be right all the time.

In the left inside pocket of his newly-purchased, finely-tailored pinstripe suit jacket, John Caudwell carried his own personal copy of the newly signed contract with Nakamura Corporation. In the expensive buff envelope next to his new Mont Blanc fountain pen, a gift from Mister Nakamura himself, was the answer to all his prayers and the source of his ongoing worries. John had just sold his idea, a prototype three-dimensional music and video player, to the Nakamura Corporation. They had paid, at the current exchange rate, just over fourteen million pounds, plus a two percent royalty on every unit sold. Sales projections from Nakamura had indicated that in the first year alone they expected to sell over one hundred and fifty million units worldwide. At the equivalent price of sixty pounds per unit, this would give John in the region of one hundred and forty million pounds in royalties in his first year. As production costs fell, given the huge numbers of units produced by the Japanese factories, the price to the customer would fall. Cheaper units would then generate greater sales, which would boost John's earnings even further.

That was a colossal sum of money for an ordinary working man from Southern Scotland. Given that John had only just quit his mind-numbingly boring job in a plastics factory, where he stood at a machine for eight hours solid and worked three shifts a week; he had pulled off quite a coup. Although his newly-acquired expensive Accountant had warned him that Her Majesty's Exchequer would want a large share of his hard-earned income.

Spreading the contract out on the table, John looked at the piece of paper that had just made him richer than his wildest dreams. Still, he was confused. Looking blankly at a piece of paper that was worth fourteen million pounds, John couldn't believe how complicated his life had become in such a short space of time. It had been just over a year since he had woken up one morning with a blinding headache and ideas in his head for the most fantastic machines he had ever dreamt of. Having served an apprenticeship as a motor mechanic in his youth, before joining the police force, John had a pretty good idea as to what was and was not technologically possible. And, the ideas and blueprints running through his mind were just too fantastical to be technologically viable in his lifetime, or even on this planet.

Current technology was producing large cumbersome video cassette recorders and the first word processing machines that everyone said would soon make typewriters obsolete. But, John had visions of huge networks that everyone on Earth could be connected to by small computers in their homes. That was the stuff of science fiction writers surely, he had convinced himself. He visualised homes where a central computer could control and coordinate all the automated functions of the household. Central heating, light switches, drawing the curtains, even robotic cleaning machines that would operate when the householders were not at home.

All these visions flashed through John's mind. But, more disturbing were the visions he had about military hardware. He saw in his mind's eye vast warships in space with weapons of unbelievably destructive ability at their command. They could travel billions and billions of kilometres in the blink of an eye. They had weapons that could lay waste to cities and wipe out entire populations. But, the most troubling of his visions was of a weapon that he seemed to have called a Trionic Cannon. John had never in his life heard of such a thing.

Being a relatively level-headed and unimaginative child, he had never dwelt on science fiction or little green men or Martian invaders, which made this sudden splash of scientific creativity all the more troubling. John had been far more interested in cars and mechanical machines when he had been younger, not Death Rays and Space Rockets.

Unknown to John, the night before the raging headache, his son, Billy, had implanted the Mind Profile of one of Garmauria's greatest scientists and inventors into his brain. Billy had scoured the historical records and archives and found a rich industrialist named Mallor Sharpal. Sharpal had been a technological genius who had been at the forefront of Trion technology and had subsequently made a huge fortune providing weapons systems to the military. Sharpal had developed and built the first proto-type Trionic Cannon.

It was the visions of the Trionic Cannon that really troubled John. He knew it was fantastical, but his mind also showed him equations and mathematical proofs that looked oddly familiar, and at the same time troublingly realistic. On Earth, John knew that the military had Hydrogen bombs that could wipe out huge cities, but this Trionic Cannon could vapourise entire planets in a few short moments; this weapon was several orders of magnitude more destructive than H-Bombs.

Formulating a theory was one thing. Building an actual weapon was something else entirely. That took huge amounts of money, skilled people, top class research and production facilities and a great deal of time. Even then, there was no guarantee that a functioning weapon would be the end result. And, if he did successfully produce this weapon, what would he do with it? He couldn't let any of the world's national Government's anywhere near that kind of destructive technology. The Earth would be vapourised in under a week. Still, the challenge of building the weapon gnawed at John's mind.

The satisfaction of simply achieving that outcome would be immense, he considered as he jingled the ice cubes in his glass absent-mindedly. Perhaps, there was some peaceful use for such a weapon, he mused for a moment, but quickly realised that it was wishful thinking on his part. Running his fingers distractedly over the contract, John Caudwell considered that he had achieved quite enough for one day.

Not bad for an ex-plastics factory worker, John Caudwell thought and slipped the contract safely back into his jacket pocket. Then, smiling, he raised his glass of watered down cola to the reflection of himself that stared back from the mirror behind the bar, and took one long, last drink before leaving.

Not bad at all.

Chapter 14

<u>The Imperial Palace, Bardan</u>

    Ambassador (to the Court of Her Imperial Majesty, Lullina, the Grand Empress of the Bardomil) Diadran Zhannell was a Hubbart. The long, gloomy face and the pale green skin marked her out as a member of a species that specialised in the complex intricacies of diplomacy and negotiation. For many centuries the Hubbart had acted as go-betweens and facilitators in some of the most tortuous and complicated peace negotiations and treaties in a three galaxy area. However, it was her previous experience heading up the peace delegation at the end of the last Bardomil-Ganthoran war that had ably suited Diadran for the position as the Universal Alliance's Ambassador to the Bardomil Empire.

    The summons to the Imperial Palace had been as mystifying to Diadran as it had been sudden in its appearance. It had been almost a year since she had presented her diplomatic credentials at the Imperial Palace to the High Chamberlain; who had dismissed her with a less than courteous snort. But, Diadran knew, that was very often the way with diplomatic life. A great deal of time was taken up with long periods of tedium and waiting that was then broken by short periods of intense activity. The Bardomil court would be no different than the dozens of other diplomatic missions to which Diadran had been attached. Diplomatic friendships and favours ebbed and flowed like the tides of the sea. You could be in favour one day and a diplomatic pariah the next.

    Not that such 'inconsistencies' ever bothered a seasoned diplomat such as Diadran Zhannell. She knew she would be out of favour on Bardan after First Admiral Caudwell had effectively annihilated an entire Bardomil Imperial Fleet with two Star-Cruisers and half a dozen Explorers. The Empress could not come straight out and make waves for the Alliance Ambassador; that would mean admitting to a horrendous defeat. And, neither defeat nor weakness was something that the Bardomil Empire could afford to admit to. There were too many rebelliously-minded species eager to use force to try and press their claims for independence from the strangle-hold of the Empire. The Bardomil did not wish to see these species seeking support, comfort or military assistance from the technologically-advanced Alliance. Thus, the Thexxian Separatist disaster was shielded from the bulk of the Bardomil Empire's population.

    Most of the other diplomatic legations on Bardan, however, were well aware of the Bardomil Fleet's disastrous encounter with First Admiral Caudwell. The news spread around the Quadrant like wildfire encouraging several species to rebel against the Empire, which had led to bloody and ruthless suppression. Now, things seemed to have settled down for the moment and matters were returning to a degree of diplomatic normality. The rebellions had been crushed, the usual round of military-frontier skirmishes with the Universal Alliance was settling down and there appeared to be no further aggressive actions from the Ganthoran Empire or the Horvath Unity. The frontiers seemed to be relatively stable which would allow for diplomacy, and espionage, to return to the Diplomatic Quarter of Bardan's Capital City, Thurrus.

Having been called to the Imperial Palace, Diadran quickly checked, through diplomatic channels, that no hostile military episodes had taken place. The Ganthoran and Horvath Ambassadors had reported that the frontiers were quiet as had First Admiral Caudwell's Staff.

Summoned by an Imperial Messenger from the High Chamberlain's Office, and escorted by two of the sinister black-clad Imperial Bodyguards, Diadran had made her way to the Imperial Palace where she had been instructed to wait by a polite yet firm Imperial Equerry in an exquisite white uniform. Diadran had expected to be kept waiting for several hours before being seen by a minor functionary on whatever matter had arisen in the Imperial Court. Diadran was both surprised and alarmed to have been kept waiting for barely a few minutes before the High Chamberlain had swung open the huge onyx doors to the Imperial Reception Chamber.

"Ambassador Zhannell!?" the once derisively-snorting Chamberlain had politely requested confirmation of her identity in a voice that would have echoed around the city.

"Yes, sir," she responded with the formal politeness that was required of her.

Let the games commence, Diadran thought to herself as the High Chamberlain bowed lowly to summon her into the Imperial Presence.

Stepping into the huge, cavernous Reception Chamber, shadowed by the rotund figure of the High Chamberlain, Diadran Zhannell forced herself not to be intimidated by the sheer size and grandeur of the place. She had seen many Reception Chambers in her career, but this was by far the biggest and most imposing. The row of huge onyx columns, that supported a beautifully frescoed and gilded ceiling, stood almost fifteen metres in height. Stationed at each column, Imperial Bodyguards stood in their menacing black uniforms with their weapons fully-charged. Standing to attention with their darkened visors down and locked, the Bodyguards made Diadran shiver involuntarily as she walked slowly across the hard, shiny floor. Hearing her soft shoes scuffing an echo in the Reception Chamber, Diadran focussed on keeping her breathing regular and under control as she approached the imposing sight of the Empress herself in full majesty perched on the huge Onyx Throne.

Surrounded by a gaggle of courtiers, many in military uniform, there seemed to be polite laughter and merriment in an atmosphere of dread and terror. The Empress, herself, the centre of attention, smiled happily as she appeared to regale the company with amusing anecdotes.

Then, suddenly from behind Diadran, something rapped heavily on the floor three times, startling her to a halt.

"Your Imperial Majesty the Ambassador of the Universal Alliance Her Excellency Diadran Zhannell!" the High Chamberlain bellowed his deep rich voice echoing around the Reception Chamber.

"Ah, Ambassador Zhannell," the Empress said brightly, gracefully drifting down from her perch on the Onyx throne her left arm extended.

"Your Imperial Majesty," Diadran bowed low in recognition of the Bardomil Head of State.

"We have been most remiss of you Ambassador," the Empress smiled sweetly, extending her left hand for the Ambassador to receive, "our High Chamberlain has neglected to inform us of your arrival," the Empress lied.

"Your Majesty is most gracious," Diadran acknowledged the diplomatic falsehood making sure she kept her gaze downcast in the Imperial presence, as she received the hand and touched it to her brow.

"Come let us walk together," the Empress instructed, allowing Diadran to rise from her bow.

The Empress extended her right hand inviting Diadran to support it with her left hand as they walked away from the group of courtiers.

"We really have been most remiss of you, Ambassador," the Empress smiled with sweet insincerity when they were out of earshot of the others, "we must make amends for our tardiness in receiving you."

"Majesty," Diadran began, "it is of no account..." she continued trying not to notice the jet black eyes that glared maliciously and disconcertingly from the otherwise angelic face.

Diadran knew that the genetic flaw in the Empress' DNA was unique to the Bardomil Imperial family. The orbs of the Empress' eyes were pure black although it apparently presented her with no difficulty in her vision.

"Ah, Ambassador," the Empress interrupted as they walked slowly to the huge bay windows that overlooked the formal garden of the Imperial Palace, "you are a realist as most Hubbarts are; we thank you for your indulgence."

"Majesty," Diadran replied feeling the cold clammy bite of the Empress' skin on the back of her own hand.

"You know, we are both realists and we ourselves do find soldiers to be the most tedious creatures imaginable," the Empress whispered almost conspiratorially.

"Majesty," Diadran gave the non-committal diplomatic response wondering where this impromptu conversation was going to lead.

Despite being in a more informal setting, Diadran knew that this was still the Head of State who commanded a military machine with tens of millions of war vessels. And, accordingly, Diadran knew that she could trust the Empress about as far as she could throw one of First Admiral Caudwell's colossal Star-Destroyers in the atmosphere of a heavy gravity planet.

"Yes, they are all bombast and bluster and braying about the good of the Empire," the Empress continued as they passed out onto the formal garden terraces, "but we are both realists, we both know that only peace and diplomacy will allow the Empire and the Alliance to flourish."

A peace overture, Diadran thought, trying to read the subtext of what the Empress was saying. Why now? Diadran cudgelled her brains for a hidden agenda. Whatever was going on, Diadran could not fathom the objective. She was, however, certain that First Admiral Caudwell would be able to spot the Empress' hidden intentions. Diadran had known many military leaders, but that young flame-haired human had a knowledge and understanding of grand strategy that was well beyond his years.

"Yes, Majesty" Diadran replied formally as she was struck by the sheer scale and beauty of the formal gardens that seemed to stretch to the deep green twilight horizon of Bardan.

"Our soldiers don't understand that, they have no vision," the Empress continued, "They only know how to kill and destroy things. Is this true with your Alliance soldiers?"

Now, probing for information, Diadran thought.

"I do not believe so, Majesty," Diadran knew she would have to be careful how she handled this, "our Alliance is made up of many diverse species and cultures, but mostly they seek peace and trade," Diadran held out the opportunity to bring the possibility of trade talks as well as military and political negotiation.

"Ah," the Empress smiled softly, "our warriors may build an Empire, but it is our merchants and traders that hold it together."

"Your Majesty is very wise," Diadran flattered as she watched the deep red orb of the Bardomil sun begin to dip towards the horizon.

"Peace and prosperity is what we also seek," the Empress said softly, "Like most species we both fear those things that we do not understand."

Well, that'll be about the closest we ever hear to an apology for the year of frontier skirmishing that had cost hundreds of ships and thousands of lives, Diadran cynically speculated.

"Then we must work together to learn about each other and banish that fear," Diadran said politely.

"It is good that we have spoken of such things; we must speak again of such matters very soon" the Empress announced, "now please leave us; we shall instruct the High Chamberlain to move your legation to more suitable and luxurious quarters more befitting of your status."

"Your Majesty is too kind," Diadran released the Empress' hand and bowed.

"We shall speak again of these matters soon," the Empress promised.

"I shall await your pleasure," Diadran bowed once more, backing away from the Imperial presence and returning into the Reception Chamber relieved to be out of the firing line.

When Diadran Zhannell had disappeared from sight, the looming dark figure of the Captain of Bodyguards stepped out into the terraces behind the Empress.

"Well?" the Empress demanded, her attention drawn to the dazzling sunset.

"The emitter weapon was dispatched early this morning," Captain Sudrus reported, "It should be in orbit around the Earth's Sun in twenty-five days," he reported.

"How long is that in Alliance time?" the Empress asked.

"Just under seven hundred of their Earth hours," Sudrus replied.

"Excellent," the Empress smiled viciously, "by the time the weapon goes off no one will be able to connect the solar flare to the Bardomil Empire. It's a beautiful sunset isn't it, Sudrus?" she added softly.

"Yes, Majesty," the sinister Captain of Bodyguards replied in agreement.

Chapter 15

The Star-Cruiser Aquarius

Marilla Thapes paced anxiously up and down the corridor outside Briefing Room One. Breathing in slowly she puffed heavily trying to force down the butterflies that seemed to be running rampage in her stomach. Despite having had nothing to eat for nearly five hours, Marilla still felt like throwing up as she constantly rehearsed her presentation in her mind. This was the big one, she told herself as she continued to pace nervously. Second Admiral Lokkrien was chairing the briefing, and as she paced, Marilla knew that what she had was pretty flimsy. Her weeks of investigation had produced nothing of any significance that would justify her ongoing use of time. But, the idea that the Bardomil had developed and produced some kind of emitter weapon gnawed at her mind. The instinct was so strong that she felt she could almost taste it. Still wrestling with the idea, Marilla was interrupted by the voice of Karap Sownus.

"Right, Marilla, don't be nervous," the gently smiling Sownus said.

"Sir!" Marilla yelped caught by surprise and snapped to attention.

"In we go now, remember to salute," Sownus said and ushered Marilla towards the grey force-shielded door of the famous Briefing Room One.

Clutching her folios to her chest, Marilla stepped through the force-shielding, her heart hammering in her chest and her throat feeling dry.

Inside Briefing Room One, Marilla was surprised to find just how small the room where First Admiral Caudwell outlined his plans was. Expecting something much grander and more impressive, a part of Marilla Thapes was rather disappointed. In the pale grey painted Briefing Room a table for only four or five people was dominated by the First Admiral's high-backed chair. Occupying the seat was Second Admiral Marrhus Lokkrien the Bardomil who was the effective second-in-command of the whole Universal Alliance military. And, as she registered the presence of Admiral Lokkrien, Marilla realised that there was no one else present. The other Departmental Heads had been dismissed prior to Marilla's arrival.

"Sir," she snapped to attention and stumbled as the precious folios started to drop from her sweaty-palmed grip.

"At ease, Technician Thapes," Lokkrien said calmly returning the salute without standing up.

"Get yourself sorted out Marilla and start in your own time," Sownus instructed from behind her before taking a seat next to Lokkrien.

BENNING

Fumbling with the folios, Marilla was aware of the steely gaze of the Second Admiral who was beginning to show signs of irritation. Taking a deep breath, Marilla focussed on her folios and made sure that they were in the right order. When she was ready she stood to attention once again.

"Proceed," Marrhus Lokkrien intoned professionally.

"Gentlemen," Marilla began nervously, "I believe that the Bardomil have developed and produced an emitter weapon that generates massive solar flares and that they are intending to deploy it somewhere against the Alliance."

"Well, that's quite a claim, Technician," Lokkrien interrupted, "I trust that you can substantiate it?"

"Yes, sir; I have evidence that supports that hypothesis," Marilla said nervously.

Marilla Thapes had been warned that Marrhus Lokkrien was a highly sceptical individual. Dozens of seemingly stupendous claims like Marilla's emerged from various departments every week, and Lokkrien's sharp incisive mind was well-honed at separating the wheat from the chaff.

"If I may, sir?" Marilla asked.

With a gesture, Lokkrien indicated his assent and leaned forward, elbows lodged on the table top.

Slipping the first folio onto the red, square plate, Marilla passed her hand over the white control panel to operate the projectors. A moment later, the projector image cleared to show the faces of two Xanath; one considerably older than the other.

"Master Sammut Claggit, to the left, sir, and his assistant, known to us as Marrut Bem," Marilla introduced the two dead weapons specialists, "Master Claggit was an expert in magnetic field manipulation who worked at the Bardomil Imperial Academy of Sciences, Peace and Friendship; both were found dead under mysterious circumstances."

"How mysterious?" Lokkrien asked.

"Both were killed in a hunting accident according to Bardomil video news broadcasts," Marilla explained, "But, Master Claggit was known to be a non-carnivore with a weak heart who stood vehemently against blood sports."

With a brief shrug, Lokkrien indicated for Marilla to continue.

"Scanning the scientific literature, the thrust of Sammut Claggit's work was in manipulating the magnetic fields of planets to make them inhabitable for colonists or for military installations; however, a month ago, a massive solar flare incinerated the planet of Collizon in the Artreaus system," Marilla paused and changed the folio sheet.

THE BURNING SUN

The new image showed a three-dimensional image of the planet of Collizon being swamped by the massive super charged solar flare.

"Data from the *Vasco Da Gama* indicates that this was not a naturally occurring phenomenon," Marilla continued as the image of Collizon was scorched, "the yellow dwarf star at the heart of the system was not in its natural cycle to produce flares," Marilla added.

Turning her attention away from Lokkrien's stern gaze, Marilla focussed on the image in front of her.

"The yellow dwarf in the Artreaus system is too young and immature to naturally produce so destructive a flare," Marilla continued as the atmosphere of Collizon finally collapsed on the image leaving a glowing cinder floating in space, "the episode, according to both intelligence operative and long-range scanner sources was witnessed by the Bardomil Empress."

"Empress Lullina was there at the time?" Lokkrien suddenly perked up, "Just passing through or was she waiting for it to happen?"

"The Imperial Fighter Carrier Taurai was stationed in the Artreaus system for nearly four hours before the flare mysteriously erupted," Marilla indicated as the Collizon image disappeared.

"Go on, Technician Thapes," Lokkrien said, now captivated by the presentation.

"I had a word with the people at Theoretical Weapons who said that the Garmaurians had been using bursts of high-intensity Lissian radiation to create very small-scale solar flares for many centuries; they used them for entertainment rather like pyrotechnics," Marilla reported, "But, the mechanisms that they used were large and cumbersome and could only be operated from the largest of the Star-Destroyers. The Bardomil currently do not have a ship of sufficient size to carry such equipment and the *Vasco Da Gama* data indicates no vessels of any significant size were in the immediate vicinity of the Artreaus yellow dwarf at the time of the solar eruption."

"So, we have a mystery on our hands?" Lokkrien asked.

"It would appear so, sir," Marilla responded, "I paid a visit to Professor Xanfar, our foremost authority on Lissian radiation, and asked if it were possible to make something smaller that would emit Lissian. Her answer was non-committal; however, she did indicate that it was not beyond the realms of possibility for someone to construct something that could deliver a short-duration high-intensity pulse."

"What might this contraption look like Technician Thapes?" Lokkrien asked.

"Professor Xanfar indicated that such a mechanism could be as small as thirty centimetres in diameter and still deliver enough Lissian radiation to cause a major solar flare," Marilla replied, "shape and composition are still unknown, sir."

"With those dimensions, our scanners would never see it, sir," Sownus commented, "Unless they were deliberately looking for something of that size."

"Well, so far we've got a very nice theory, Technician," Lokkrien said pensively, "Do you have any physical evidence that I can hang my hat on here?"

"I believe that we may have, sir," Marilla replied setting down a new folio sheet on the projector.

The image that appeared showed a Bardomil M-Cruiser amongst some turning and tumbling rocks being attacked by the unmistakable darting shapes of Alliance Eagles.

"This, sir, is the enhanced data from 'The Clements Incident' on the edge of the Nezadir galaxy," Marilla began as the M-Cruiser tried to make a slow and ponderous turn whilst being harried by the smaller and more agile Eagle fighters.

"The long range data from the Magellan indicates that this solitary M-Cruiser was picking up, apparently examining and then discarding rocks close in dimension to the suggestion of Professor Xanfar," Marilla said knowing that the link was going to be tenuous at best.

"Are you suggesting that this M-Cruiser was launching this weapon?" Lokkrien asked.

"It is a possible explanation for an otherwise inexplicable incident," Marilla winced inside as she knew it was the best answer that she could give.

On the image, the final run by the Eagle that would destroy the M-Cruiser was just beginning. As the four explosions from the rapid-fire pulsar-cannons blossomed from the top of the M-Cruiser, Marilla slowed the image down.

"I'm magnifying the M-Cruiser's forward air lock, sir," Marilla manipulated the image to focus on the rectangular door-like structure, "the crew have just ejected this particular structure," she indicated a small rock-like image that seemed to drift forwards.

"Slowing down the image, sir," Marilla manipulated the scene once more, "the structure is drifting forward," she commented, "the M-Cruiser starts to explode," she indicated as a bright flash began to impinge upon the image, "and, here, the structure seems to move to the right under its own propulsion," Marilla commentated as the structure moved rapidly to the right for a few frames before being swallowed up in the flash of the explosion.

"Is that it, Technician Thapes?" Lokkrien asked calmly.

"Yes, sir, that is the extent of our data, but we have..." Marilla began to explain anxiously.

"No, Technician," Lokkrien held up his hand to stop Marilla, "I believe I've seen enough, thank you for your time, dismissed," Lokkrien ordered.

Stopping the projector, Marilla recovered her folio sheets and saluted the Second Admiral before scampering rapidly to the doorway. Passing through the force-shielding, Marilla cursed herself for not having more convincing evidence. Stamping her foot in frustration, she set off, leaden-footed to the Intelligence Offices where she suspected that she would be back monitoring signal traffic in a few more hours. The big chance had come and gone, Marilla thought, and fought back the urge to weep. It was going to be a long walk back to the Intelligence Offices for Marilla Thapes.

And, a very quick return to obscurity.

BENNING

Chapter 16

<u>Planet Earth</u>

The music was loud in the school assembly hall that now doubled as a dance floor for the evening's entertainment. The flashing strobe lights in the heavy darkness seemed to accentuate the sweaty faces of the dancers as they writhed and gyrated to what was, according to the cool kids at the school, the popular music of the day. The illicit consumption of alcohol at the local bars and hostelries, the ones that didn't question how old their patrons were, added to the beaming flushed faces and the enthusiasm of the dancing. But, as was traditional, the segregation of the genders was scrupulously upheld. The young ladies, dressed to look older than they actually were, congregated on one side of the room; whilst the young men, full of bravado and cheap spirits were rigidly corralled by convention on the other.

The bravest of the young men had already made their moves on the prettier of the young women; running the gauntlet of rejection and public humiliation to claim their prize or make a hasty exit with even redder faces. Meanwhile, the more cautious and reserved held firmly to their own stag-groups discussing matters far more important whilst furtively glancing at potential dance partners as they attempted to summon up the courage to make an approach. The less attractive young women, the wallflowers, would smile shyly at their potential beau's trying to hide their growing desperation, hoping that someone would at least ask them to dance just once.

The more adventurous and amorous pairings were already quietly cloistered in the darkened recesses of the assembly hall, where the flashing lights hardly ever shone. Already, the teachers, who doubled as chaperones for the night; were ferreting out kissing and groping couples and they were being reluctantly dragged, with much protest, back onto the dance floor. The ever-vigilant adults hovered and prowled the margins of the dance floor seeking out the hormonally-charged teenage miscreants in an endeavour to maintain at least a semblance of decorum.

In this furnace-hot atmosphere of sweat, cheap perfume, after shave, alcohol and desperation, a steely-eyed sober yet boiling angry Billy Caudwell slipped un-noticed into the cauldron. Scanning the room quickly, he found the source of his rage standing amongst a group of older friends next to the door to the senior study room.

"Emma, a word," Billy smiled with wicked insincerity as he gently took hold of the provocatively-dressed young woman's elbow and jostled her efficiently into the open study room, pushing the door closed behind them.

The loud THUD-THUD-THUD of the heavy drum-beat music was instantly muffled as Emma was firmly ushered into the brightly lit lounge from the darkened, flashing dance floor.

"Billy!" the outraged Emma Wallace protested, "What's going on here!?" she demanded as she was guided gently to one of the study tables.

"I could ask you exactly the same question," Billy said with icy calm, "Where were you when I turned up at your door to pick you up?"

In the well-furnished, but deserted study room, Emma suddenly felt the stifling tension in the air generated by the angry Billy sweep over her like tidal wave. Caught unawares, she had not expected to be challenged about ditching Billy without telling him, and going out to the dance with someone else. She had expected Billy, like all of the others she considered to be wimps and mummy's boys, to simply slink away and whine to his mother and his other little loser friends. In that split-second of surprise, Emma suddenly realised that this particular mummy's boy was not going to slink away. Deep in the recesses of Emma's mind, the primal animal knew that this young man was different. He was going to stand up to her until he got the truth. As that realisation dawned in her mind, the germ of an idea was planted that, perhaps, she had made a colossal mistake.

Looking into the grey-blue eyes of the angry young man in front of her, she saw the hurt and the icy anger, but, most unnervingly she saw a hard-edged ruthlessness that she had never seen in him before. Instinctively, she knew that she could never sweet talk and patronise her way out of the situation. She knew that she had to bluster and attack, hoping that he would cave in as all the other men she knew had done when a woman raised her voice in scorn.

"Where was I!? Where was I!?" Emma snapped, "YOU are NOT my father, I don't have to explain anything to you Billy Caudwell. I've got my own life!"

"Spare me the modern, independent woman speech," Billy cut her short, "It doesn't justify plain old-fashioned bad manners, dear!"

"I am not your 'dear' Billy," Emma bristled, "I am!"

"If you want respect, DEAR," Billy emphasised the insult as he cut her off once more, "then you will earn it by showing respect. Now where were you when I turned up at your door and was left feeling like an idiot!?"

For a moment, an astounded Emma bit her tongue, her face reddening with anger at the challenge.

"I decided that I wanted to go to the dance with Micky Stewart, that's all," Emma retorted defiantly crossing her arms over her chest, "I am old enough to make my own decisions you know, and I am entitled to change my mind!"

"You came here with Micky Stewart?" an astonished Billy stammered.

For a moment, Billy was taken aback and stood in shocked silence at the realisation that she had not only stood him up, but she had done so in favour of the young man who had attacked his stand-in Jedithram Prust. That realisation stung him like a very hard slap to the face and hardened his resolve.

"Whom I choose to go out with is none of your business Billy Caudwell!" she bristled jutting her chin out with defiance.

For a moment, Billy composed himself from the shock and then pressed on into the attack with renewed vigour.

"You can go out with whomever you like, Miss Wallace, but you do not agree to go out with me and leave me standing looking like a total prat in front of your father at your front door. Is that clear lady?" Billy hissed icily.

"Don't you dare talk to me like I'm a five-year-old!" Emma bridled pointing her finger at the enraged Billy.

"Well, maybe you should stop behaving like one," Billy retorted, "and learn some manners while you're at it!"

"There's absolutely nothing wrong with my manners. Mister Caudwell!" Emma snarled dangerously.

"No there isn't; at least nothing that learning some consideration for other people wouldn't cure!" Billy refused to back down.

"I don't any advice from jealous, immature little boys!" Emma spat contemptuously taking a new tack in the exchange.

For many years Emma had watched the women in her family control and manipulate their men with scorn and derision. It was a practice almost as old as the human species, and Emma was quickly becoming a skilled practitioner.

"Jealous!?" Billy replied, "Jealous of what?"

"You're jealous because I chose to come here with Micky, now go away and grow up Caudwell!" Emma barbed.

"What!? Jealous of Micky Mouse!? The biggest lying, cheating rat-bag in the school," Billy replied shakily; she had hit a raw nerve, "If that's who you want, good luck to you; but don't come crying to me when he's finished with you and ditches you for someone else!"

"Oh really!?" Emma crowed triumphantly realising that she had drawn metaphorical blood, "you hypocrite, Caudwell, pretending to be my friend so you could make a pass at me, you're just like all the others; after only one thing, at least Micky's a real man, not like you!" she stung.

"Hypocrite is it!?" Billy rallied; he was far from beaten yet, "it didn't stop you stringing me along and using me as a buck-shee math tutor. So, I'd be really careful about who you're calling a hypocrite, Miss Wallace!"

"Why you..." Emma seethed, "I did not string you along..."

"'Oh, Billy,'" he mocked her wheedling tone of the last night he had helped with her maths in her room, "'let's wait until the school dance, then we can start going out properly, OK?' I think you could safely call that stringing someone along."

"Look, we were never going out, Billy," Emma defended weakly, "I've changed my mind about you, that's all. So, I don't know what you're whining about."

"It's called consideration for other people, Emma Wallace," Billy attacked again, "something you obviously don't have, unless, of course, you want something from them. You're a user, Emma Wallace, a dirty, selfish, arrogant little user; just like Micky Stewart, so you're well met, the pair of you."

Turning on his heel, Billy headed towards the door.

"Now, just one minute mister high-and-mighty Caudwell!" Emma burst out.

"No, Emma, we're done here!" Billy snapped contemptuously turning back to the enraged young woman.

"Hey," a new voice sounded as the door opened allowing a deafening flood of screeching lyrics and heavy drumbeat to flood the savage tension of the study room.

"What's going on here?" the newly arrived Micky, heavily made up in his New Romantic outfit, questioned; two glasses of something clear and fizzy splashed in his hands.

"Nothing at all," Billy replied turning back to the door and finding a group of Micky 's garishly-dressed, laughing and cavorting, drunken friends blocking the doorway.

"You alright babe, this guy giving you trouble?" Stewart asked the red-faced Emma.

"Nothing I can't handle; he's just being a jerk!" Emma barbed.

"Is that right, babe?" Micky asked, stepping into Billy's path, "You being a jerk, Caudwell?" he asked, setting the two glasses down on one of the study tables nearby.

"Get out of my way, Micky," Billy said calmly.

"Oh, I don't think so, Caudwell," Micky Stewart smiled malevolently, confident of the support of his group of friends behind him, "maybe you should apologise to the lady."

"Yes, Billy," Emma smiled, "maybe you should apologise."

"Pity there aren't any ladies in here," Billy met Micky's sneering gaze.

"Now, Caudwell," Micky said menacingly, "that's not a nice thing to say about my new girlfriend is it?" Micky moved close to Billy until the two young men were almost nose to nose.

"Like I said," Billy replied calmly to Micky's heavily powdered face, "pity there aren't any ladies in here."

From behind Micky Stewart one of his friends let out an involuntary gasp as the tension rose another several degrees.

"I said apologise, Caudwell!" Micky demanded viciously.

"Get knotted, Micky," Billy replied and stepped aside to pass the obstruction.

"I said apologise!" Micky grabbed Billy's left arm and pushed him backwards causing Billy to stumble as he narrowly missed a chair.

"And, I said get knotted; now, if you want to make something off it, come on, face-to-face, not from behind like a coward," Billy challenged after recovering his balance, "otherwise, get out of my way."

"Careful, Micky," a male voice spoke from behind Micky.

"You know, I really don't like you, you little ginger weasel," Micky said with an insincere smile, "I think that maybe we should teach you some manners, Caudwell."

Slowly, all four of Micky Stewart's male friends started to spread out menacingly from the doorway to form a shallow semi-circle in front of Billy. Calmly, Billy scrutinised the four young men. The memories and experiences of Teg Portan quickly registered and categorised the four new potential combatants. All four of them were red-flushed with alcohol and not prepared for a fight. They would all take part enthusiastically in a drunken beat-up if the target wasn't resisting. But, they had no real motivation to take part in a fight where they could potentially get hurt. The real trouble was going to be Micky, not the hangers-on. So, Billy quickly formed a plan with the realisation that if he hurt Micky badly enough, these others would back off. And, already Billy knew that at least one of these hangers-on knew what he was capable of.

Micky had pushed the dispute beyond a verbal solution. Now, he was planning to settle it on his terms, with his friends behind him. Billy, with all the experience and knowledge of close-quarter combat from the long-dead Garmaurian First Admiral, knew that Micky either had to resort to violence or lose face with those same friends.

"I don't think I need to learn anything from someone who wears more lipstick than his so-called 'girlfriend'." Billy spat the last word contemptuously in an attempt to enrage his opponent.

The tactic of enraging Micky was working, as Billy noticed the momentary flash of anger in his opponent's eyes. Always watch the eyes, the dead Garmaurian commander's memory flashed through Billy's mind. If he's going to do something stupid, you'll see it in the eyes first. Billy also knew that an angry opponent was a careless and clumsy opponent. It didn't matter how much bigger or stronger he was, if he wasn't focussed, he was vulnerable.

"Oh yeah," Micky snarled, "well, at least I've got a girlfriend, loser!"

"Tell me, Micky," Billy asked with a deliberate smile, "are you really interested in her, or are you just after her eye-liner?" Billy smiled.

"Oh, very funny, Caudwell," Micky smiled, "try laughing this one off," he drew back his hand and bunched a fist.

Here we go, Billy thought as he steeled himself for action. The memories of Teg Portan, the Garmaurian First Admiral, taught him not to panic in a hand to hand combat situation. Stay calm, stay focussed and be ready to respond when a weakness presents itself, the dead Garmaurians lifetime of experience had counselled.

An instant later, the bunched fist was hurtling towards Billy Caudwell's face. But, with the speed of a striking cobra, Billy lifted his left hand and caught the flying fist in his palm; his fingers closing quickly around it. The force-shielding of Billy's Personal Environment Suit deflected the thrust of the blow back into Micky's hand and wrist. The savage impact immediately fractured all four of the bones at the base of Micky's right hand. To Micky, it felt just like he had just punched a brick wall. The searing, shooting agony of the fractures lanced up into his brain, drawing a yell of pain from the injured assailant.

It took very little effort from Billy to twist and squeeze the damaged hand forcing the shrieking Micky to buckle to his knees in front of his horrified friends.

"You want some too, boys?" Billy glared at the four hangers-on, who now stood frozen as their leader yelped with pain, the tears of anguish beginning to cut a path through the caked on make-up on his cheeks.

"Let him go, you bully, you're hurting him!" Emma protested and felt the complaint choked off in her throat as she caught sight of Billy's eyes.

Emma had never known real fear and terror in her young life. But looking into Billy's hard, ice-cold, grey-blue eyes made her gasp with fright. These were the eyes of a killer. Not the kind, generous and helping eyes of the Billy who had patiently tried to explain those equations to her. Kneeling down, trying to comfort her injured boyfriend, Emma realised that she had made the most horrible mistake.

BENNING

With no expression on his face, Billy dropped the damaged hand; producing another yelp of agony from Micky who cradled his crushed and broken fingers protectively. Without a backwards glance, Billy walked calmly away from his fallen enemy. Micky's friends stared anxiously at the victor of the short and brutal fight as he approached, and slowly and silently made way for him. Passing through their frightened make-shift line, Billy walked to the door, disappearing back into the loud banging and flashing maelstrom of the school dance.

Cradling her injured and agonised boyfriend, Emma watched Billy step through the line of Micky's friends. As he walked to the door, Emma felt the hatred and fear of him well up inside her. That hatred was for someone who had ruthlessly exposed her failings, her dishonesty, and her contempt for other human beings. She had expected him to simply skulk away in a huff and never speak to her again like all the other losers she had used and abused. But, this young man had forced her to look at her own reflection and her own misdeeds. He had told her the truth about herself, and she hated him for that, almost as much as she hated herself for having been found out.

As he slipped back to the school dance, a new feeling welled up inside Emma Wallace. It was something she had never expected to feel about Billy Caudwell.

It was a feeling of grudging respect.

THE BURNING SUN

Chapter 17

The Star-Cruiser Aquarius

"Ambassador Zhannell, what a pleasure to finally meet you!" Billy Caudwell welcomed the Ambassador to Bardan into his Quarters with an outstretched hand.

"First Admiral? Erm, the pleasure is all mine," Diadran Zhannell took the offered hand, slightly surprised by the warmth and sincerity of the greeting.

"Please, take a seat," Billy smiled indicating the chair in front of the curved 'S' shaped couch that was firmly jammed against the large viewing window, "something to drink, perhaps?"

"Oh, no...no thank you, First Admiral," Diadran held up her hand in refusal as she sat down on the offered chair.

For a moment, Diadran stared in wonderment at just how Spartan and un-cluttered the Private Quarters of the Supreme Military Commander of the Universal Alliance actually were. In the dim light of the room, Diadran could see a small work-desk and chair beneath a bright light, a simple standard-issue storage locker, two chairs, the 'S' shaped couch and a matching table. The immediate impressions on Diadran were that either this was someone who shunned shows of ostentation or it was someone who preferred to live away from the flagship Aquarius.

"Well, I see you've escaped from the lion's den unscathed," Billy entered what he called 'Diplomatic Mode'.

As Supreme Military Commander, Billy was having to rapidly learn and cultivate the social skills required of a politician and a diplomat. It was not a task he took to readily; however, the quest to forge his Universal Alliance was a strong and powerful motivation.

"Yes, First Admiral, life can be, shall we say, 'interesting' on Bardan," Diadran smiled starting to feel very at ease in Billy's company.

"I can well imagine," Billy smiled taking his seat on the couch behind the table, "Is our friend Lullina still as eccentric as ever?"

"Oh yes, very much so," Diadran had to agree; "she is a very dangerous creature and should have a 'handle with care' sign round her neck."

"Oh, I can well believe it," Billy laughed politely, "I have several Second and Third Admirals who might benefit from the same," he quipped.

"It seems we all have those same problems," Diadran smiled.

"So," Billy brought the conversation round to the business of the day, "what is our friend Lullina up to?" he asked.

"Well, First Admiral," Diadran sat forward in her seat, "I had quite an enlightening little conversation with Her Imperial Majesty a few days ago."

"So, she's stopped ignoring you?" Billy asked.

"Indeed," Diadran commented, "and in this little conversation she seemed to be putting out hints of a possible peace," she let the implications sink into the mind of the Supreme Military Commander.

"Why should Empress Lullina suddenly be interested in peace with the Universal Alliance?" Billy asked the million-pound question.

"That, First Admiral, is a question that has taxed my wits also," Diadran replied, "but, the hints were being dropped and couched in the appropriate language of a possible peace offer."

"Hmm," Billy mused for a few moments, leaning back on the couch, "the political situation on Bardan is stable," Billy said remembering the most recent briefing from Karap Sownus.

"There is no sign of any rebellious activity within the Empire," Diadran added.

"And, there seems to be no significant military activity on either the Ganthoran or Horvan frontiers. So, the question is still why does she need peace with the Alliance?" Billy mused.

"I know it might sound stupid, but, perhaps, just perhaps, the Bardomil are starting to accept the idea of the Alliance's existence and are looking to start trading with us?" Diadran speculated.

"It's a possibility; but, I don't think it's very likely," Billy replied, "the Thexxian issue has still to be considered."

The enmity between the Bardomil and the Thexxians was still too deep-seated; that combined with the military defeat the Bardomil had suffered at Billy's hands made a serious peace offer an unlikely prospect in the First Admiral's mind.

"We could certainly use some stability on at least one of our frontiers." Diadran suggested.

"That's very true," Billy replied.

The Alliance Fleet was already badly overstretched trying to protect frontiers against the major Imperial powers of both the Ganthorans and the Bardomil. The Alliance needed time to integrate a host of new species and to train their military in the use of the advanced Garmaurian technology that was the bedrock of the Fleet. Some degree of peace and stability would be a God-send, but Billy suspected that the price might be a bit too rich for his blood.

"So, we at least have to explore the possibility?" Diadran asked.

"I'm not rejecting it completely," Billy replied, "just keep it as an exploration at this stage."

"That sounds fair enough, First Admiral, we commit ourselves to nothing and see how the hand plays out," Diadran sought clarification.

"Yes, I'm sorry; I simply don't trust Lullina," Billy shrugged.

"Understood, loud and clear," Diadran smiled delighted that she at least had won the chance to explore a potential peace scenario.

"Good," Billy replied standing up, "now, if you'd care to join me for dinner, Ambassador; my Senior Staff Officers are quite eager to meet someone who has spoken to the Bardomil Empress," Billy smiled.

"But, of course, First Admiral, I'd be delighted. I do enjoy the company of men in uniform," she smiled cheekily.

"And, I do believe that Admiral Schremmell proposes to sing a Hubbart love ballad in your honour," Billy explained.

Half rising to her feet, Diadran sat down once again. The thought of a low, droning Hubbart love ballad made her mind recoil in horror at the prospect of having to smile fixedly through the ordeal.

"You know, First Admiral," she smiled weakly, "I think I might just take that drink you offered me earlier."

"What would you like Ambassador?" Billy asked stepping over to the Synthesiser unit built into the wall next to the couch.

"Hubbart Brandy," Diadran said anxiously steeling herself for the approaching trial.

"A large one, please," she added with a shudder.

BENNING

Chapter 18

<u>Planet Earth</u>

"Look, Micky, stop it!" Emma Wallace protested pushing Micky Stewart's uninjured hand away from the hem of her fashionably-short skirt.

In the weeks since the school dance, it had been more a point of pride and principle for Emma to continue the relationship with Micky than through any particular attraction. Micky was a Monitor at school, he had a car, and the other girls were bitterly jealous of her for having Micky as a boyfriend. And, having totally alienated Billy Caudwell, she certainly wasn't going to give him the pleasure of saying 'I-told-you-so'.

"Come on, Ems, don't be shy," Micky smiled kissing Emma's neck once more and sliding his left hand down over her buttocks towards the skirt hem once more.

"No Micky!" Emma protested again, pushing Micky fully away from her, onto the ground, "I don't want to!"

Angrily, Emma fastened the two open buttons of her blouse and sat up on the sofa before trying to locate her discarded shoes.

"What's the matter now, Ems?" Micky asked concernedly picking up his discarded sweatshirt from the coffee table in front of the sofa.

"I just...I just...just don't want to, that's all," she flustered finding one of her pink high-heeled shoes beneath the coffee table.

"OKAY, Ems, what's going on here?" Micky sighed resignedly sitting down on one of the armchairs that stood at right angles to the coffee table.

For the first time in over a fortnight, Micky's parents had gone out for the evening, leaving him alone in the house. And, Micky had planned to make the best of the situation. Now, once again, his partner had developed a case of cold feet when it came to physical intimacy.

"What do you mean, 'what's going on here'?" Emma bristled.

"Just what I said," Micky replied, "you come over here dressed to the nines, a little bit of smooching, getting me all wound up, and suddenly you're all cold and giving me 'I don't want to'. So, what's the story, Ems?"

For a moment, Emma was silent as she racked her brains for a response and realised that she was totally out of her depth here.

"That's all you men ever think about isn't it!?" she snapped, gambling that the best form of defence was attack.

"And, whadda ya want me to think of, Ems!?" Micky yelled in response, "You're a beautiful girl, giving me all the green light signals. Did you think I wanted you to come over tonight to play Scrabble!?"

"Well, I certainly didn't come over here for you to try to rape me!!" Emma snapped, resorting to her last line of defence.

"Oh, I tried to rape you with a broken hand? Grow up, you stupid, immature little brat!" Micky replied angrily.

"Oh, 'stupid, immature brat', so that's it, is it, Micky?" Emma snarled standing up, driving her foot angrily into her other shoe, "different story when you're trying to get into my blouse, eh?"

"Hey, no one forced you, Ems!" Micky stood up pointing to Emma accusingly.

"God knows what I ever saw in you Micky Stewart!?" Emma snapped, lifting her jacket from the armchair opposite to Micky's.

"Well, an older boyfriend, someone with a car, to take you out drinking and dancing, with a bit of teasing practice for good measure, eh, Ems?" Micky barbed.

"Will you stop calling me that!?" Emma yelled.

"What? 'Ems' or 'tease'!?" Micky pressed home the advantage.

Stunned to silence once more, Emma jammed on her jacket and stomped over to the hallway to retrieve her bag.

"I'll just have to tell all the girls at school what you're like," Emma tried a new line of attack, "you're an animal, a sex maniac!"

"Oh, please do," Micky smiled, "the girlies like a bad boy," he followed her to the hallway, "they'll be queuing up outside my door," he added indicating the red painted doorway.

"No they won't," Emma replied huffily, "you think you're the best thing since sliced bread, Micky Stewart, but, let me tell you something; you're not,"

"Well, let's face it, I can do better for myself than a spoilt, immature little tease like you," Micky smiled sensing he was winning the argument, "I only went with you to annoy that loser Caudwell; otherwise, I wouldn't have touched you with a ten foot bargepole."

"Why you!!" Emma snarled, losing all reason, and aimed a vicious slap at Micky's face.

"Temper, temper, Princess!" Micky replied catching the flying right hand with his uninjured left, "yeah, the poor sap really fancied you, maybe you can go back to him and he'll take you on as second-hand goods!"

"You...!" Emma snarled angrily and tried to slap Micky again.

But, even all the strength in her right arm was not enough to overcome Micky's left.

"Oh yes Ems, you've got a bit of a reputation as a tease, so go ahead, do your worst; no one will ever believe you, Emma-No-Mates," Micky barbed.

BENNING

"They'll believe me when I tell them that you tried to rape me!" Emma snapped icily, determined to get the last word in.

Unfortunately, for Emma, it was a taunt too far.

The triumphant smile vanished from Micky's face faster than snow on a hot day. The look of anger and outrage that replaced it made Emma realise that she had stepped over the line. But, it was too late.

The pressure around Emma's right wrist loosened for just a fraction of a second before a heavy open-handed slap connected on her head above her right ear. With a yelp, Emma stumbled backwards, losing her balance, before another heavy back-handed slap connected with the left side of her head. Reeling from the two savage and painful blows Emma was pushed against the brightly decorated hallway wall. Trying to recover her balance, Emma felt a tight constricting band clamp around her throat partly blocking her windpipe.

Gasping from the two blows and now struggling to breathe Emma was able to look up and see the hate-twisted face of Micky Stewart pushed up close to hers, and realised that he had his left hand fixed tightly round her throat.

"You go right ahead, Ems," the twisted face hissed chillingly, his dark brown eyes as empty and hollow as Billy Caudwell's had been in the Study Room, "Tell everyone how I tried to rape you, the little teaser, the manipulator, the liar, after you got all tarted-up like a dog's dinner and went round to be alone with your boyfriend who was in pain with the broken hand," Micky held up his bandaged right hand, "and when they've finished laughing at you, Ems, if they don't lock you up, I'll come looking for you," Micky threatened with deathly calm.

Struggling for breath, Emma Wallace knew that this was no idle threat. She had seen murder in the eyes of Micky Stewart and felt the terror of that realisation seep into every nerve and fibre of her body.

"Look, Micky I'm sorry, I was just kidding," Emma gasped, her face reddening with congestion.

"No, Ems, you don't joke about things like that," Micky hissed viciously.

Calmly, Micky Stewart released his grip on the terrified Emma's throat. And, finally able to breathe once more, Emma slowly slid down to the floor, shivering with fear and shock. Still gasping, and too terrified to scream, Emma felt the heavy impact of her bag hitting her, causing her to raise her hands and arms protectively.

"There's your bag!" Micky snapped.

A moment later, Emma felt the smothering blanket of her overcoat being thrown over her as she tried to struggle to her feet. For a split-second, she panicked fearing some further attack, or worse. She simply wanted to escape and get as far away from the house as possible; so she started to scramble towards the blocked doorway.

"There's your coat!" the malevolent voice hissed as the front door was flung open next to her.

Grabbing her bag and coat, Emma tried to crawl to the open doorway to the perceived safety of the dark chilled street, when she felt a heavy impact on her posterior. The blow from Micky's foot propelled her out into the night, where she landed on her face, half in and half out of the door. Another well aimed kick shoved her fully out of the doorway and onto the concrete paving slabs, where she landed heavily.

"Don't ever show your face around me again, Wallace!" Micky snarled and slammed the wooden door shut.

In the darkness of the driveway, still shaking with terror and relief, Emma Wallace struggled slowly to her feet. With tears running down her face, Emma tried, unsuccessfully, to slide her arms into the sleeves of her overcoat. She found that she was unable to keep her hand steady long enough to thread it into the narrow sleeve opening, and gave up trying. Wrapping her overcoat around her arm and bag, Emma Wallace stumbled out into the night.

"Oh God, Billy, what have I done?" she mumbled to herself and sobbed quietly in the darkness.

BENNING

Chapter 19

The Bardomil Imperial Fighter Carrier Taurai

General Grattus Darrien sat uneasily in the chair at the large Conference Table. The 'invitation', bearing the Imperial Crest, which had summoned him to this little gathering, was one that Grattus knew he could not ignore. And, what a gathering it was turning out to be, the commander of the Bardomil Twenty-Sixth Rogandus Imperial Fleet considered as he scrutinised the other five generals around the table.

Two of them were immediately recognisable as Methrien and Glabbrus; two of the worst sadists ever to put on an Imperial uniform. A third, named Terfall he knew only by sight, whilst the other two were unknowns to Grattus. Six Fleet commanders being summoned to the Empress' flagship could only mean one thing, Grattus speculated, and that was a major military campaign. The where, when and against whom, Grattus considered, was something that they were all just about to find out.

Eying each other warily, the Generals said nothing as they waited in the heavy oppressive atmosphere of the Conference Room for someone to tell them what was going on. The dull drone of the heavy electro-magnetic generators that drove the Taurai supplied the already crippling tension in the room with a nerve-shredding constant. Looking cautiously at the other Generals, Grattus could see that they were scrutinising him too. Not that he would consider any of them friends. The Empress took great delight in playing her Generals off one another. It was a successful strategy that kept her Fleet commanders plotting and scheming against each other rather than her. Unfortunately, in the mind of Grattus Darrien, the time spent in 'politicking' was time that could be far better spent preparing the Rogandus Fleet for battle. But, that was the hard reality of the Bardomil military, Grattus understood. Covering one's own back was just as important a skill as actually being able to soldier and defeat the enemies of the Empire.

Sitting back on the seat, a wary eye clamped on his rivals, Grattus sighed. But, no sooner had the breath passed his lips than the Conference Room door burst open. Instinctively, Grattus leapt to his feet in the expectation of the Empress herself sweeping majestically into the room. Instead a squad of eight black-clad Imperial Bodyguards marched purposefully through the doorway and took up strategic positions against the Conference Room wall. The other startled Generals also leapt to their feet whilst Grattus reached for the blaster-pistol at his right hip. Feeling the empty holster, Grattus realised that he had been compelled to surrender the weapon when coming aboard the Taurai. Only Imperial Bodyguards were allowed to carry arms on the Empress' flagship.

The other Generals fearing, as Grattus did, an immediate execution began to remonstrate and complain. It was not unknown for the Empress to gather up those who had displeased her and allow the Imperial Bodyguard a spot of live target practice. But, as the black-clad guards took their stations, Grattus recognised one of the two figures who swept in behind the security squad.

"Good evening, gentlemen," Captain Sudrus stepped smartly to the lectern at the head of the large Conference Table, "if you would please take your seats," he instructed.

Still stunned, and slightly relieved not to be in the midst of a fusillade of blaster-bolts, the Generals nervously re-took their seats. Staying silent, Grattus waited for what was about to enfold.

"Gentlemen you have been summoned by the Empress to take part in the most glorious campaign in the history of the Bardomil Empire," Sudrus began.

'Glorious campaign' was usually a euphemism for 'bloodbath', Grattus considered as his mind slipped smoothly into the tone of the lecture that was about to follow.

"Her Majesty, the Empress, has decided that the time has come for the so-called Universal Alliance to understand the true might of the Bardomil Empire," Sudrus continued.

At the mention of the words 'Universal Alliance', Grattus suddenly brightened up. Since the defeat of General Sarvin's Bardomil Ninth Sarmitha Imperial Fleet by Caudwell, a large number of Bardomil Generals wished to try and avenge their comrades. With the commanders of six Imperial Fleets gathered in the Conference Room, one of them was going to have his chance. Leaning forward on his seat Grattus banged the table with the flat of his hand to show his appreciation. Quickly, the other Generals, not wishing to appear out of step in their loyalty to the Empress, followed suit.

"Gentlemen, if you please," Sudrus raised his hands to placate the table thumpers, "I applaud your eagerness to vanquish our enemy, but there is much preparation to be done," he shouted over the noise of table banging.

For a few seconds, the table banging continued, and when the Generals felt that they had shown sufficient loyalty, it petered out.

"Gentlemen, your loyalty is duly noted," Sudrus got down to the business of the briefing, "Junior Fleet Officer Batarrien will now outline the strategic situation," Sudrus gave way on the lectern to the handsome young Officer who had presented the idea to the Empress.

Another courtier, Grattus thought to himself as he watched the handsome, well dressed young Officer take the lectern. There had been a long and less than distinguished procession of Imperial favourites who had expounded their particular strategies over the years. However, Grattus, eager for the chance to take on Caudwell was prepared to listen to what this particular Imperial 'pet' had to say.

"Gentlemen, it is an honour to be here..." Batarrien began.

"Get on with it, boy!" the gruff General Glabbrus interjected.

Glabbrus, a solid, muscular slab of a creature was nobody's fool and did not suffer fools gladly.

"As I was saying, it is an honour to be here," Batarrien replied, unshaken by the General's rude outburst, "having completed a political and demographic study of the Universal Alliance..."

"Sometime today would be nice!" Glabbrus baited once more.

"Very well, General, if you do not wish to be part of this glorious campaign, I shall inform her Majesty of your reticence to participate," Batarrien smiled icily.

The tension in the room, already intolerably high went up several more notches at the insult.

"Are you calling me a coward, boy!?" a dangerously enraged Glabbrus hissed, raising his considerable frame from the seat that he occupied.

"Well, sir," Batarrien said confidently, "if your last performance against the Horvath is any indication, then I'm surprised that the Empress would want you on this expedition."

"What do you mean by that, boy!?" Glabbrus bunched his fists ready to strike.

This was a dangerous situation for young Batarrien. One of Glabbrus' favourite pastimes was to take sharpened metal spikes and drive them into the skulls of prisoners with his bare hands. Glabbrus was well able to kill with one blow.

"Well, I believe that they call you 'clean-pair-of-heels' on Horvan," Batarrien did some baiting of his own.

"Why you..." the incensed Glabbrus tried to clamber over the table to get to the lectern.

No sooner had Glabbrus moved than an Imperial Bodyguard struck the irate General with a stinging blow on the back of the head with a pistol. The General, stunned by the blow, stumbled and landed on his back on the

94

table top. The barrel of the black-uniformed Bodyguard's pistol pressed against the General's nose quelled any further aggressive outbursts.

Well, well, well, you seem to have some guts, Junior Fleet Officer Batarrien, Grattus considered as Glabbrus took his seat once more under the close guidance of a pistol-wielding Imperial Bodyguard. Watching the temporarily defeated General take his seat, Grattus knew that Glabbrus would not let the insult pass, and, no matter how long it took, he would kill Batarrien one day.

"As I was saying," Batarrien began again, cool as a cucumber, "I have carried out a political and demographic study of the Universal Alliance and have found a weakness."

Now Grattus was very definitely interested in what the young Officer had to say. Sitting forward, his elbows on the table, Grattus watched as the young Officer activated the Display Screen and studied the image that appeared on the table surface. The illustration seemed to be a two-dimensional schematic of the territory held by the Universal Alliance.

"Here, Gentlemen we have the current extent of the territories of the so-called Universal Alliance," Batarrien began, "we have the New Thexxia bloc highlighted in red," he added as one half of the Alliance schematic flashed a pale red, "the Colos bloc in yellow, the Ganthoran frontier in blue and our own frontier in white," the young Officer activated the various controls to illuminate the appropriate sectors.

"And, here Gentlemen, we have our objective," Batarrien indicated showing the five vulnerable systems in bright green, "we have the Praxos system; uninhabited," Batarrien informed, highlighting the system in orange, "the Terran system with one inhabited planet; not part of the Alliance," the orange highlight moved to the next system, "next, the Sidionas system; two inhabited planets currently at war with each other and not members of the Alliance," the orange highlight moved forward again, "then Botar; uninhabited and finally, the Sykith system with one inhabited planet; not part of the Alliance."

For a moment, a stunned silence fell over the room. Batarrien had just described a virtually undefended corridor through the heart of the Universal Alliance.

"Junior Officer," Grattus piped up, "this is all well and good, but surely their frontiers with us and the Ganthorans are heavily policed?"

"A very good strategic question, General," the young Officer praised, "and the answer to it is 'not really'. From our last reconnaissance sweeps, Intelligence indicates that the bulk of the Alliance's military forces are committed to establishing and protecting colonies in the new Thexxia sector. We believe that Alliance Admiral Chulling has five of their Star-Cruiser craft to defend the Praxos frontier."

"Turthus Chulling?" Grattus asked, "I've fought against him, he's a slippery one, he's clever and he has no shortage of courage," Grattus had to admit his admiration for the Thexxian-born Admiral.

"But what of Caudwell?" one of the unknown Generals asked.

"Caudwell will be distracted by a diversion, General Trathar," Batarrien replied.

"What kind of diversion?" the new General, Trathar, asked.

"That is confidential General," Batarrien replied with the famous Bardomil military euphemism for 'I-don't-really-know'.

The constant secrecy and back-covering were a source of annoyance for Grattus. The Bardomil military seemed to exist on the basis of the left hand not knowing what the right hand was doing. It was all part of the Empress' divide and rule policy. Unfortunately, the lack of shared information had more than once caused a Bardomil defeat. However, the Empress valued control of her Generals far more than she valued the lives of Bardomil soldiers.

"So, we are to attack the Alliance through the Praxos system?" General Methrien asked.

"Yes, General," Batarrien replied and changed the image on the Conference table surface.

Looking at the thin, cadaverous features of General Methrien, Grattus knew that despite being one of the cruellest and most savage of commanders, Methrien was also very tactically and strategically aware.

"Her Imperial Majesty has drawn up a plan of attack," Batarrien instructed as the Conference Table image showed a schematic of an invasion route, "gentlemen, the Praxos campaign," he added with the drama of a professional actor.

Grattus, like all the other Generals, had to stand up to look at the full extent of the plan.

The image showed a map through the five systems. A huge white line tipped by an arrow indicated the path of advance for the invasion force. Branching off from the large white line, narrower arrow-headed lines indicated where garrisons of Bardomil troops were to be established along the invasion route.

Nodding quietly, Grattus had to admit that the plan looked tactically sound. But, like all soldiers, he knew that plans were one thing and what the enemy did was something entirely different. Very rarely did an enemy conform to the planners' expectations. And, as Grattus Darrien scanned the invasion plan, he began to second guess what Chulling and Caudwell would do to resist the attack.

"It's very nice, Junior Officer," General Methrien was first to speak, "but to implement this plan it will require close to two million troops and their supplies."

"Very astute of you, General," Batarrien replied, "and this is only phase one. Her Imperial Majesty is committing five million soldiers to the campaign," he added proudly.

Once more the Generals murmured amongst themselves at the boldness and sheer scale of the plan.

"I don't see any occupation force for Planet Terra," a chastened and angry Glabbrus returned to the conversation.

"Terra is of no consequence, General," young Batarrien replied.

"No consequence? No consequence, Junior Officer? Terra is Caudwell's home planet. There are over five billion humans on that world. It's an ideal staging post for a counter-offensive, and we're just going to bye-pass it?" Glabbrus persisted.

"Her Majesty assures me that Terra will be taken care of by other means," Captain Sudrus said darkly, which stifled any further discussion on the matter.

"You said five million troops," Grattus commented, "with say two million to hold this 'corridor' and split the Alliance, do we deploy the rest against the Ganthorans?" he asked.

"No General, they will be required for phase two," Batarrien smiled and changed the Conference Table graphic.

The graphic for phase two showed a line of white squares on the left of the newly conquered 'corridor' whilst to the right, three vast white blocks showed large arrow-headed lines plunging deeply into Alliance territory and converging on the planet of New Thexxia.

"So, we're finally going after the Thexxians!?" General Methrien cheered loudly.

"Yes, General," Batarrien smiled, "we stabilise the Ganthoran frontier and isolate the Colos bloc before eliminating the Thexxians once and for all."

"And what do our planners think the Colos planets will be doing as we tear the heart out of the Alliance?" the other unknown General spoke.

"General Mardak, Her Majesty believes that the internal political instability amongst the planets around Colos will make a decisive military response highly unlikely," Batarrien replied, "our political analysts predict that the Colos bloc will sue for peace before the Thexxians are eliminated."

"That seems a very optimistic reading of the situation, Junior Officer," Methrien commented.

"No," Glabbrus insisted," there's no real fight in the Colosians; they're traders and merchants, not warriors," he added.

"Comments, Gentlemen?" Batarrien asked.

"It looks very nice on graphics and charts," Methrien spoke up again, "but supplying this kind of campaign will be a logistical nightmare."

"Her Majesty has committed two hundred and ten thousand transport vessels to the campaign with a further thirty thousand support transports every day," Batarrien replied.

Once again the Generals fell silent as they contemplated the sheer scale of the endeavour.

"That's a big undertaking Junior Officer," Grattus asked, "Do we really have the capacity to maintain that level of ongoing support?"

"Her Majesty has assured me that every effort will be expended to support this campaign," Sudrus intervened.

"The conquest of the 'corridor' and the elimination of the Thexxians will effectively remove the Universal Alliance as a threat to the Empire," Batarrien continued, "When the Alliance collapses, we will step in and conquer all of their territory."

"And, their technology," Methrien pointed out.

"Yes, General, we can copy and mass produce their technology and that will make us invincible," Batarrien smiled.

For a moment, the Generals fell silent as each one savoured the thought of invincibility and conquest with a few old scores settled in the bargain as well.

"Yes, Gentlemen, the Ganthorans would be defeated, the Horvath would be exterminated like the Thexxians and the riches of the unclaimed territories would be ours for the taking," Batarrien offered them a dream of limitless Imperial expansion.

"So, Junior Officer," Grattus asked the big question, "who is to be given the honour of commanding this expedition of yours?"

"Why General Darrien," Batarrien smiled, "that would be you, of course."

For a moment, Grattus stood stunned to silence as the enormity of what he was being asked to do started to sink in. It was a very big request indeed. Six full Imperial Fleets; nearly a quarter of a million transports and nearly seven million personnel was a big responsibility. If he was successful, the name Grattus Darrien would be the most famous in the Empire. In his mind's eye he saw fame, fortune, wealth, honours and power heaped upon his head by a grateful Empress.

Still not quite able to believe his luck he mumbled, "Long live the Empress!"

Chapter 20

<u>Planet Earth</u>

"Billy, phone!" Elizabeth Caudwell called from the living room.

Amongst the boxes and clutter of his bedroom, Billy Caudwell was attempting to pack away the treasured items that had to survive the ruthless cull of personal possessions that made up the move to the new house. With two days to go to the house move, Billy was excited at the prospect of the new property. All through his early childhood years he had stayed in police accommodations, which required that he move house every two years to fit in with his father's new postings. The stay at their most recent house had been five years, since his father had left the force; that was much longer than he had been accustomed to. The house the Caudwell's were leaving was damp and cold and Billy had never really felt any physical warmth or a psychological sense of belonging in the run-down Council-rented property. Now, with the new house, Billy felt that, at long last, he might actually have somewhere he could call home.

Despite all of his travels across the universe, Billy felt that this would be somewhere he could feel grounded and secure, even if it was only going to be for a short while. A home on Earth was at least preferable to the nomadic existence of the First Admiral of the Universal Alliance. Living in the Private Quarters next to the War Room aboard the Aquarius, or the Commanding Officer's quarters aboard a Star-Destroyer, no matter how luxurious, was not the same as having your own roof over your head or your own four walls surrounding you. There was just no comparison in the mind of Billy to having a home.

Trotting down the open-plan staircase, Billy took the ultra-modern phone receiver from his mother's outstretched hand. Around him, the living room was pretty much in the same state of disruption and disarray as his own room. Open boxes littered the ancient carpet that was soon to be discarded as his mother returned to wrapping the myriad of ornaments and family photos that would survive to be transported to the new house.

"Hello?" Billy said calmly placing the cold plastic receiver to his ear.

"Hello, Billy, it's Emma," a tinny-sounding, nervous voice greeted him on the other end of the line.

Immediately, Billy's expression shifted from calm to annoyance.

"I was under the impression that we had nothing further to say to each other," Billy said with that edge of annoyance manifesting.

"Billy, I need to talk to you..." Emma stammered.

"Well, I don't need to talk to you; goodbye," Billy said tersely.

"Please, Billy, hear me out," Emma pleaded her voice cracking with emotion, "I broke up with Micky last week, he was just using me to…"

"Well, that's too bad Emma; but, sorry I'm not in the-shoulder-to-cry-on business any more, go and whine to one of your girlfriends." Billy snapped.

"Look, Billy, this isn't easy for me…" Emma responded sharply.

"Really, oh boo-hoo," Billy mocked, "didn't your mummy tell you, life isn't easy, Princess; welcome to the real world."

"I didn't have to call you, you know?" Emma responded her temper rising.

"Oh, that's right, doing me a big favour speaking to me are you? It's funny how I don't feel blessed at hearing the sound of your voice" Billy barbed.

"I didn't mean it like that," Emma protested, "I didn't have to phone you, you know?"

"Yes, you did," Billy replied pragmatically, "you had to phone me because you want something; that's usually the only time I ever hear from you," he added, "well, bad luck, I only do maths tuition for my friends now. If you've got anything to say then get on with it, I'm busy."

"Billy," Emma paused, swallowing her pride, "I'm trying to say that I was wrong and that I'm sorry."

"Really," Billy sighed, "you're sorry are you? OK, why?" he challenged.

"What do you mean?" Emma quizzed, taken aback.

"It's very simple; you say you're sorry, I'm asking you why," Billy replied.

"Billy, I've said I'm sorry," Emma snapped, thrown back in confusion.

"And, I want to know why," Billy interrupted ruthlessly.

"Because, I was wrong…" Emma stammered still reeling from the question.

"And, it took you four weeks to realise that, did it?" Billy probed.

"Look, I was angry and upset…" Emma protested.

"About what?" Billy challenged again, "Someone standing up to you? Calling you on your bad manners and dishonesty? Boy, are you in for a disappointing lifetime, lady!" he added.

"I'm trying to apologise so that we can be friends again," Emma blurted.

"Well, I don't need your so-called friendship, Emma Wallace. I had a bellyful of it at the dance," Billy said icily, "now if you've got nothing more…"

"Okay, Okay!" Emma interrupted, "I was wrong. I treated you badly. I shouldn't have said all those stupid, horrible things. I apologise. I'm really sorry, Billy," she pleaded.

"No, I'm sorry; that's not good enough. I don't believe you," Billy replied calmly, "You have no integrity; your word is worthless and I simply don't trust you."

"You could give me another chance?" Emma said softly.

"Why would I want to do that?" Billy asked.

"Because everyone deserves a second chance," she replied hopefully.

"No they don't," Billy responded, "second chances have to be earned they're not simply a right."

For a moment the line went silent; the static crackling in Billy's ear.

"I've really blown it, haven't I, Billy?" Emma said sadly.

"Blown what?" Billy asked.

"Our friendship," she replied.

"Don't make me laugh" Billy snorted, "there was never any real friendship between us,"

"That's not true!" Emma protested.

"Yes, it is, Emma," Billy cut in remorselessly, "I was a convenient shoulder to cry on when it suited you, a back-up plan for the school dance and a handy maths tutor to get you through the pre-Quals."

"No!" Emma protested loudly, "That just simply isn't true!"

"Really?" Billy snapped, "Then, please, tell me one thing, just one thing that you ever did for your old and dear friend Billy Caudwell!?"

"Well..." Emma blurted, "There was..." the line fell silent once more.

"There was nothing, Emma Wallace," Billy responded, "Friendships are about give and take, and that doesn't mean you doing all the taking."

"I'm really sorry, Billy," Emma said dejectedly and hung up the receiver.

"You all right there, Billy?" his mother said quietly, looking up from the box she was packing as he gently replaced the receiver.

"Just putting out the garbage, mum," he replied softly and climbed slowly back up the staircase.

THE BURNING SUN

Chapter 21

The Star-Cruiser Aquarius

Intelligence Technician, Junior Grade, Marilla Thapes, sat alone, in utter silence contemplating the Display Screen on the table in front of her in the Intelligence Section's Bardomil Desk. It had been another long and frustrating duty shift for Marilla. She knew, just knew, that the Bardomil had deployed some kind of emitter weapon. Every instinct in her body told her that somewhere out there, in the depths of space, a Bardomil weapon was pointed like a pulsar-pistol at the proverbial head of some life-bearing planet. The question was; where they would deploy it? The video signal from the Explorer-Class Science Ship Magellan had shown her that something had been launched from the Bardomil incursion close to the frontier. To all the Scanner Interpretation people it had looked like a small rock, with a high metallic content, not unlike many trillions of other small rocks in that sector.

Looking carefully at the data once more, Marilla could clearly see 'the rock' being jettisoned by the damaged M-Cruiser before it disappeared in a huge blinding fireball. The debris from the blast was scattered in all directions. Yet, Marilla still believed that this 'rock' was moving under its own propulsion. Again and again, Marilla watched the few fractions of a second before the fireball, where 'the rock' seemed to move quickly away. Rubbing her tired eyes once more, Marilla was starting to doubt the evidence of her own vision. Was she really seeing an object moving of its own volition or was she simply imagining it, she asked herself. She couldn't possibly have gotten it so badly wrong, she challenged herself. And, to stand up in front of Admiral Lokkrien and get it wrong stung Marilla even further. Further, the look in Senior Intelligence Officer Sownus' eyes told her that her opportunity to shine was about to come to an end. The normally philosophical Marilla Thapes would have usually taken the disappointment in her stride, but this time, she knew, that this was her one and only chance to impress the top brass. But, she had blown it.

Again, she took the heavily magnified image forward, one frame at a time. The fuzzy image of 'the rock' seemed to be pushed slowly away from the M-Cruiser as the Alliance pulsar-bolts slammed into its hull.

"Towards me...towards me...towards me..." Marilla tracked 'the rock' on each individual frame until suddenly it blurred for two frames as it moved off quickly to the right.

"Yes, it definitely changed direction," Marilla hissed to herself.

"It's the first sign of madness you know, Technician Thapes?" a voice said from beside her.

Turning quickly, Marilla noticed the two small golden stars of a Second Admiral on the lower left sleeve of the uniform next to her.

"Sir!" Marilla barked and sprang to her feet, her chair falling to the floor and clattering behind her.

"At ease, Technician," the familiar voice of Marrhus Lokkrien consoled.

"Sir!" Marilla rested into the 'at ease' position waiting for the dressing down she felt that Lokkrien would inevitably deliver.

"Do you really believe that my old friends on Bardan have created this emitter weapon?" Lokkrien asked calmly.

"Yes, sir, the evidence indicates..." Marilla began a further regimentally-correct report.

"The evidence indicates only the possibility, Technician Thapes," Lokkrien cut across her, stifling Marilla's flow of words.

For a long nerve-shredding moment, Lokkrien let his view sink into Marilla Thapes' mind.

"You have nothing but speculation and supposition, Technician Thapes," Lokkrien added, "However, I happen to think that you might be on the right track."

"Sir?" Marilla looked in astonishment at the Second Admiral.

"What you suppose and conjecture, Technician Thapes, works in very well with what I happen to know about how the Bardomil Empire operates," Lokkrien continued, setting up Marilla's chair once more.

"And, sir, I..." Marilla started to speak once again and then gave up the ghost, "I have nothing to add other than what I presented earlier," her shoulders slumped in resignation.

"Your reasoning and logic are correct, Technician Thapes, your technique is somewhat lacking," Lokkrien announced pulling another chair up and sitting down, "sit," he ordered.

Nervously, Marilla sat slowly down on the chair that Lokkrien had retrieved for her.

"I don't understand, sir?" Marilla puzzled.

"Let's look at what we have and do a bit more speculating," Lokkrien suggested, "The Empress has had the weapons expert Claggit and his assistant killed; that's standard procedure for the Empire. Aliens are not considered intelligent enough to create the weapons that win glorious victories, only Bardomil scientists do that. So, Claggit and his little friend are removed, do you follow me?"

Still mystified by what Lokkrien was talking about, Marilla stared open-mouthed at the Second Admiral and nodded.

"This tells us that our Bardomil friends have a weapon made by Master Claggit and being a magnetic field specialist, we can assume that the weapon works on those principles," Lokkrien continued to the confused Marilla.

"We are now also assuming that the Empress has tested this weapon in the Artreaus system, which was chosen for a specific reason. Now, what might that reason be, Technician Thapes?" Lokkrien asked.

"Well, I'd say because it bore certain similarities to where the weapon is intended to ultimately be used?" Marilla speculated.

"Now, Technician Thapes, you're getting the hang of it," Lokkrien praised.

"So, the Bardomil would target this weapon at an enemy planet, would they not?" Lokkrien asked.

"Well, yes sir," Marilla replied.

"And, this planet would have to be a life-bearing enemy planet, would it not?" Lokkrien asked.

"Yes, sir," Marilla replied, "There's no point in scorching an empty piece of rock."

"So, how many life-bearing planets were there in the Artreaus system, Technician Thapes?" Lokkrien continued.

"Just the one, sir, Collizon," Marilla answered.

"This weapon supposedly created a super-charged plasma stream from the star at the centre of the Artreaus system. So, what kind of star does the Artreaus system have?" Lokkrien questioned.

"It's a yellow dwarf, sir," Marilla provided the information from her own memory.

"And, how far was Collizon from that yellow dwarf?" Lokkrien continued.

"About one hundred and fifty million kilometres, sir," Marilla replied.

"So, Collizon, a fairly unremarkable planet in a back water system in the depths of the Bardomil Empire was wiped out to test this weapon, why Technician Thapes?" Lokkrien asked.

"Same answer as before, sir, because it has some similarity to where the Bardomil want to attack," Marilla responded.

Wondering where the line of constant questioning was going, Marilla managed to forget that Marrhus Lokkrien was a Bardomil; the traditional enemy of her Thexxian blood. As a Bardomil, Marilla distrusted and was wary of the Second Admiral. Yet, as a Second Admiral, Marilla knew that she not only had to obey his orders, but she also had developed a rather reluctant admiration for him. He didn't have to travel through the Aquarius to sit with her in the Intelligence Section. He didn't have to explain that he shared her suspicions. And, he surely didn't have to sit down and try to work out what he thought was happening with her.

"So, we are looking for a system with a yellow dwarf star and a life-bearing planet some one hundred and fifty million kilometres away from it," Lokkrien theorised, "Do we have such a system in our territory?"

"We have several systems that are similar to Artreaus in Alliance held space, Admiral," Marilla replied, "But, none of them lie on the predicted course of the weapon," she added sadly.

"Show me," Lokkrien asked.

With a few deft stabs at the portable keypad, Marilla called up the three-dimensional schematic of the course that she had projected from the encounter with the Clements. From that location, Marilla had extrapolated a path that stretched all the way through Alliance held territory to the unclaimed systems beyond New Thexxia.

"There is nothing on that course even remotely similar to Artreaus, sir," Marilla said reluctantly.

"Then, obviously, this weapon must be taking another route," Lokkrien replied, staring at the schematic.

"Because it has independent propulsion capability," Marilla added, suddenly feeling rather stupid for not considering that option when she herself had suggested it based on her video analysis.

"Precisely," Lokkrien smiled, "so, how many systems do we have in Alliance space with a yellow dwarf star and a life-bearing planet at one hundred and fifty million kilometres distant?" Lokkrien asked.

Tapping on her keypad once more, Marilla dismissed the flawed projected course image and accessed the Astrophysical database.

"Three systems sir: Stegmar, Terra and Palyon," Marilla replied innocently.

Marrhus Lokkrien flinched in his seat as if he'd been shot by a pulsar-pistol at the realisation that had just struck him.

"Technician Thapes, if you were a vain and arrogant Bardomil Empress who had just lost an entire Imperial Fleet to First Admiral Caudwell, how would you take personal revenge for that?" Lokkrien said calmly, the tension in the conversation racking up several notches as Marilla listened.

"I'd be mighty angry, sir, and I'd want to kill him?" Marilla said speculatively.

"But, to kill him, you'd have to get through the entire Alliance Fleet, so what's the next best thing?"

"I'd want to kill his family, sir!" the realisation suddenly struck Marilla, "and his family and his whole human species are on Terra!"

"And, we have a surveillance asset close to Terra," Lokkrien answered grabbing the keypad from Marilla.

Quickly, Lokkrien tapped in his personal code and was connected to the Ranger that orbited over Planet Earth to monitor and shelter Billy Caudwell's double, Technician Jedithram Prust. A moment later, the face of the Commander of the surveillance Ranger appeared on a two dimensional projection on the Display Screen.

"Admiral, it's an honour, sir; how can we be of service to you?" the nervous Thexxian Ship Commander stammered.

"Scan the yellow dwarf star at the heart of the Terran system, quickly," Lokkrien barked the command.

"But, sir..." the Ship Commander stammered again.

"Just do it!" Lokkrien snarled.

"Yes, sir!" the Ship Commander yelped like a frightened schoolboy and his image vanished to be replaced by that of the burning yellow orb of the Earth's sun.

"Scanning, sir," the disembodied voice continued.

Looking anxiously at the yellow star at the heart of the Terran system, Lokkrien could see nothing out of the ordinary. The sun seemed to be just the same as thousands of other yellow dwarves he had personally encountered in his career.

"Sir, we're picking up a massive increase in Lissian radiation emissions from the star," the voice of the Ship Commander broke over the image, "but, this star doesn't produce any Lissian..." he added in confusion.

"No, no, no, no!" Lokkrien hissed through gritted teeth as he watched the yellow dwarf closely.

"There sir, top right," Marilla instructed, drawing Lokkrien's attention to an area of the star that seemed to be turning a deeper orange colour.

"Oh no, you do not," Lokkrien challenged the image as the orange patch seemed to convulse.

Slowly, at first, the great orange blister on the surface of the sun began to spread as the Bardomil weapon destabilised the magnetic polarity of the star. With growing horror, Thapes and Lokkrien sat motionless as the blister quickly expanded and then suddenly burst, throwing great spumes of solar material out into space. The long, snaking finger-like tendrils seethed out into the darkness of space and began their journey towards the unsuspecting blue planet that lay just a shade less than one hundred and fifty million kilometres away.

"Sir, it's..." the horrified Marilla announced pointing to the image.

"Yes, I know Technician Thapes, I can see it," Lokkrien replied, stabbing the keypad once again, "Ship Commander get the First Admiral off that planet immediately!"

"But, sir..." the Ship Commander replied, "I don't have the authority to..." he pleaded for understanding.

"Never mind," Marrhus Lokkrien interrupted the Ship Commander as he watched more and more solar material spewing out from the sun, "How long did it take to destroy Collizon, Technician Thapes?"

"About two Terran hours," Marilla replied still staring aghast at the drama unfolding on the Display Screen.

Tapping the keypad again, Lokkrien began to bark orders.

"Ship Commander," Lokkrien contacted the 'Captain' of the Aquarius, "make ready for immediate Trion Drive to the Terran system."

"Acknowledged," the Aquarius Ship Commander replied professionally having learned not to question orders.

"Senior Intelligence Officer Sownus," Lokkrien tapped the keypad once more, "report to the War Room immediately."

"Sir, acknowledging," the familiar voice of Karap Sownus responded, "Do we have a problem?"

"That Bardomil emitter weapon Technician Thapes told us about has just activated in the Terran system," Lokkrien answered.

"But, the First Admiral..." Sownus suddenly realised the significance, "on my way," he added.

"Technician Thapes," Lokkrien broke Marilla out of her morbid fascination with the great plumes of super-heated plasma hurtling away from the Terran sun, "you're with me," Lokkrien ordered.

"Sir!" Marilla barked, snapping out of her fascination.

"Come on, we have to get to Terra and secure the First Admiral before it's too late," Lokkrien announced and dashed off towards the nearest Teleport station.

Marilla Thapes was close behind.

THE BURNING SUN

Chapter 22

<u>Planet Earth</u>

Elizabeth Caudwell, nursing her cup of scalding hot tea, sat on the battered brown family sofa for the last time and contemplated the worn and untidy street that had been her home for the last five years. When this particular tea break was over, the long-serving family sofa was being consigned to the local rubbish dump. The new house in the country was almost ready. It had taken Elizabeth several weeks to get it just right, but now she was happy with it. And, now it was nearly time to move in to the new property. The lease agreement on their current home, a Council property, was due to expire in three days. The decorators were due to finish the new kitchen the day after tomorrow giving the Caudwell's a full day to settle into the new property before surrendering the keys and rent book of their old home. Everything in the new house was new, and, to John Caudwell's mind, just a little bit too expensive for his tastes. But, Elizabeth didn't care. She had always wanted a home that she had designed and decorated to her tastes and specifications. She had grown tired of living in rented houses where a landlord's rules stifled her creative and decorative aspirations. The money in the bank from her writing now made those aspirations a reality and she was going to let her imagination run riot.

Outside the large living room window, the young removal men were kicking a wad of newspaper around like a football on the narrow front lawn that Billy had hated mowing. It had been a thankless task for young Billy. The lawn was more weed than grass, and every mowing seemed to produce more weeds and dandelions to be culled with a hand held trowel. That was one job Billy certainly wouldn't miss, Elizabeth considered, sipping the scalding sweet liquid from the dark blue mug. The noise from the rowdy young removal men distracted Elizabeth from her thoughts for a moment. An older man, tough overweight and world weary, the gang leader, perched precariously on the three bar fence that divided the asphalt public footway from their front lawn. Smoking a rolled up cigarette, the gang leader smiled and nodded to Elizabeth who smiled in reply. The gang leader had recognised her from the portrait on the back cover of her book. Like hundreds of thousands of husbands and fathers he had secretly read "My Lost Little Angel". He himself had lost a child of a few days, many years before, and had felt the anger, outrage and powerlessness. Elizabeth's book had helped his wife, even these many years later, and gave him a window into what she had never really been able to explain to him.

Thus, when the football playing young men's language became a bit colourful, the older man would bark them into a more restrained respectful vocabulary. However, the florid language of a few vigorous, scuffling young men was not likely to be a major distraction this day. The real worry of Elizabeth Caudwell lay in an innocuous brown envelope that lay on the sofa next to her. Elizabeth Caudwell had read the very polite very formal letter nearly a dozen times. It had been over two hours since the tired and footsore postman had delivered the large, neatly addressed, brown envelope with the foreign stamps in the top right hand corner. The stamps had borne the legend of the U.S. Post Office with the postal mark of New York City. Now, this was indeed glamorous and exciting for the girl who was brought up in a former mining village in Southern Scotland.

As a little girl she had dreamed of seeing exotic places like New York, with the Empire State Building and Central Park.

But, those had just been the stupid fantasies of a silly little girl alone, in a room she shared with two sisters, dreaming of a better life in the dim and distant future. Now, here it was in front of her, in black and white, something she had always dreamed of; an all expenses paid invitation to visit New York City, and to discuss possible publication of her book. An invitation signed by the President of the Publishing House himself; a signature she couldn't quite make out, but the typescript beneath said Bertram Millinghouse the Third, President.

Well, it looks like you've really arrived now, Elizabeth had considered, reading the text of the letter, part of her not quite believing that it was real. But, the invitation to travel to New York City was very, very real indeed. The letter with the brash, multi-coloured letterhead that announced that it was from Millinghouse Publications did indeed invite her to a meeting with the Vice-President of Fiction, a Mister Lindstrom, seven days from the date of the letter. Looking at her watch, Elizabeth had realised that the letter had taken three days to arrive. She had four days to make up her mind and get to New York. More importantly, she had to find a way to tell John and Billy just as they were moving into their new home.

The decision to go was purely academic and Mr Teddington had said in the past that it might be a good idea for her to do some book signings in the United States. Yes, but she wasn't going to sign books she reminded herself. And, she suspected, that Mr Teddington wouldn't be too happy about her speaking to a rival publisher considering the investment he had already made in her. No, she corrected herself she would go to New York, but politely and firmly tell Millinghouse Publications, that she was not looking for a new publisher. She would go to New York, see all the sights she had always dreamed of seeing, visit the big department stores she had read about in the glossy magazines, and then come home again to her brand new house. It would be a simple straightforward business trip with a great deal of sightseeing and no complications.

After all, she had worked hard for what she had achieved, so she deserved a little bit of 'me' time to herself, Elizabeth considered. She didn't need to be tied to the house, to be at everyone's beck and call. She was going to have a life for herself.

John and Billy would just have to get used to that, she decided.

Chapter 23

<u>Planet Earth</u>

"Billy!" Emma Wallace called out in the middle of the playground, "Billy! Wait up!" she called, pushing her way through the straggle of students slowly making their way to the tower block building.

Struggling to keep her shoulder bag in place, Emma jostled and pushed her way, breathlessly, forward until she had caught up with Billy Caudwell.

"Billy, I really need..." She said panting with exertion.

"I told you last night, I've got nothing to say to you!" Billy snapped with hurt irritation, striding on towards the heavy safety glass doors of the building.

"Billy, please," Emma protested trying to keep up whilst wrestling with her shoulder strap, "look, I know I've messed up big time..."

"Look," Billy snapped, stopping and turning to face Emma, "get outta my face. I want nothing to do with you!" he barked and strode angrily off into the darkened maw of the building.

Emma, however, was not the kind of girl to give up so easily. Hitching up her shoulder bag determinedly, she dashed after Billy into the cool darkness of the ground floor corridor. In the hallway, three streams of foot traffic merged. Those coming down from upper floor classrooms and out of the building, those entering and heading up to classrooms, and those heading for classrooms on the ground floor mingled and barged their way to their appointed destinations.

Sharing the first two periods of Biology with Billy, Emma knew exactly where he would be going and moved rapidly to intercept pushing through the traffic streams. Catching Billy just before he entered the classroom, Emma barged Billy aside and pushed him into the well beneath the stairs.

"Look, Mister Billy Caudwell, I know I've messed up and I'm sorry!" Emma said determinedly.

"Go away, Emma, I've told you before..." Billy remonstrated with her at the same time causing a huge distraction amongst the puzzled students.

"Oh...fudge!" an exasperated Emma finally conceded the row, threw caution to the wind and grabbing Billy's tie; she pulled his head towards her, as she planted her lips squarely against his.

Locked in a passionate kiss, Billy was taken completely by surprise and unable to resist. His eyes bugging wide with astonishment, Billy found himself in the embrace and unable to escape. Flapping his arms weakly, he held his breath and tried to make sense of what was happening.

In the corridor, students were cheering, yelling and applauding. "You go, grrrrl!" a female voice called out as Emma pulled Billy closer.

"Come on you two, take it home with you tonight!" a male teacher barked, interrupting the kiss.

Gasping for breath and blushing to his hair roots, Billy stared in astonishment at Emma.

"What..." he gasped, unable to form a coherent sentence let alone an explanation in his own mind.

"Come on, Billy; I know I messed up big time, but just give me a chance, please?" she begged.

For a moment, Billy was torn. Part of him wanted to push her away whilst another part wanted her to kiss him again. With a defeated sigh he nodded his acceptance and tried to speak.

"Just shush, and get into class, we'll talk about it later," Emma whispered, with a smile, pressing her forefinger up against his lips to silence him.

"Come on you two lovebirds, get a move on!" the teacher jostled Billy away from the stairwell.

Half turning to speak to Emma, the teacher moved Billy on towards the traffic stream. And, as Billy struggled towards the Biology lab door, Emma cheekily pinched his bottom.

"Hey!" Billy protested, smiling broadly.

"Move it, sweet cheeks," Emma whispered seductively in his ear.

"Come on, get in here or I'll send you to detention," the female Biology teacher called from the classroom door as Billy stumbled into the lab.

Taking his seat at the end of the front bench in the Biology Class, as the other students straggled into the room Billy turned a quick glance to Emma and winked craftily. Emma, sitting at another bench, smiled broadly and replied with her own cheeky wink making Billy smile and blush. He felt the surge of heat on his face as he diverted his attention to the attractive young woman who was to teach this days' first lesson.

"Right come on, settle down," the young, petite blonde woman in the white lab coat barked in agitation at the tardy students still chattering and meandering their way into her classroom.

Mrs Sheena Collier, Billy speculated, could be no more than twenty-five or twenty-six. He had seen an old school orchestra image of a younger version of her taken only eight years before. Assuming she had been eighteen at the time, he could calculate her age and how long she had been teaching at the school, if this had been her first post.

"Come on, Angela, we haven't got all day," Mrs Collier scolded one of Billy's dawdling classmates as she finally found her seat at the back bench of the lab.

When the last of the students had straggled their way to their appointed places, Mrs Collier strode up to the oblong chalkboard and began to write.

"Today, we will be continuing with..." she began, as she wrote the letters P-H-O-T, the chalk squealing against the slate board, "Photosynthesis."

Almost as one, the class groaned, good-naturedly. Mrs Collier was a popular young teacher; the boys, including Billy, fancied her, whilst all the girls wanted to be like the stylish, confident young woman.

With a deep sigh, Billy glanced at the clock next to the door, it read nine-oh-five and the class would be in the lab until ten thirty. Mentally, he resigned himself to the hour and a half of being spoon fed how plants made food and oxygen out of carbon dioxide and water. Quietly, he smiled to himself wishing he could show Mrs Collier some of the plant species on other worlds that could move around, communicate, and eat flesh. But, that part of his double-life had to remain secret and that meant that those botanical delights would be hidden from the young woman.

It was at that moment of Billy's resignation that seven blinding flashes shattered the early morning tedium of the laboratory.

Instinctively, Billy Caudwell knew the materialisation flashes from the Teleport and his mind recoiled in shock from the realisation that his carefully constructed cover was about to be blown.

A moment later, three blue and four black uniformed figures materialised from the blinding flashes.

Three Fleet Officers and four Landing Troopers, the standard Security Detail, had materialised in the middle of the classroom. Billy immediately recognised Marrhus Lokkrien and Karap Sownus with a young, female Thexxian Intelligence Technician. The Landing Troopers, the close combat specialists of the Alliance, were a pair of Thexxians and two tall reptile-like Icharians.

A chorus of stunned gasps, screams and cries of astonishment greeted the new unexpected arrivals.

"First Admiral..." the anxious figure of Marrhus Lokkrien, standing in front of him at his bench was the first to speak.

"What is the meaning of this?" Sheena Collier blustered as she strode determinedly from in front of the chalkboard.

THE BURNING SUN

The Landing Trooper closest to her, sensing her hostility and aggression, raised the spindly butt of the seven-barrelled pulsar-rifle to violently pacify the advancing teacher.

With his lizard face set in a determined stare the young Icharian Landing Trooper prepared to knock the teacher to the ground.

"TROOPER! Stand down!" Billy barked, his cover now well and truly blown.

Instantly, the Trooper snapped to attention with Sheena Collier cowering nervously against the chalkboard, her arms crossed in front of her face. Billy had to admit that the young teacher did have courage, but a reptilian soldier brandishing a weapon had taken the wind from her sails.

"This had better be good, Admiral Lokkrien," Billy hissed viciously.

Over the last year, he had taken considerable care to ensure that his other life would remain hidden and now Marrhus Lokkrien had managed to destroy all of that effort in the blink of an eye.

"What's going on here, Caudwell?" Mrs Collier asked nervously from the chalkboard starting to regain her normal stance.

"Just...just...just stay where you are and be quiet, Miss," Billy said firmly in a tone that brooked no arguments.

Glancing over to Emma, he could see her staring back at him in astonishment and terror. Closing his eyes, Billy banged his fist down on the bench-top with frustration and anger.

"Now, explain Admiral," Billy turned his attention back to the three blue uniformed Fleet Officers as the Landing Troopers took stations covering the door and windows.

"Sir," Karap Sownus stepped forwards, "my apologies, but we had no choice but to interrupt you," Sownus began, "we have to get you away from this planet quickly."

"What's happened?" Billy asked anxiously, knowing that the solid, reliable and level-headed Karap Sownus did not press the panic button without very good reason.

"Sir," Lokkrien intervened, "we believe that the Bardomil have activated a weapon in close proximity to your Sun and that a massive solar flare has been released that will destroy this planet."

"Marrhus, are you quite sure?" Billy replied not quite able to believe what he was hearing.

"Yes, unfortunately we are, sir," the young Intelligence Technician, Marilla Thapes, entered the conversation, "we had suspicions that such a weapon had been created, but it was only within the last hour that we have had positive confirmation when the weapon was activated."

"And, this thing will destroy the entire planet?" the hard-headed part of his mind that was Teg Portan came crashing to the fore.

"Yes, sir," Marilla Thapes replied, "we estimate in less than two hours the super-charged and super-heated plasma will enter the Terran atmosphere."

"Okay, how do we stop it?" Billy asked starting to grasp the enormity of the situation.

"The simple answer is that we can't, sir. I'm sorry," Lokkrien replied.

"No, Admiral, my family and everything that I know and love is on this planet; there has to be a way," Billy said his jaw set firm with determination.

"We can evacuate you and your family, sir," the ever-realistic Lokkrien said.

"Unacceptable!" Billy Caudwell barked again, "I will not abandon this planet with everyone on it and skulk away like a coward!"

"Sir," Lokkrien countered, "we cannot afford to lose you, I'm sorry, sir, but we cannot save this planet."

"No, I will not hear of it," Billy replied, "we have the ability to shield and protect New Thexxia; we can do it here!" Billy said adamantly rising from his stool and stabbing his forefinger onto the bench top.

"The planetary defences around New Thexxia were built by the Garmaurians along with the facility; it would take us weeks to set up a similar defence system on this planet and we have less than two hours," Lokkrien tried to reason with the distraught Billy, "I'm sorry, sir, it can't be done."

"What about shielding?" Billy grasped at straws, "bring in the big Star-Destroyers and throw a shield over the planet."

"Sir," Marilla Thapes answered, "the Engineers Corps calculated that the suspected test firing of the weapon in the Artreaus system produced an energy release in the region of one hundred million billion of your Hiroshima-type atomic weapons."

"The Star-Destroyers themselves would be very lucky to survive that kind of blast," Lokkrien added.

"But, they might survive?" Billy grasped at another straw lifting a pencil from the bench top.

"Sir," Lokkrien insisted "you have to be realistic about this..."

"No, Admiral, we have to explore and exhaust every possibility!" Billy snapped in reply, "and that's an order!" he added snapping the pencil in his frustration.

"Yes, sir!" Lokkrien snapped to attention, as Billy caught sight of the snapped pencil in his hand.

For a moment Marilla Thapes stared at the pencil point in Billy's hand and a strange idea sparked in her head.

"And, what do we do about these civilians, sir?" Sownus asked quietly drawing Billy out of his thoughts.

"We take them with us," Billy ordered, "We can deal with the fall out if the planet survives."

"Yes, sir," Sownus responded, "I'll teleport them to the Containment Cells and..."

"They are not prisoners, Karap," Billy interrupted, "take them up to the Observation Deck and give them the VIP treatment."

"Sir," Sownus replied and signalled the waiting vessel in orbit above the planet.

"Marrhus," Billy turned to Lokkrien, "lock this place up just in case, no one will come looking for another hour and a half and if we haven't stopped this flare by then there probably won't be anyone to look anyway," Billy instructed, "Crisis Conference in the War Room."

"Sir," Sownus acknowledged and relayed the instructions.

Turning to Emma, Billy smiled weakly to the astonished schoolgirl who looked at him with a mixture of curiosity and horror. With a shrug of resignation he shook his head slowly and disappeared in a blinding flash of light.

As the students and their teacher waited for whatever fate the classmate they knew as Billy Caudwell had decided for them, the Sun at the heart of the solar system erupted. The huge outpouring of super-heated plasma spewed forth from the surface of the yellow dwarf star like huge fibrous burning tendrils that snaked and slithered their way towards the defenceless planet just over one hundred and fifty million kilometres away.

A distance it would span in less than two hours.

Chapter 24

Planet Earth

For John Caudwell, the high-pressure spray of the shower smashed onto his exhausted body like the Niagara Falls. The cascade of cool refreshing water seethed and flowed remorselessly over every square inch of skin; washing away the stresses, aches and weariness of the last twenty-four hours that he had spent in his loft workshop. His body was aching, and even his short fair hair felt weary, but his head was still spinning from the elation of what he had just achieved.

The proto-type beam that he had initially thought to be a piece of pure science-fiction had actually worked. Up in his loft, there was a standard red concrete house brick with a gaping black-rimmed and scorched hole torn from the centre of it. Still too hot for the human hand to touch, John had abandoned the brick to cool down whilst he took a shower and tried to clear his head. He had developed what could be a weapon with potentially awesome power and destructive potential. And, in the wrong hands, that power could be used for evil and malicious purposes. John knew that he had to be careful with what he did with this mechanism. He knew that he had to think.

The obvious solution would have been not to have built the machine, but the scientist and engineer within John knew that if such a device could be built then he had to build it. Now, he had a prototype weapon on his hands, and a great deal of further work to do for the weapon to become functional anywhere outside his own loft. There were so many issues to resolve with the mechanism before anyone could even consider deploying it in the field.

The principle of the prototype was simple enough. John had designed an energy discharge device that took a small laser beam and caused the frequency of the light to rapidly fluctuate. A basic laser beam, at a steady frequency, was harmless, and even the most powerful lasers could cause no damage. However, John had installed a cheap and simple condenser behind the lens of the laser beam. With a few simple modifications, the condenser temporarily stored the laser energy and stimulated the particles of the beam to rapidly modulate their frequency through a cycle of narrow frequency ranges. This frequency modulation gave the beam, when it was eventually discharged, the pulsing effect that John had theorised. It was this pulsing effect that made the beam so destructive.

The part of his mind that was the Garmaurian industrialist, Mallor Sharpal, understood Trion Theory, and that to stimulate Trions beyond a certain range of frequencies had catastrophically destructive consequences. John understood much of what his mind told him about Trion Theory, and for that reason he had kept the frequency range of his new weapon to very precise and limited parameters. In fact, the beauty of his new weapon, if any aspect of the destructive power of a weapon could be considered to be beautiful, was that it was self-regulating. When the pulsing beam of the weapon struck an object, whether organic or inorganic, the Trions at the point of contact would be agitated by the pulse effect. If the frequency range of the pulse was outside the Trionic frequency range of the object, then the object would remain largely unscathed.

If, however, the Trionic frequency of the object was within the parameters of the pulse, then the damage caused would be proportional to the intensity of the beam. In a low-intensity beam, the Trions within the object would become agitated, and start to rupture their Trionic Bonds as far as the intensity of the beam permitted. The lower the intensity of the beam, the easier it would be for the Trions of the target object to absorb the energy being expended towards them. Like a bullet hitting a stone wall, the energy would be absorbed by the structure. The rupturing of the Trionic Bonds would release its own destructive energy against the atomic structure of the target object, causing damage and destruction.

What John had to be careful of was setting the intensity of the weapon too high or the frequency range too broad. Setting the intensity too high would cause the pulse to pass through every solid object it came into contact with like a knife through butter. To set the frequency range too broad would create a chain-reaction through the Trionic structure of the object it struck, which would agitate and disrupt the Trions around it. That could be the air or water or whatever the object was in contact with, and, theoretically, the chain reaction would be too powerful to stop. What would, happen in that situation was anyone's guess. It was a circumstance, John did not really want to consider.

The frequency ranges and the intensity of the discharged beam could be experimented with to make best use of the Trionic properties of the objects being targeted, but the biggest stumbling block was going to be a power source. To discharge the weapon once, John had drained four normal sized car batteries. He had considered using the mains supply, but rejected the idea. If this weapon was going to be effective, it would have to be portable and usable in a hand-held format, perhaps, a pistol or a rifle. To anchor it to one fixed point with a power supply would create something like an artillery gun. But, John knew that artillery with this kind of weapon was far too destructive for the human species to have access to.

BENNING

As the water from the cooling and refreshing shower ran down his back and legs, John considered that he could perhaps adjust the settings of the weapon to allow it to be fired by a small battery like the ones in the portable music players that were coming onto the market. That then presented a problem of reloading the weapon after the initial discharge. When he had been at the police college, they had trained on the old Lee-Enfield bolt-action rifles. Perhaps he could design something along those lines, where the bolt action ejected a battery-like power source similar to the spent cartridge of the rifle. That would, of course, litter any battlefield with nasty acid-based batteries. Even with re-chargeable batteries, the weapon would most probably only fire once. What he needed was a reliable, high-powered, portable energy cell with the capacity of one of those new nuclear reactors; essentially a nuclear battery.

A nuclear battery, John mused, as the cooling soothing water seethed across his face and chest.

Where on Earth would I get a nuclear battery?

THE BURNING SUN

Chapter 25

The War Room, Star-Cruiser Aquarius

Ten minutes later, Billy Caudwell convened his Crisis Conference in the cavernous War Room. Around the massive War Table, Billy had hurriedly assembled the brightest and the best that were aboard the flagship Aquarius. Marrhus Lokkrien, Karap Sownus and Marilla Thapes were joined by specialists from the Fleet Engineers Corps, who all sat anxiously around the table.

The noise of communications traffic and the murmur of conversation amongst the hordes of Officers and Technicians that populated the banks of consoles around the War Table, only just managed to drown the suppressed anxiety that hung like a dark blanket over the Conference attendees. First Admiral Caudwell was fighting for his home-world, his family, and everything he held dear in this life. He was anxious and irritable, and no one around the War Table wished to feel the wrath of an angered Supreme Commander.

"So," Billy opened the proceedings standing, arms forded, at the War Table, "what are our options?"

Having been challenged for suggestions, the conference fell disconcertingly silent.

"Come on!" Billy badgered, "I've got the finest brains in the Alliance here and no one has any ideas?"

Again, the conference fell into silence as eyes were averted from the agitated Supreme Commander. After what seemed like an eternity Marrhus Lokkrien spoke.

"Sir," Lokkrien was always careful to begin with the honorific in front of subordinates, "I'm sorry, but there is just no way that we can put anything in place in the limited time that we have."

"The best we can do, sir," Karap Sownus continued the argument, "is to try to save what we can in the time available..."

"As I said before," Billy barked angrily, "that is not an option!" he slammed his fist down on the edge of the War Table, "I will not play God as to who lives and who gets left behind. I want ideas as to how we protect that planet!"

Again the conference fell into an awkward silence.

"Any ideas!?" Billy pleaded with a long drawn out sigh of desperation while he ran his left hand through his hair as if it might draw some fresh inspiration from his brain.

BENNING

After a few more moments of strained silence, Marilla Thapes piped up.

"Well, sir," Marilla said nervously, "when I was very young, my mother used to take me out into the country," she began and was aware of all eyes now being turned on her.

"Yes, go on," Billy implored, prepared to grasp at anything.

"Well, sir," she licked her lips nervously, "we used to sit underneath this waterfall, sir, but there was this huge rock that stuck out from the cliff face above us and split the falling water so we were perfectly dry even though we were underneath tons and tons of liquid."

"Technician Thapes, please don't be so..." Sownus started to scold the presumptuous subordinate.

"No, Karap," Billy interrupted the Senior Intelligence Officer, "she might just have something there," his mind sparked with an idea.

"So, you sat under this big waterfall?" Billy questioned, "and this large rock, you describe deflected the water away from you and your mother?"

"Yes, sir," Marilla said nervously under the silent scowl of Karap Sownus.

"A breakwater, or something like a breakwater," Billy began to postulate excitedly, "far enough away from the planet, could deflect the plasma out into space and not harm Earth?"

Again, the conference fell silent.

"Can we do it?" Billy asked the Senior Engineering Officer pointedly.

"I doubt it, sir," the stocky Senior Engineer replied, "there are all sorts of variables to be considered..." he continued.

"What would we need to make it happen?" Billy questioned the Engineer excitedly, "Could our force-shielding concentrated in a small area deflect the plasma away?"

"Well, sir," the Engineer thought, "theoretically, we'd need a very heavily strengthened force-shield focussed and concentrated to a very precise angle..."

"Right, the force-shielding on the Black Rose is pretty tough and it can be focussed to a needle point," Billy jumped in, "what else?"

"We'd need a massive power source to bolster the shielding," the Engineer said warily, "far more than we could generate from a Star-Destroyer."

"What about if we linked the force-shielding of several Star-Destroyers together and fed power to the point of the force-shielding that way?" another Engineering Officer piped up, much to the annoyance of the Senior Engineer.

"Can it be done?" Billy probed his enthusiasm building.

"Well, yes, sir," the Engineer had to concede, "we can feed power along the force-shielding to other vessels, but there are so many..."

"So, we can boost force-shields from more than one source?" Billy pressed home his enthusiastic questioning.

"Yes, sir," the Engineer confirmed, "but there are so many other variables such as the angles of deflection and the distance so that plasma doesn't creep round the shielding and strike the planet anyway,"

"That's just a set of simple math problems," Billy dismissed the concerns almost out of hand.

"Even with all the Star-Destroyers, they just won't be able to provide a constant supply of power without blowing up, sir," the Engineer continued almost pleadingly.

"I can split the shielding on the Black Rose and concentrate power on the incoming plasma waves, where it's most needed, that's simple enough," Billy countered.

"But, that would require a control mechanism that can react quicker than anyone's reflexes, sir," the Engineer argued.

"Oh, I have a solution for that," Billy responded realising he would have to use the thought-command function on his PES linked directly to the controls of the Black Rose.

"I think what the Senior Engineer is trying to say, sir, is that it's never been done before," Lokkrien interjected.

"Then, it's high time we tried it Admiral Lokkrien," Billy countered, "if the Bardomil have this weapon we're going to need some kind of solution to it," he added as a justification.

"But, sir....." Lokkrien challenged again.

"No 'buts', Admiral," Billy silenced the opposition, "we draw every resource we need here, bring in all five of the Star-Destroyers," he ordered Lokkrien.

"Senior Engineer, get the force-shielding from those Star-Destroyers linked up as soon as possible, and get onto the computer models and work out the math," Billy ordered the Senior Engineer, "any questions?"

The conference, brow-beaten by Billy's enthusiasm and tenacity remained silent.

"Good," Billy acknowledged, "get this solution sorted and meet back here in thirty minutes; dismissed."

Silently, the conference personnel set off to their appointed tasks, all except Lokkrien.

"I take it you have some objections, Marrhus?" Billy dropped into a more informal tone with his friend when everyone had left.

"Oh, you better bet I do," Lokkrien challenged, "are you seriously going to risk five Star-Destroyers and their crews for this planet?" he bridled.

"No, of course I'm not, don't be stupid, Marrhus," Billy replied, "I'm putting you in charge of the Star-Destroyers and if the force-shielding isn't enough, you get the ships out of here and leave me."

"LEAVE...you!" Lokkrien spoke the first word slightly too loudly for the acoustic tolerances of the War Room, "what do you mean, leave you!?" he hissed the question.

"Who did you think was going to pilot the Black Rose, Marrhus?" Billy said calmly, "it's my shuttle and my home-world if anything goes wrong you get the Star-Destroyers out of here to safety."

"Are you out of your mind?" Lokkrien began to protest.

"Actually, no," Billy replied, "it's the most logical and most pragmatic answer; I'm the best pilot for the Black Rose."

"But, you could get yourself killed!" Lokkrien protested.

"Do you really think I could live with myself if I abandoned my family along with everyone and everything down on that planet to be fried?" Billy asked and walked away.

Lokkrien stood dumbstruck next to the War Table. The man who had left his wife and sons back on Bardan knew only too well the pain and anguish of that kind of loss.

"Sir!" one of the Technicians called out from the Communications section of the console.

"What is it?" Billy stopped and half-turned to face the direction of the calling Technician.

"Message from Admiral Chulling from Second Fleet, priority," the Technician highlighted the urgency of the message.

"Put it on the View Screen," Billy ordered, and one of the two-dimensional Screens was initiated, projecting up from the War Room floor.

The View Screen image crackled with static for a second, and then the face of a middle-aged Thexxian in a blue uniform appeared.

"Admiral Chulling, what seems to be the problem?" Billy asked, hoping that this interruption would soon pass.

"Sir," the Thexxian began, "our Scanners are picking up a very large concentration of Bardomil vessels approaching the Nezadir frontier."

"What kind of vessels?" Billy asked, his suspicions rising as he walked slowly back to the War Table and Marrhus Lokkrien.

"From our preliminary analysis, it looks like a very substantial military strike force of three, possibly four, full Imperial Fleets and a secondary, larger, supply flotilla," Chulling responded.

"A large supply flotilla means that wherever they're going they intend to stay a while," Lokkrien commented quietly.

"Do you have a projected course and destination for this force?" Billy asked.

Secretly, Billy began to pray that it was just another round of exercises that the sabre-rattling Bardomil carried out close to frontiers to worry the defenders. But, in the back of his mind, the part of his consciousness that was Teg Portan was ringing alarm bells. A threat to Earth from a Bardomil secret weapon and then the appearance of a large military force was far from coincidental.

"Not as yet, sir," Chulling replied, "we have them on an approach to the Colos sector."

"It can't be Colos they're after, it's far too heavily defended," Lokkrien speculated quietly, "manoeuvres, maybe?"

"No, it won't be Colos," Billy said darkly, as a very nasty scenario started to play out in his mind.

"What then?" Lokkrien asked, sensing the sudden change in his commander's mood.

"Admiral Chulling?" Billy returned to the Thexxian on the View Screen.

"Sir!" the Thexxian Second Admiral responded.

"What forces can you scratch together right now to get to the Praxos system?" Billy asked.

"Praxos? What's going on?" Lokkrien asked quietly.

"Maybe five Star-Cruisers, the Memphis, Sherman, Light Brigade, Sontara and Ticonderoga, sir," a confused Chulling replied, "the system's uninhabited, so we don't have much in the vicinity."

"Which is exactly what the Bardomil planned for," Billy whispered to himself and drew a heavy breath, "it's not enough," he started to drum his fist on the edge of the War Table as he worked the problem in his mind.

"How big is this Bardomil strike force? Three, maybe four, full Imperial Fleets?" Billy sought clarification.

"Yes, sir," Admiral Chulling confirmed.

"Nine Imperial Fighter Carriers per Fleet gives thirty six Carriers, around one hundred M-Cruisers and a full complement of Harpoons and Flying Devils," Billy mused.

"That's an Invasion Fleet, sir," Lokkrien opined, "We can't protect Earth and defend against this attack."

"That is precisely what we're going to do!" Billy hissed viciously, his eyes flashing with anger, "Admiral," he turned back to the View Screen, "when will this Bardomil force be at the Praxos system?"

"Calculating, sir," the Thexxian replied and looked off screen to one of his aides.

"About thirty minutes, sir," a disembodied voice said quietly from Chulling's location.

"At current speed around half an hour, First Admiral," Chulling repeated.

"Admiral Lokkrien, pull together any and every fighting vessel we can spare and send it to the Praxos system. Have Scanners watch for any movement from the Ganthorans," Billy began, "Admiral Chulling, I want you to take everything you can scrape together to the Praxos system and expect an immediate attack."

"Yes, sir!" Admiral Chulling snapped.

"And, Admiral," Billy stressed the next point heavily, "you have to hold that system."

"Yes, sir," Chulling replied.

"I mean, whatever the cost, Admiral; it is absolutely imperative that we hold this force at Praxos," Billy emphasised, "I will personally bring whatever reinforcements we can muster to support and relieve you when we can; the fate of the Alliance depends upon you holding out until we can get to you."

"Yes, sir!" a slightly confused Chulling barked and the Screen image dissolved.

"What about the Star-Destroyers? We can't tie them to Earth whilst we're fighting at Praxos?" Lokkrien asked.

"We can and we will!" Billy said determinedly; conversation over.

"But, what's so important about Praxos? There's nothing there!" Lokkrien asked confused by the conversation he had just witnessed.

"What system is next to Praxos?" Billy asked.

"Well, Terra?" Lokkrien scrambled through his memory.

"Next to Terra is Sidionas, next to Sidionas is Botar and next to Botar is Sykith, and what's next to Sykith?" Billy queried.

"Sykith is our Ganthoran frontier!" Lokkrien gasped, the significance of the Bardomil attack location suddenly becoming clear in his mind, "it's a corridor through the entire Alliance."

"If they cut us in two, the whole Alliance falls apart; so, I suggest Admiral Lokkrien, that you round up every battlewagon, bath tub, row boat and canoe you can find, and send them to Chulling at Praxos," Billy ordered.

"What about the Star-Destroyers, sir?" Lokkrien asked again, "they'll need them."

"Bring them here," Billy ordered, stepping away from the War Table, "and pray that we can finish up here and make it to Praxos on time," he said softly to himself, setting off to the Landing Bay where the Black Rose waited for him.

Stunned by the realisation of just how precarious the situation had become, Lokkrien took a deep breath, calmed his nerves and began to issue orders to the War Room.

BENNING

Chapter 26

The Star-Cruiser Aquarius

Emma Wallace sat alone in one of the quietest corners of the Observation Deck. Above her, the great transparent cupola gave her a clear view of the stars against the infinite darkness of space. However, the immeasurable vastness of space was far from her thoughts. Her classmates, wary of her through her association with Billy Caudwell, stared at her anxiously and whispered amongst themselves. Never had Emma felt so lonely and confused as she sat by herself amongst the strange alien foliage in a huge, hangar-like Observation Deck of a spacecraft millions of kilometres from Earth.

Crouched against the base of a low wall structure that seemed to pen in some strange alien plants that could move of their own volition, Emma racked her brains to try to understand what was happening. Life had seemed so straightforward for Emma when she had gone to school that morning. Now, it had become her worst nightmare. From the moment those strange creatures had appeared in front of Billy from the bright flashes of light, Emma had been ostracised by her classmates. Since the entire class had disappeared from the school, and had re-appeared on this spaceship, no one had spoken to her except missus Collier. Even then it had been a fear-filled and angry interrogation to which Emma had no answers to offer. No one was speaking to her and everyone was avoiding her like she had some deadly dangerous disease. She had never felt so frightened and alone. And, right now, she really needed someone to explain to her just what was going on.

"Hello, there," a bright cheerful voice chimed from above Emma.

Looking up, Emma saw a short humanoid alien with olive skin, pink eyes and one nostril, carrying what looked like a plate or a tray, smiling at her. Shuffling sideways, the terrified Emma tried to get away from the alien creature.

"It's all right," the creature said soothingly, "I'm not here to harm you."

Wide eyed, Emma tried to shuffle further away but found herself hemmed in by another wall structure.

"I suppose you'll be hungry?" the alien asked crouching down and offering Emma what looked like pink circular cakes from the tray, "it's all right they're not poisoned," the alien said and popped one of the cakes into its mouth.

THE BURNING SUN

Jamming herself into her corner, Emma drew up her knees and wrapped her arms around them, her ultimate defensive barrier.

"They call me Tarissa," the alien said, "I'm a Communications Technician," she smiled, "what do they call you?"

"Em...Em...Emma Wallace," Emma mumbled still terrified of the entity in the pale blue overall that crouched in front of her.

"Yes, it's all a bit confusing for you isn't it Emma Wallace," the alien called Tarissa knelt down, "I'll tell you what, I'll explain to you what I know and we'll take things from there, all right?"

With a frightened nod, Emma pulled her arms closer around her knees and agreed to the compromise.

"Well, Emma Wallace, you are aboard the Star-Cruiser Aquarius, the flagship of the Universal Alliance Fleet," Tarissa began, "we are about sixty million kilometres from your home planet."

"Wh...Wh...Why?" Emma managed to stammer the question.

"Why are you here?" Tarissa clarified, "Well, we couldn't leave you down on Terra after you had seen our people with the First Admiral, but it's all right, we'll get you back just as soon as we can," she smiled.

"F...F...First Admiral?" Emma puzzled.

"Yes, First Admiral Caudwell; aren't you the human female who mates with him?" Tarissa asked.

Shocked and stunned, Emma blushed at the suggestion. With her head reeling she tried to comprehend what the alien was saying to her.

"No, we don't...you know...mate," Emma said with quiet anxiety and deep embarrassment.

"Well, if he was interested in me, Emma Wallace, I would mate with him," Tarissa smiled, "you sure you don't want something to eat?" she slipped another cake into her mouth and offered the tray once more.

Carefully, Emma stretched out her hand and took one of the delicacies on the tray. Breaking a small corner from the cake, Emma slipped a small portion into her mouth. Immediately, the strong flavours of chocolate, orange and rum burst onto her taste-buds. Surprised by the delicious taste, Emma broke a larger piece from the offering and began to eat.

"That's nice isn't it?" Tarissa smiled helping herself to another, "it's one of the First Admiral's favourites."

"So, Billy is this First Admiral?" Emma asked nervously, nibbling at another corner of cake.

Looking to her right, Emma became aware of the sound of laughter. Many of her classmates were already involved in conversation with other creatures in pale blue uniforms. One of her classmates, a shy boy named

James, was smiling broadly enraptured by a young adult male alien with a long gloomy face. The blue overalled creature was swooping and diving with his hands as if he were describing a fighter combat. Missus Collier was laughing with a slightly older adult male who had a face like a bird of prey, and another girl, named Caroline, seemed to be laughing whilst trying to explain something to another young adult female of Tarissa'a species.

"Yes, First Admiral Caudwell has been our commander for nearly a year now, since the Alliance was founded," Tarissa explained.

"But...Billy...he's just...well, he's just...a boy, really," Emma smiled starting to feel a little more comfortable and happy.

"Well, to your species he's just a child; but, to the Alliance he's our most important Senior Officer," Tarissa replied offering Emma another cake.

"But, he's just...Billy," Emma smiled starting to feel a warm sensation in her limbs and a bit dizzy as she munched into the offered delicacy.

"Appearances can be deceptive, Emma Wallace," Tarissa smiled, "if he has chosen you to be his mate, then I'd be very proud."

"Oh yes, I'm very proud," Emma mumbled jokingly through a mouthful of cake scattering crumbs onto the floor.

Around her the laughter seemed to be increasing in volume. Smiling broadly, Emma looked round once more to see James trying to follow the fighter combat, missus Collier laughing slightly more loudly than would be considered appropriate back on Earth and Caroline was trying to show the alien that was with her some Highland Dance steps. As Emma watched her classmates engaged in ever more animated conversations, she noticed that the pink cakes were everywhere. The overalled creatures all had trays of the delicious delicacies and the humans seemed to be enjoying eating them in large numbers.

Then, it dawned on Emma, but far too late, that she had already consumed two full cakes. Staring at the cake she held in the palm of her hand, she shifted her open mouthed gaze to Tarissa who smiled and seemed to become blurred. Shaking her head, Emma realised that the cakes must be drugged, but how could the aliens be immune from it, she puzzled. Staring over to her classmates once more, she saw James collapse and be caught by the gloomy-faced pilot who lowered him gently to the ground.

Turning her attention back to Tarissa, Emma saw the uniformed creature fade in and out of focus and felt her hand on her shoulder.

"Emma Wallace! Emma Wallace! Are you all right?" her voice seemed to echo as if it were from far away.

Then, closing her eyes, Emma gently passed out.

"Right, Tarissa get her to a Restraint Seat on Hospital Deck three," an Officer ordered, "it's going to get rough out there and the First Admiral does not want them to get injured," the voice added as Tarissa bodily lifted Emma from the floor as if she weighed no more than a dried leaf.

BENNING

Chapter 27

The Black Rose

Settling comfortably into the single, high-backed chair in the Command Cabin of the Black Rose, Billy Caudwell felt the familiar tingle down his spine as the microscopic machines in his Personal Environment Suit linked with the Mind Control Systems of his shuttle craft. In front of him, the newly modified control panels stood like an island amongst a sea of grey and silver. The three Display Screens had been activated and were being constantly updated direct from the Data Consoles in the War Room of the Aquarius. All the manual controls and instruments aboard the Black Rose had been carefully stowed behind their bulkheads leaving the Command Cabin with a feeling of emptiness and inactivity.

For Billy, the distraction of the various monitors and control mechanisms was something that he simply did not require. He needed his mind clear and focussed on the job at hand. At stake was the fate of his home-world and every living thing on that planet. With wave after wave of super-heated plasma hurtling towards him, he knew that he had to judge and anticipate their movements as well as direct the energy from the massive Proto-Star reactors to the force-shielding generated by the Star-Destroyers that anchored this particular umbrella in space. The Black Rose, Billy knew, was the tip of the umbrella, and it was up to him to switch the power from one sector of the protective force-shielding to the other in response to the oncoming waves of super-heated plasma.

The central of the three Display Screens looked like one of the arcade games he had played when he was younger. Pale blue graphic lines converged to a point in the near distance creating five long triangular sections that formed a five-sided pyramid on his screen. The apex or point of the graphic pyramid he knew was himself and the Black Rose. His viewpoint was from the base looking towards the apex. To his left, the second Display Screen indicated the power drainage on the massive Proto-Star generators aboard the five, huge octagonal-shaped Star-Destroyers that formed each corner of the pyramid's base. As Billy scanned the five twitching vertical bar charts, he understood that there was very little demand being put on the generators at present. However, in the heat of the action, these bar charts would spring upwards on his screen as he drew vast amounts of power from the generators. The generators were linked through the force-shielding so that he could draw power from more than one source as the situation demanded. But, he knew that he had to be careful. If he overloaded one generator, then the whole pyramid-like umbrella would collapse and the Earth would be swamped by super-hearted plasma. The crews aboard the Star-Destroyers would also be vulnerable and reliant on either Emergency Escape or their own force-shielding. There were nearly one hundred and fifty thousand crew members aboard each Star-Destroyer. Almost seven hundred and fifty thousand Alliance soldiers plus the billons of creatures on Earth were depending on him to get it right. If he got it wrong, however, Billy knew that he would be the first to die. The force-shielding on the Black Rose was being heavily reinforced by the power drawn from the generators aboard the Star-Destroyers. If that power failed, Billy and the Black Rose would be vapourised in an instant.

The third Display Screen, on his right, was the most important of the three. This gave Billy a graphic representation of the super-heated plasma as it streamed towards his position. He could rapidly switch the graphic image from a top to a side view of the advancing plasma streams, giving him a form of three-dimensional image that would allow him to anticipate where the hottest and heaviest concentrations were. He could then divert additional power from one sector to another as rapidly as possible to deflect the incoming plasma away from the Earth.

It all sounded so simple and straightforward in theory. The reality, however, was very much unknown territory. There were so many things that could potentially go wrong, Billy considered, as he waited for clearance from one of the huge Hangar Decks of the Aquarius. One of the generators could malfunction, the engineers might have miscalculated on the field strength required or the distance to deflect the material away from the planet or he might just be that fraction of a second too slow in dealing with a burst of plasma that would overwhelm the whole mechanism.

There were just too many unknown variables; but yet, here he was about to risk his life on the longest of long shots he had experienced to date. The part of his mind that was Teg Portan recoiled in horror from what he was about to attempt. The cold, hard-headed logic of Garmauria's last Supreme Military Commander knew that the odds were just too heavily stacked against him, and that the sensible and correct choice was to walk away from the situation. He could evacuate his parents and family plus a few hundred thousand others, and, perhaps, a few token species of wildlife, domesticated animals, and plants. But, in his heart of hearts, Billy knew that he could not walk away from this. He had to try to save his home, his family and all of the other people on the Earth. If he did not, he knew that he would never be able to face himself in the mirror ever again. For that and for his home and family, he was ready to risk his life. He did not feel particularly heroic or noble in his actions. He was, he convinced himself, simply doing what hundreds, maybe thousands of generations of people had done before him.

In fact, he felt quite calm about the whole episode. This was mainly due to the effects of the Personal Environment Suit. Under normal circumstances he would be scared to death. But, the tens of thousands of microscopic machines in the PES, being attuned to his bodily functions, had detected the massive increase in blood pressure and hormonal activity. Having been designed to keep the body of the wearer at optimal performance levels, the PES had flooded his body with chemicals and radiation to counter-act these effects. So, even though he knew he was frightened, Billy did not experience the adverse physiological and psychological effects of his own fear. This would allow him to remain calm and focussed, able to perform to the very best of his abilities when normally he would be dissolving in terror. However, more important than the technological support of the PES, Billy also had the wisdom and experience of Teg Portan in is armoury. The decades of experience of the now-dead Garmaurian were more important to Billy than all of the vessels in the Alliance Fleet. Portan had been in more than a few dangerous situations in his long and illustrious career. And, Billy knew that he could rely on those instincts and memories in a crisis.

"Spearhead One, Spearhead One," the voice of the Flight Controller broke into his consciousness, "you are cleared for launch."

"Acknowledged," Billy gave the simple one word response and activated the two Thrust-Engines that propelled the Black Rose when she was not using the Trion Drive. Gently, the Black Rose lifted about a metre from the grey metal deck and began to drift towards the great gaping maw of the Hangar Deck Access Door. This is it, Billy thought, no going back now. Taking a deep breath, he gently exhaled a long slow controlled breath and eased the Black Rose forward with his Thought Commands.

"Good luck, and, God Speed, Spearhead One," the Flight Controller's voice pushed Billy out into the cold hostile darkness of space.

THE BURNING SUN

Chapter 28

The Praxos System

Turthus Chulling, Second Admiral and Commander of the Universal Alliance's Second Fleet paced confidently around the War Room of the Star-Cruiser Memphis. The emergence of the Star-Cruiser Caractacus from the Trionic Web now gave Chulling a formidable fighting force. In the short space of time since he had spoken to First Admiral Caudwell, his original rag-tag flotilla of five Star-Cruisers had mushroomed to a healthy two Fleet Carriers, the New Thexxia and the Leonidas, with a further fifteen Star-Cruisers to bolster the ranks.

For Chulling this was a force that could more than match the Bardomil invasion fleet that was approaching. After all, First Admiral Caudwell had eliminated a full Bardomil Imperial Fleet with two Star-Cruisers and six Explorers. And, although Chulling did not consider himself to be the tactical or strategic equal of First Admiral Caudwell, twenty Star-Cruisers and two Fleet Carriers could surely hold off four Bardomil Imperial Fleets. Looking at the arithmetic, certainly the Alliance was going to be outnumbered, but that seemed to be par for the course. The advantage of the Alliance's force-shielding would surely make the coming battle a foregone conclusion.

Once more, Chulling worked the numbers in his mind and reached the same conclusion; that it was going to be a turkey-shoot. The four Imperial Fleets would bring almost forty Imperial Fighter Carriers each with around one hundred and fifty of the single-seat Harpoon fighters and fifty of the dangerous Flying Devil gunships. Of all the vessels the Bardomil could field, Chulling really wished that the Alliance had something that could match the Flying Devil. But, wishing didn't win any battles, Chulling knew as he tallied up close to eight thousand Bardomil fighter craft. The protective screen for the vulnerable Imperial Fighter Carriers would bring around one hundred of the gull-winged M-Cruisers to the battle. But, given their primary function, Chulling suspected that they would play a very minor role in the contest. Once again, it would be a defensive battle where the Alliance could hunker down behind the force-shielding and annihilate the waves of Bardomil fighters that would be thrown at them.

With the two Alliance Fleet Carriers each bringing one thousand of the single-seat Eagle fighters plus each Star-Cruiser bringing sixty Eagle fighters, they were going to be outnumbered slightly more than two to one. But, with the Harpoons and Flying Devils eliminated, the Eagles and Star-Cruisers could harry and pursue the M-Cruisers and Imperial Fighter

Carriers back to the main invasion force and then start killing an awful lot more of the Bardomil. And, as a Thexxian, Chulling had a lot of scores to settle with the Bardomil.

Setting aside his thoughts on the impending battle, Chulling turned his attention to the War Room of the Memphis. The six Staff Officers of Second Fleet were all present and correct around the War Table. They seemed quietly confident and quite relaxed given the situation. Most of them he had known for many years, sharing the hardships and troubles of the Thexxian Exodus. They too were eager to kill large numbers of Bardomil, and they waited expectantly for his orders to allow them to do just that. In the War Room itself, expectations were high amongst the personnel who populated the consoles that fed the information into this battle centre, with an edge of quiet confidence that lay over the usual pre-battle anxieties.

Turthus Chulling was just nodding his personal satisfaction to himself when a voice called out from the consoles that flanked the War Table.

"The enemy are now within long range video scanner capability, sir!" the Scanner Technician reported.

"Excellent," Chulling replied, "let's have a look at our guests, activate War Table please."

A moment later, the entire War Room was plunged into darkness with only the harsh lighting of the War Table to allow Chulling and his staff to see the tiniest detail on the projected image as the battle progressed. Above the War Table, a large image flickered for a few moments and then cleared to show a three-dimensional representation of the approaching Bardomil force.

Chulling saw exactly what he had expected to see in the approaching Bardomil dispositions. Two large groups of space vessels were approaching the Praxos system. The first group would be the strike force, Chulling considered, whilst the second, much larger, group would be the actual invasion forces with their supplies in tow. Lifting the Manipulator control in his right hand, Chulling focussed his attention on the strike force. A straggling cordon of Flying Devil scout vessels led the fighting armada followed by more Flying Devils in a long 'V' formation to protect the main strike force. It was a classic Bardomil tactical advance. Behind the 'V' of Flying Devils, the M-Cruisers formed a circular pattern around a rectangular block of Imperial Fighter Carriers, whilst a line of Flying Devils brought up the rear.

So far, so good, Chulling considered and switched the War Table image to scrutinise the larger body. Four, long straggling columns of vessels made up the Bardomil invasion force. Thousands upon thousands of troop transport and supply ships were snaking their way towards the frontier. Each column, tens of thousands of kilometres long, consisted of two lines of troop transports flanked on each side by two lines of supply vessels.

Staggered by the sheer size of the invasion force, Chulling stepped back from the War Table to take in the sheer scale of the invasion.

"Looks like they're planning to stay a while, sir?" one of his staff Officers quipped, still awed by the scale of what was unfolding before them, as the others laughed politely.

"When we're through with them, they'll be staying permanently, as part of the scenery," another Officer quipped, drawing louder laughter.

"Scanners, do we have numbers for their troop transports?" Chulling asked, still smiling.

"Initial estimate indicates close to two hundred thousand," a Scanner Officer replied nervously.

For a moment the whole War Room seemed to draw an astonished breath as Chulling did the mental arithmetic.

"That'll be close to five million troops!" one of the staff Officers beat Chulling to the total.

Suddenly, the mood around the War Table changed as the magnitude of this support force sank into their minds. The quips immediately stopped as each of them marvelled at the enormity of it.

"They're not just planning to strike the five systems are they, sir?" a more nervous junior staff Officer asked.

"No, they're not," Chulling replied anxiously, his previous optimism rapidly receding.

"Do you think they'll go after New Thexxia?" the Officer asked.

"No, don't be stupid, the planetary defences are far too powerful," another Officer replied.

"But, the colonies aren't," a third voice chimed up reminding them all of the vulnerability of the four fledgling colonies that the Thexxians had established since the founding of the Alliance.

"They can bottle us up on New Thexxia and just keep chipping away until they find a way through," another commented gloomily.

"The five systems will be just the start," another Officer speculated amidst anxious murmuring.

"Right, gentlemen, that's enough!" Chulling stamped down ruthlessly on the spreading pessimism, "when we've all stopped wetting ourselves about the big bad bogey-man eating our heads, let's get ready to kick their backsides" he snapped and held the Officers to silence for a long moment as they shuffled anxiously.

"What's their convoy support looking like Scanners?" Chulling asked trying to sound business-like.

"Large numbers of Flying Devils, M-Cruisers, and Imperial Fighter Carriers," the Scanner Officer replied from the darkness of a now tense War Room.

"How many Fighter Carriers?" Chulling asked.

"About twenty, sir," the Scanner Officer replied.

"So, another two Imperial Fleets," Chulling speculated absent-mindedly, "Comms, get a message off to Aquarius with the size and dispositions of the enemy"

"Yes, sir," a female voice called from the darkness.

"Scanners, how long to contact?" Chulling asked.

"About six minutes, sir," the Scanner Officer replied

"Well, gentlemen," Chulling took hold of the situation, "we're expecting visitors; I suggest we give them a warm welcome."

"Sir!" the staff Officers snapped to attention.

"Let's roll out a very special welcome mat for them. Let's get the Star-Cruisers into position with Fleet Carriers to the rear," Chulling began and set down the War Table Manipulator.

"Do we launch Eagles, sir?" one of the staff Officers piped up.

"Not yet," Chulling instructed, "put the pilots on stand-by and have their machines ready for immediate launch; now go!"

"Sir," the staff Officers responded and scattered like chaff in the wind to carry out their instructions.

Turning back to the War Table image, Chulling once again marvelled at the sheer size of the Bardomil force. And, as he scrutinised the images before him he remembered a well-worn phrase often used by the First Admiral.

The bigger they come, the harder they fall.

THE BURNING SUN

Chapter 29

The Terran System

Out in front of the rapidly-advancing waves of plasma, Billy Caudwell drew the Black Rose to her designated position. To his right, Billy could view the dull orange orb of Mercury. Behind him, to his left, had he chosen to look in that direction, the deeper red of Venus would have been visible. However, one hundred and fifty kilometres behind him, the five, two-kilometre wide, octagonal Star-Destroyers that formed the base of the protective umbrella, were preparing for the forthcoming action. The crews had been briefed and everyone knew what was expected of them. The atmosphere aboard all of the Alliance vessels was tense, but calm. Arranged at their stations, in their pentagonal formation, the five huge Star-Destroyers, Colossus, Titan, Atlas, Hercules and Zeus, looked like an impenetrable wall. But, Billy and every single crew member aboard the huge slab-sided planet-killers knew that they were facing powerful forces that could sweep them away as easily as a child scattering twigs.

Aboard all five of the Star-Destroyers, the Engineers were powering up the massive Proto-Star reactors. The reactors, the size of a cathedral back on Earth were fuelled by material harvested from young stars just before they went nova. The vast amount of potential energy held within the proto-star matter was locked in heavy sealed chambers and surrounded by layer upon layer of force-shielding and safety protocols. For the upcoming battle with the super-heated plasma, the Engineers knew they would have to draw upon every ounce of energy from the huge reactors. There was no margin for error; any mistake, however small, was likely to be fatal for Billy and every crew member that waited for the plasma to arrive.

"This is Spearhead One, have reached contact position," Billy announced into the Communications Network indicating his position nearly one hundred million kilometres from the Earth.

"Roger, Spearhead One, this is Control One," the voice of Marrhus Lokkrien responded to him from the War Room of the Aquarius, "we have four minutes to contact."

"Acknowledged, Control One," Billy replied, "Do we have power from the Star-Destroyers yet?"

"Spearhead One," Lokkrien's voice sounded calm and professional, "the Star-Destroyers report full power will be available in ninety, that's niner zero seconds."

"Acknowledged," Billy replied, glad of a friendly voice, "that gives us plenty of time to test out this system."

"Roger, Spearhead One," Lokkrien replied, "the target should be entering your scanner range in ten seconds."

"Understood, Control One," Billy replied turning his attention to the third Display Screen on his right, which registered only the static icon of his own horribly exposed vessel.

Slowly, Billy counted down the seconds and in his mind's eye he saw the leading edge of the first wave of super-heated plasma snaking and twisting forwards in the blackness.

At times, the leading edge double backed on itself; spiralling like a whip as it drove relentlessly and inexorably forward like an all-consuming avalanche. And, in his mind's eye, Billy also heard the vicious howling like a wind storm that heralded some dark malevolent force.

"Control One, I have scanner contact," Billy announced as the first stream of yellow appeared on his Display Screen.

"Acknowledged, Spearhead One," Lokkrien responded, "Star-Destroyers standing by; force shield control has been set to automatic."

Calmly, Billy digested the information that the force-shielding controls had been taken off manual. When the umbrella was activated all force-shielding control would be relayed from Billy's mind aboard the Black Rose through the shielding itself to the computers aboard the Star-Destroyers. Billy, and the Alliance Fleet Engineers, knew that the split-second it took for a voice command to be relayed and reacted to by an operator could well be that split-second too late. The mind control systems aboard the Black Rose linked to the computers would give Billy and the Alliance vessels that additional edge.

"Roger, Control One," Billy replied and drew a deep breath as he prepared his mind for what was likely to be the longest, and, perhaps, the last, three minutes of his entire life.

"Spearhead One, Star-Destroyers are ready to initiate force shield umbrella," Lokkrien announced.

"Acknowledged, Control One," Billy replied turning his attention to the Central Display Screen, "can we initiate in sequence, Control One, I want to check that these sectors pan out."

Billy wanted to make sure that he knew from which Star-Destroyer he was drawing power in each sector on his Display Screen. In the heat of the action, he did not want to mistakenly try to draw power from a reactor that was already heavily committed.

"Roger, Spearhead One," Lokkrien confirmed his understanding of the situation, "commencing initiation sequence now...Sector one, Colossus."

THE BURNING SUN

On the Central Display Screen, the first sector on the top left of the image lit up. Glancing to the left Display Screen the first bar chart flickered upwards for a brief second before returning to its nominal state. Sector two, the top right of the Display Screen was lit up with power from Atlas. Sector three was bottom right of the image and lit up with power from Zeus. Sector four, the bottom sector, was powered by Titan with sector five lit up by the Star-Destroyer Hercules. With all five sectors established, Billy became aware that the great swirling mass of super heated plasma was getting very close.

Travelling at nearly seventy-five million kilometres per hour, the mass of plasma was hurtling towards the pathetically small Black Rose and the accompanying Star-Destroyers. The detectors on Earth picked up the solar flare relatively quickly. This left the Earth Governments with a hideous dilemma. The super-heated plasma was moving somewhere in the region of ten times faster than any previous solar flare. The Earth was about to be engulfed with very little warning and with no chance of any realistic defence from the surface. In capital cities throughout the world, the Doomsday Warnings went out and people struggled as best they could to reach their home and families to await the end. Unknown to the people of Earth, a lone teenager in a small space craft was all that stood between their planet and annihilation. That lone teenager was rapidly running through the mechanisms of the force-shielding umbrella. Quickly, Billy adjusted the variables, drawing power from more than one Star-Destroyer to reinforce a number of sectors on his force-shielding.

Having run the permutations, Billy just had time to draw one deep breath before the message came through from Lokkrien.

"Spearhead One, Spearhead One," Lokkrien said, "we have ten seconds to contact," he said and began the countdown.

"Acknowledged, Control One," Billy replied, "Thrust Engines to maximum," he declared.

Aboard the five Star-Destroyers, the Engineers were also setting the huge Thrust Engines to maximum. Even when at their waiting station, the huge vessels were going to need stability to hold the force-shielding umbrella in place when the plasma waves hit.

"Four...three..." Lokkrien intoned as the tension rose rapidly throughout the Star-Destroyers.

"Good Luck everybody!" Billy added.

"One...con..." Lokkrien counted down but never got to complete the count.

In the Black Rose, at the very tip of the force-shielding umbrella, Billy felt like he had been hit by an enormous sledge hammer. The massive jolt from the leading edge of the plasma wave slammed into the force-shielding around the Black Rose at the same moment that Billy fired the Thrust Engines at full forward velocity. The push from the Thrust Engines and the power to the force-shielding from the Star-Destroyers held the small space vessel in its station.

The Star-Destroyers were hit a fraction of a second later. The umbrella had survived the initial impact, but the constant demand on the Thrust Engines from stabilising their positions would mean that they could not hold the umbrella for long. As with most of the force-shielding umbrella idea, Billy was gambling that the plasma waves would pass before the Thrust Engines burned out.

Aboard the Aquarius, lodged behind the circle of five Star-Destroyers, the impact was no less ferocious. In the War Room, Lokkrien was knocked from his feet forcing him to grasp the edge of the War Table to prevent him taking an embarrassing and painful fall. Around him, anxious Officers and Technicians grabbed their consoles or any available structure to steady themselves against the shaking and shuddering of the initial concussion wave.

"Casualties and damage...report!?" Lokkrien shouted amidst the rumbling and violent shaking as he clung precariously to the War Table.

"No serious damage reported from any vessel, sir!" an Engineer responded, "all systems still performing efficiently!"

"Several minor injuries reported on Atlas and Titan, no fatalities!" another voice added.

"Let's hope it stays that way," Lokkrien muttered between gritted teeth as he held on grimly.

With the initial impact survived, Billy was now focussed on monitoring the incoming strands of plasma and powering up the force-shield sectors to deflect the danger away. Sitting rigidly in the high backed chair, Billy felt the Black Rose being buffeted and hammered by the incoming waves of super-heated plasma. With teeth gritted, he focussed on the three Display Screens his mind issuing commands to bolster each sector as required. Very quickly, Billy was under pressure as the waves of super-heated plasma hurtled towards his position. The waves were just coming in too fast for Billy to comfortably handle.

Meanwhile, in the War Room of the Aquarius, Lokkrien monitored the three-dimensional image of the situation. On the screen, Lokkrien could see the umbrella was holding its shape. Struggling to stay on his feet against the constant pounding, Lokkrien watched anxiously as the Black Rose image seemed to be engulfed by a great plume of fire. The super-heated plasma bounced away from the nose of the Black Rose giving the vessel the appearance of a fiery halo. But, the reinforced force-shielding was working as the vessel seemed to be cutting through the plasma like an arrowhead casting the fiery material off in every direction except towards Earth.

"Sir, we've lost contact with Spearhead One!" an alarmed Communications Officer called out.

"That's to be expected with all this radiation flying about; do what you can to regain contact!" Lokkrien responded loudly as he braced his legs against the War Table, "Flight Surgeon, is Spearhead One still all right!?"

"Sir, stress levels above normal, blood pressure elevated, pulse and respiratory rate rising rapidly!" the prompt medical reply cut through the shuddering impacts.

Well, at least he's still alive, and fighting, Lokkrien thought and steeled himself for the continuing ordeal.

Aboard the Black Rose, Billy Caudwell was feeling far from comfortable as the vessel was buffeted and slammed from almost all angles by the super-heated plasma waves. Billy felt that his teeth were being rattled from his jaws, and that his bones were being ground into powder through the intense pounding that the Black Rose was taking. Still, despite the brutal turbulence, Billy held firm. His attention fixed on the three Display Screens before him Billy worked the numbers and diverted power to where the force-shielding needed to be strongest. On the Central Screen, the triangular sectors lit up in rapid succession like flickering lights on a Christmas tree as the power usage bar charts danced and flickered.

But, most dangerous of all was the heat. Despite the reinforced force-shielding the temperature in the Command Cabin of the Black Rose was rising rapidly. With the force-shielding of the Personal Environment Suit set to maximum, Billy was, as yet, unaware that the temperature was climbing to dangerously high levels. The hull of the Black Rose quickly began to glow dull red as the heat built up. Meanwhile, inside the Control Cabin, Billy kept a watchful eye on the dancing bars and figures of his Display Screens as the assault from the super-heated plasma seemed to intensify. On the Display Screen, the strands of plasma seemed to thicken and become denser and more numerous as sheet after sheet of searing hot death bombarded the tiny shuttle. Judging the intensity of the bombardment by the dark areas on his Display Screen, Billy was able to anticipate where to divert the power to the deflecting force-shielding. With wave after ferocious wave of plasma hurtling towards the frail and fragile looking shuttle, Billy's mind and reflexes were only just able to keep that split-second ahead of the next scorching onslaught.

The Thought-Command mechanism built into his Personal Environment Suit provided him with those additional fractions of a second that would otherwise have been lost sending the impulses from his brain to his hands and fingers. And, it was those split-second decisions that were the difference between life and an agonising, fiery death for the young pilot of the Black Rose. But, despite the technological advantages, Billy was still finding things more than a little bit uncomfortable.

Aboard the Star-Destroyers, things were equally uncomfortable for the crews as the Engineers anxiously watched the power consumption being diverted to the force-shielding. The initial drainage on the proto-star reactors had been well within acceptable tolerances. However, now that the force-shielding was being challenged the power consumption had rocketed.

So far there had been none of the dangerous power spikes that wore at the fabric and infrastructure of the reactors. But, the Engineers knew that even greater demands would be placed on the reactors and that the chance of power spikes grew with every passing second.

Aboard the Aquarius, Lokkrien was also far from comfortable. Watching the two-dimensional display Screens that were projected up from the floor of the War Room, Lokkrien could see the same displays that Billy was monitoring. Power consumption was acceptable and the force-shielding seemed to be holding up well under the intense onslaught. Lokkrien was, however, worried about the human component in the mechanism.

"Hull temperature on Spearhead One just reached one hundred thousand degrees Kelvin!" one of the Scanner Technicians announced to the violently shaking War Room.

That's nearly one million degrees Celsius, Lokkrien calculated quickly as another savage concussion hit the Aquarius.

"What's the temperature ceiling on Spearhead One?" Lokkrien asked anxiously.

"Unknown, sir!" an Engineer replied honestly, "we've never tested Spearhead One's hull to destruction!"

"Oh, wonderful," Lokkrien muttered.

Sitting down on one of the chairs that were attached to the War Table on a curved support, Lokkrien finally gave up his dignity in favour of comfort and a degree of stability. This allowed the others at the side of the Table to also sit down. No one sat whilst the Commanding Officer stood.

"Sir," another voice interrupted his thoughts.

THE BURNING SUN

"Report!" Lokkrien interrogated the new voice.

"Sir, we're through thirty percent of the plasma streams!" the voice of a Scanner Technician reported the first piece of encouraging news.

Mentally, Lokkrien gave a small sigh of relief; that was one third of the material successfully pushed aside. The main crises would come at around forty to sixty percent and at the very end when the biggest bursts of plasma were ejected from the Sun. But, so far, so good, Lokkrien thought.

"Excellent!" Lokkrien replied, "Keep calling out those numbers!"

"Sir, Colossus, Zeus and Hercules all report huge increases in power demand," an Engineer called out.

Looking over at the bar charts on his display screens, Lokkrien could see that three of the five oscillating images were now up in the red zone for power consumption. When the images jumped into the white zone at the top of the chart there was a danger of catastrophic explosion.

"That's what we're here to do, son!" Lokkrien replied in as commanding a voice as he could muster amongst the rattling and shuddering of the War Room, quietly cursing the panicky Engineers on the Star-Destroyers who he felt were being too cautious.

Meanwhile, aboard the Star-Destroyers, the Engineers watched anxiously as the power was drained from the reactors into the force-shielding. The tons of proto-star matter, harvested from the star nurseries just before they went nova, could chain-react for tens of thousands of years before starting to deplete. Generating power was not a problem, but harnessing and controlling this wild untamed beast was a major headache. So far, the force-shielding and safety protocols around the proto-star matter were holding up. But, with the increasing demands from Billy aboard the Black Rose those force shields would be tested to their limits.

The Engineers were far from confident that the force shields could hold out for very long. If the force-shielding did fail, the Star-Destroyers would be vapourised, the proto-star matter would be liberated and there would be five new brilliantly shining stars burning close to what remained of planet Earth.

"Hull temperature on Spearhead One is now one hundred and fifty thousand degrees Kelvin, sir!" the Scanner Technician reported.

Aboard the Black Rose, Billy was starting to have trouble seeing the screens in front of him. The vibration from the pounding that the vessel's hull was receiving made it difficult for him to keep an accurate focus on the monitors that seemed to dance around and blur in his eyes. With Billy concentrating on the screens in front of him, the microscopic machines of the PES began to adjust the force-shielding around his face to compensate for the instability.

"Sector two...sector four...sector one...sector two...sector three... sector two...sector five!" Billy's mind issued instructions to the parts of the force-shielding that deflected the huge splashes of super-charged plasma away from the vessel. On his screen the triangles of each sector would light up white as the power surged through the linkages from the Star-Destroyers to strengthen the shielding where the intensity of the plasma was greatest.

For an instant, he noted that power consumption from Star-Destroyer Titan was getting dangerously high, the block rising and flickering into the red zone for a few brief moments. However, Billy knew that he had to keep focussed on the streams of plasma that were battering the hull of the Black Rose or everything would be lost.

"Passing through forty percent, sir!" the Scanner Technician indicated to the War Room.

"Flight surgeon!?" Lokkrien called for an update.

"Under very heavy stress, sir, but holding steady!!" the commanding voice replied.

"Nearly half way," Lokkrien mumbled to himself, gritting his teeth.

Back aboard the Black Rose, Billy was starting to experience a new phenomenon.

With the volume of material from the Sun steadily increasing as the Black Rose pushed it aside, a new danger was emerging. The plasma that had been pushed aside was being pushed back towards the Black Rose by the volume of the material behind it. Like a snow plough pushing through a heavy drift, the pressure from the material bouncing off the shielding was pushing a great deal of plasma back at the Black Rose. Strands of super-charged plasma were starting to filter through the shielding further down.

It took Billy several seconds to realise what was happening and that he had to step up his game further to monitor and deflect super-charged plasma from the whole shield. Expanding his view of the shielding on his centre screen, Billy knew that he had no alternative other than to increase the demands on the power generators aboard the Star-Destroyers. As a result, he had to focus his mind even more intently on the screen in front of him as he watched for the splash-back from the streams of super-charged plasma that he had already deflected away.

"Two...one...three...four...one...one...three!" the rate of instruction rapidly increased from Billy's mind to deal with the increasing splash-back.

THE BURNING SUN

The five triangles on his centre screen flickered even more rapidly as the power consumption bars of all five Star-Destroyers danced ever closer to the red zone.

"Going through fifty percent, sir," the Scanner Technician announced as the whole umbrella passed through a huge bulge in the matter stream that signalled the height of the solar eruption.

"Half way," Lokkrien mumbled to himself, "all downhill from here," he prayed.

"Power usage reaching danger levels, sir," an Engineering Technician called out amidst the shuddering and shaking.

"We're not there yet!" Lokkrien responded.

For a split-second, Lokkrien considered listening to the Engineers and abandoning the umbrella. But, having come this far, he considered, it was now becoming a matter of pride to hang on in there. If Billy Caudwell, out there in the flimsy structure of the Black Rose could hold on, then so could Marrhus Lokkrien. He was not about to abandon his commander and friend just yet.

"Flight surgeon!?" Lokkrien called for another medical update on the First Admiral.

"Extreme stress, sir, heart rate and blood pressure dangerously elevated! He can't hold out for very much longer sir!" the Flight Surgeon replied.

"Oh, yes he can!" Lokkrien replied as another violent shudder rattled through the Aquarius.

"Passing through sixty percent, sir!" the Scanner Technician announced as the bulge in the plasma stream started to tail off.

"Just the tail to go," Lokkrien prayed as the hammering of the Aquarius continued unabated.

Out on the Black Rose, Billy began to notice that the intensity of the plasma stream was starting to reduce. The splash-back problem was starting to decrease. It looked like the major crisis had passed, but he knew that he could not let his concentration lapse for one single moment. Still jammed heavily into his seat by the intensity of the pounding, Billy tilted his head to the left, eyes still focussed on the screens, to achieve some relief for his aching neck muscles.

"Two......one......three......one......four!" the command rate was starting to decrease and the power demands from the Star-Destroyers was beginning to drop down below the red zone.

The buffeting and shaking of the Black Rose was still continuing, but Billy was starting to feel like the end was in sight. Still the great snaking, writhing stream of super-charged plasma just kept coming at him.

"Come on, Billy! Come on!" he urged himself to focus on the work ahead.

Starting to feel dizzy, he tried to shake his head and stared hard at the central screen.

"One.............five..............two..............three" he illuminated the sectors on his central screen as the flood of plasma slammed into the force-shielding once again.

"Through seventy...and seventy-five percent, sir!" the Scanner Technician updated anyone who was listening.

"Nearly there! Come on, Billy!" Lokkrien hissed through clenched teeth as the pounding of the flagship continued.

Aboard the Star-Destroyers, the concerned Engineers were starting to feel slightly happier as power demands seemed to be reducing back to below the dangerous levels of the major crisis. Their main worries now turned to the structural damage that the intense pounding would have caused to the enormous vessels.

"Eighty...eighty-five...ninety percent, sir!" the Scanner Technician kept the updates coming.

"Nearly there, nearly there, nearly there," Lokkrien mumbled as he steeled himself for the final burst that was the dying convulsion of the solar eruption.

Aboard the Black Rose, Billy could see the final great wall of plasma hurtling towards the point of the umbrella on his screen. Breathing heavily, he tried to focus, but found his vision blurring as the screen seemed to fade in and out. An instant later, he felt that the Control Cabin of the Black Rose was starting to spin.

"No!" he yelled feebly as he gave one last desperate, supreme effort to focus on the screens.

Then everything went black.

"I'm sorry," he heard a faint voice, his own voice, sighing in despair as he finally lost consciousness.

Chapter 30

The Praxos System

Just as Billy Caudwell was about to enter the streams of super-charged plasma, Turthus Chulling was scrutinising the approaching Bardomil strike force as it made the final approach to the Praxos frontier. On the War Table image, the Alliance formation of twenty Star-Cruisers stood in a diamond shaped pattern with the two larger Fleet Carriers safely tucked behind.

"The enemy have just crossed the frontier, sir!" a Scanner Officer announced as Chulling watched the first of the Flying Devils cross the faint white line that defined the boundary of Alliance space.

"Comms, send them the standard challenge," Chulling ordered knowing that the Bardomil would either ignore his message or reply with their usual degree of haughty arrogance.

"Sir," the Communications Officer responded and began the official challenge to the invasion of Alliance space.

"WATO," Chulling then called upon the Weapons and Tactical Officer who hovered close to the War Table.

"Sir," the WATO responded.

"Get the pulsar-cannons in the turrets warmed up, but don't fire until I give the command," Chulling said absent-mindedly as he watched the images of the Bardomil vessels cross into Alliance territory.

"Yes, sir," the WATO replied and went to his duty.

"Comms?" Chulling asked if any response had been received.

"Nothing, sir, no response, sir," the Comms Officer responded just as Chulling had expected.

"Very well," Chulling began.

"The enemy are in scanner range, should we block them, sir?" a Scanner Technician asked.

"No, let them have a good look at us," Chulling ordered.

Suddenly, on the War Table image, the Bardomil formation drew to a halt and held stations.

Well, here we go, Chulling thought, they'll arrange themselves into battle formation and then we can all begin.

But, as Chulling watched the Bardomil formation, he saw something strange happening.

As he had expected he saw the leading Flying Devils start to return to their Fighter Carriers, where they would refuel and join their comrades for the approaching battle. The Imperial Fighter Carriers, with their protective

M-Cruiser screen, were moving forward to launch their Harpoon and Flying Devil complements. All well and good, Chulling thought. Except that all of the M-Cruisers were now detaching themselves from their defensive positions around the Imperial Fighter Carriers. This was something new, Chulling considered, as he watched the M-Cruisers move forward to the front line of the Bardomil formation.

"Comms? Are we listening in?" Chulling asked, trying to fathom some explanation for this new Bardomil tactic.

"No, sir, enemy communications are being scrambled," the Comms Officer said almost apologetically.

"Try to crack them Comms," Chulling ordered, still mystified as to what the enemy were planning to do with their M-Cruisers.

"Yes, sir," the Comms Officer responded, wondering if it were even possible to crack the Bardomil Fleet Codes.

Still puzzled by the appearance of the M-Cruisers moving forward, Chulling racked his tactical brains as to what his Bardomil opposite number was trying to achieve. He couldn't possibly be planning to attack with his M-Cruisers completely unsupported, Chulling speculated. If the high-yield pulsar-cannons aboard the Star-Cruisers didn't get them, then the Eagle fighters would rip them to shreds. And, surely they weren't going to stand toe-to-toe with the Alliance's Star-Cruisers and try to slug it out with their laser weapons against the force-shielding and high-yield pulsar-cannons. That was just plain suicide. It just didn't make any sense to Chulling.

"Enemy launching fighters!" a Scanner Officer called out.

Looking closely at the War Table image, Chulling saw the tiny specks of Harpoon and Flying Devil fighters emerging from the bays of the Imperial Fighter Carriers.

"That's more like it," Chulling said to himself softly, "the more the merrier," he smiled.

An attack by the massed formation of M-Cruisers was going to require close support protection from smaller, faster and more agile fighter craft. They would, however, simply be more targets for the guns of the Eagles as they lay safely behind the force-shielding of the Star-Cruisers, Chulling considered.

"Are the enemy within range?" Chulling asked speculatively.

"Negative, sir," the WATO replied almost nonchalantly.

The effective range of the high-yield pulsar-cannons aboard the Memphis was greater than the laser weapons of the M-Cruisers and as a result the WATO felt quite safe.

"Enemy fighters still launching, sir," the Scanner Officer repeated indicating that a large force was being marshalled and assembled.

At the War Table, Chulling shook his head and speculated that surely the Bardomil could not hope to overwhelm his position with sheer weight of numbers. Their total lack of regard for the lives of their soldiers was legendary, but the sacrifices had always had some purpose. To Chulling, this looked just like pointless slaughter.

But, as Chulling watched the great horde of fighters and gunships taking up their formations, he noticed that the front line of M-Cruisers was beginning to cluster into groups. Puzzled, Chulling took up the Manipulator in his right hand and zoomed into one of the clusters. Three M-Cruisers seemed to be holding a tight formation as they began to move forward.

"Enemy M-Cruisers moving forward, sir," a Scanner Technician confirmed what Chulling had already seen.

Switching back to a wider view of the M-Cruisers that had begun to advance Chulling noted that all but a single, solitary enemy vessel was in a three craft formation. Thirty of the perplexing formations were advancing on his line, still way out of normal range and with no Harpoon or Flying Devil support.

"Open fire when they get in range and..." Chulling began to order the WATO turning away from the War Table.

"Enemy opening fire!" the same Scanner Technician yelled.

"Wha...?" Chulling started to yell in astonishment when it suddenly felt like the Memphis had run into a very powerful force shield.

Flung off his feet, Chulling was hurtled backwards from the War Table against the grey painted wall.

"Get the shielding up! Get the shielding up!" Chulling yelled amidst the carnage in the War Room.

Around him, people were being flung from their posts as consoles fizzled and sparked amongst billowing acrid smoke as the alarms blared.

"Return fire, WATO!" Chulling ordered, cursing himself for his complacency.

Whatever had happened, Chulling realised that the Bardomil had developed some kind of new weapon. The enemy had been quite active in the year since First Admiral Caudwell had humbled an entire Bardomil Imperial Fleet with two Star-Cruisers. And, now Chulling's formation was going to pay the price for it.

"Returning fire!" the WATO yelled.

Clambering back to his feet, Chulling stared hard at the three vessel formations that approached his position.

"Force-shielding initiated!" an Engineering Officer called out as the War Room personnel began to recover their wits and take their stations once more.

"Maximum intensity!" Chulling ordered, "damage!?" he demanded.

"Two of our high-yield turrets have been destroyed, sir, a third is damaged and out of action!" the Engineering Officer replied.

"Casualties!?" Chulling demanded as the anger and outrage swept over him.

He knew he had been complacent. It was the deadliest sin of a battlefield commander and he cursed himself for underestimating his enemy's capabilities. But, he also knew that the time for recriminations would be later. He had to hold his position until First Admiral Caudwell could bring reinforcements.

"We have eighty-six dead, sir," the Flight Surgeon Technician said darkly, "with one hundred and ninety wounded reported so far."

For a moment, Chulling stood in stunned silence as the figures challenged his consciousness. The loss of nearly three hundred from a complement of two thousand was a big blow, especially when the ship was supposed to have the most advanced force-shielding capability in the universe.

The War Room also stood silent for a moment as the severity of the blow sank in.

"Sir, the flotilla is also reporting damage and casualties!" a Comms Officer reported.

"Serious?" Chulling dragged himself back to the dangerous situation he knew he now faced.

"Marlborough, Ticonderoga and Devastator reporting loss of main power, Perilous and Agamemnon report weapons control systems inoperative," the Engineering Officer added to the already disastrous news.

The Bardomil first strike had been utterly devastating. Almost all of the Alliance ships had been hit, with significant damage inflicted upon more than half. It had been a bad mistake by Chulling assuming that the Bardomil were out of range of his ships. Now, nearly three thousand people had been killed with three times as many wounded swamping the Hospital Decks.

"Tell the other ships to give them cover under their force-shielding," Chulling ordered, knowing that he had no alternative other than to weaken the force-shielding of his other ships to protect his lame ducks.

"Sir," the WATO brought yet more bad news, "we've lost nearly a third of our high-yield guns," he reported, "they targeted our turrets."

Chulling closed his eyes and sighed for a moment. Then, he steeled himself to take charge of this unfolding disaster.

"Keep what we've still got, firing, WATO, and launch half of our Eagles," he ordered.

With a nod, the WATO went to his duty.

Chulling knew that he needed to launch his single-seat fighters to keep the M-Cruisers, with their devastating new weapons, away from his formation. Looking at the War Table image, he could see the Bardomil Harpoons and Flying Devils forming up into their Big Wing formations for just that eventuality. The Bardomil Big Wing was their classical 'V' shaped flying wedge with a heavily reinforced right wing. When the formations engaged the weight of numbers on the right flank would simply sweep round and encircle the enemy's formation.

"Very good," Chulling cursed his opposite number at the realisation of the Bardomil commander's tactics.

Someone in the Bardomil force knew what he or she was doing. This neatly set trap would force the Alliance Eagles to challenge the M-Cruisers allowing the Flying Devils and Harpoons to isolate them from their Carrier ships. And, Chulling knew that he might have no alternative other than to sacrifice all or most of his Eagles to buy time to repair his own damage and for First Admiral Caudwell to bring reinforcements. Hold at all costs, the First Admiral had said and Chulling knew that there would be some hard fighting to be done before help could arrive.

However, Chulling was unaware that this current disaster could have been much worse. The Bardomil commander, Grattus Darrien, had targeted the Alliance weapons systems unaware that the Star-Cruisers were unshielded. Had he known that, the Bardomil weapons would have been targeted at engines and power plants with fatal consequences for the Alliance.

"Eagles launching!" the WATO intoned as Chulling watched the small fighter craft emerge from the launching bays of his own flotilla.

Still watching the images of the ragged chain of advancing M-Cruisers, Chulling saw the faint yellow streaks of high-yield pulsar-bolts smash into several of the Bardomil craft. Each hit was fatal, reducing the gull-winged spacecraft to debris in a cataclysm of red roaring devastation. The Alliance formation was, at least, hitting back, Chulling comforted himself, but noticed that only eighteen of the one hundred M-Cruisers had fallen to the Alliance's guns. The Alliance high-yield pulsar-cannons required a full fifteen seconds to cool down before they could be fired again.

As the pulsar-cannons cooled, the Bardomil M-Cruisers continued their advance. Watching the War Table image, Chulling noticed the M-Cruisers were once again forming into their three vessel formations.

With the three components of the formation flying perilously close to each other, the tell-tale tiny yellow streams of laser fire seemed to meet, cross and combine as the M-Cruisers fired simultaneously. Then, having fired their weapons, the three craft split up and resumed their independent advances upon the Alliance positions.

"So, that's how they're doing it," Chulling said to himself reluctantly having to admire the sheer simplicity of the solutions that the Bardomil had discovered to the problem of penetrating the Alliance's force-shielding.

It was a very easy process to treble the capacity of their existing laser weapons through some simple mechanism and re-focus the reinforced beams towards their targets. Having lost the advantage of force-shielding, the Alliance vessels were now vulnerable to the weight of numbers that the Bardomil possessed. But, in this new innovative tactic, Chulling immediately spotted a weakness.

"WATO?" he beckoned the Weapons and Tactical Officer over to the War Table just as another Bardomil combined laser bolt struck the Memphis.

Inside the Alliance Star-Cruiser it felt as if someone had struck the hull with a massive sledge hammer. The concussion from the Bardomil weapon shook the force shielded Star-Cruiser heavily causing further damage to already weakened systems and structures. It gave Chulling no comfort to realise that every other ship in his flotilla was undergoing a similar ordeal.

Clinging tenaciously to the edge of the War Table, Chulling indicated to the WATO what he had just discovered.

"See, they cluster in threes before they fire," he indicated to the WATO who nodded his understanding, "that's why they're hammering us," he added as another bolt struck causing him to lurch along the War Table edge.

"Take the Tactical Computers offline and go to manual firing," Chulling ordered, "divide the enemy force into sectors and target them as they begin to cluster."

Taking the Tactical Computers off line would give target selection responsibility back to the high-yield pulsar-cannons' gunners. The Tactical Computers had not been programmed to read the increased threat potential of the M-Cruisers taking up their new and innovative three vessel formation. The old parameters of distance, weapon range, weapon strength, and the other variables that the Tactical Computers calculated hundreds of times every second were now redundant in the face of this new tactic.

"You understand what I'm saying, WATO!?" Chulling asked as the Memphis shook once more.

"Yes, sir," the WATO replied, "It'll take time to re-programme all the tactical computers!"

"We don't have that time!" Chulling instructed, "Go to manual firing and target them as they cluster!"

"Sir!" the WATO barked and dashed back to his console.

For the first time since the engagement had begun, Chulling was starting to feel like he had some control over the events that were unfolding. He had caught a break by discovering the Bardomil innovation; now he had to make use of the knowledge.

"All Eagles launched and in formation," the WATO announced.

Looking at the War Table image, Chulling used the Manipulator to change the perspective and see the squadrons in their holding stations, circling behind the Alliance force-shielding. With another deft flick of his fingers, the Manipulator changed the image to that of the advancing M-Cruisers who dodged and weaved their way through the fusillades of Alliance high-yield pulsar-bolts. As Chulling watched another M-Cruiser was struck. The left gull-wing was torn off by the passing white-hot pulsar-bolt. The vessel survived the bolt strike, but Chulling knew it would play no further part in this day's combat. It wasn't a 'kill' for the hard-pressed gunners to celebrate, but one less M-Cruiser in the battle was always a blessing.

"Tactical Computers are now offline, sir," the WATO announced.

"Excellent; order the gunners to fire, but only when those M-Cruisers start clustering," he ordered the WATO, "Engineers, how long until Ticonderoga, Devastator and Marlborough can get underway?"

"Marlborough is back in the firing line, Devastator is running final tests and Ticonderoga reports another ten minutes," the Engineering Officer reported.

"Very well," Chulling replied, "right, WATO, let's get those Eagles in there to chase off those M-Cruisers," Chulling ordered feeling bullish once more at the prospect of handing out little punishment for a change.

Operating the Manipulator once more, Chulling showed a blue highlighted course for the Eagles on the War Table image.

"Send them out in a pincer attack, WATO, and try to get them in behind those M-Cruisers to cut off their line of retreat," Chulling instructed, indicating with his free hand how the Eagles should get behind the enemy before attacking.

"Understood, sir," the WATO replied, "but what about the Harpoons and Flying Devils?"

"It's going to be hit and run, WATO," Chulling explained, "get in there, hit them hard and get out before the Big Wing closes on them."

"Yes, sir," the WATO responded.

"Sir," the Scanner Officer chimed, "the enemy are bringing up their reserves from the convoy."

For a moment, Chulling tried to comprehend what had just been said. The Bardomil commander was committing his reserves to the fight. The additional M-Cruisers coming forward would mean that even if the Eagles could beat off this attack, there would be new ships to pound at his already fragile line once the Flying Devils and Harpoons had chased the Alliance fighters away. With a deep sigh, Chulling knew that he had only one course of action open to him or his flotilla would be bombarded to space dust where they stood.

"Engineers," Chulling called out, "I want all ships ready for Trion Drive in ten minutes," he ordered, "if Ticonderoga isn't ready by then, abandon and destroy her. Is that clear?"

"Clear, sir" the Engineering Officer confirmed the order.

"Sir," the WATO interrupted, "pulsar-cannons ready."

"In your own time, WATO, in your own time," Chulling ordered and concentrated on the line of advancing M-Cruisers once again.

"Opening fire, sir," the WATO confirmed the order.

For a long moment nothing seemed to happen as Chulling watched the advancing M-Cruisers. Then suddenly, the M-Cruisers began to cluster in their three vessel formation in preparation to fire at the Alliance positions.

With several groups of M-Cruisers coming into position, the Alliance gunners opened fire. Moments later, the white-hot pulsar-bolts seethed downrange towards their intended targets. Many of the three vessel formations, already committed to firing, had no way of escaping. Chulling watched calmly as one trio of M-Cruisers sustained a direct hit and disappeared in a huge fireball of death and destruction. Four more formations suffered the same fate within moments of the first strike sending great plumes of fiery destruction in every direction. Two more trios managed to see the oncoming harbingers of death and devastation and attempted to break formation. However, it was far too late. With one of the three vessels struck by the hurtling pulsar-bolt, the massive feedback built up in the link between the vessels reached back through their power connection and annihilated the other two ships.

Within seconds, twenty one M-Cruisers had been consigned to a fiery oblivion. But, Chulling noted with some disappointment that more pulsar-bolts had missed their targets than had hit. Removing the Tactical Computers from the equation had reduced the accuracy of the gunnery. Having become reliant on the computerised targeting systems, the Alliance gunners had become rusty in their target practice. The simple rules of their original training had long become faded memories. Once again, Chulling considered that his complacency had let his flotilla down in the heat of battle.

With the pulsar-cannons now cooling, Chulling watched as the two Eagle formations rapidly closed the gap towards the advancing M-Cruisers.

With a weather eye to the Harpoons and Flying Devil formations that were trying to close the gap on their M-Cruiser comrades, Chulling gauged that it was going to be a close run thing. The speedier and more agile Eagles were closing the distance, but the Bardomil fighters were in closer proximity. The War Table image showed that the Alliance fighters would arrive first, but with only a few seconds to spare. Chulling wondered just how much damage they could do in those precious seconds. Broadening out his War Table view, Chulling could see the Bardomil reserves hurtling through the lanes of the invasion convoy to reinforce the front line strike fleets. There was no way they could reach the front line M-Cruisers before the Eagles, but they could add their weight to the next, inevitable, round of pounding on his position.

"Ready to fire again, sir," the WATO announced.

With a brief nod, Chulling waited for the next salvo of high-yield pulsar-bolts to go streaking downrange to shatter more M-Cruisers. Once again, a short delay heralded the full force of the Alliance guns. Three more trios of M-Cruisers were destroyed in the red, fiery blooms that meant death for the Bardomil crews. It was a disappointing haul in the mind of Chulling, who angrily turned to the WATO.

"Anticipate them!" he yelled, "fire at where they're going to be, not where they are!"

"Yes, sir," the nervous WATO replied, now painfully aware of just how out-of-practice the Alliance gunners had become.

"Eagles approaching enemy formations, sir," the chastened WATO called out.

"Cease fire on the turrets," Chulling ordered and diverted his attention to the two pincers of Eagle fighters that were about to smash into the flanks of the M-Cruiser advance.

Holding his breath with anticipation, Chulling counted down the seconds until the first volleys from the low-yield rapid-firing pulsar-cannons tore into the undefended hulls of the approaching M-Cruisers. The wedge-shaped Eagle fighters with the high tail planes, for supreme manoeuvrability, hurtled forward into the attack. With their low-yield pulsar-cannons stuttering at the rate of five bolts per second, the swarms of Eagles very quickly began to tear chunks from the hulls of the slow and lumbering gull-winged M-Cruisers. However, Chulling knew that it would take several hits on an M-Cruiser to cause it serious damage. Once again, Chulling cursed the Alliance for not having a heavy weapon gunship like the Bardomil Flying Devil. The speedy and agile Eagles could sting and harry the M-Cruisers, but they needed greater firepower to do real damage to them.

The Eagle pilots, however, were taking to their task with relish. From both flanks, the Eagles scythed through the M-Cruiser formation, strafing across their hulls as they zipped past their opponents. With virtually no self-defence capability, the M-Cruisers could do very little except absorb the punishment that the Eagles were handing out. And, despite the Eagles' lack of real firepower, Chulling noticed that two M-Cruisers were suffering severe damage. On one the vulnerable gull-wing was starting to fold up under the impacts from an Eagle's pulsar-cannons. A second M-Cruiser was casting debris, flame and dead crew members out into space from the concerted attacks of three Eagles.

But, the joy of an unprotected enemy under their guns was to be short lived.

The great horde of Flying Devils and Harpoons was rapidly approaching their position. The Flight Controllers aboard the two Fleet Carriers and the Star-Cruisers began to issue instructions to extricate their charges from the combat zone. The Alliance left pincer was withdrawn first, the great right wing of the Bardomil fighter force looming large on the Scanner screens. The Eagle pilots on the left wing, took their chances at one last strafe on the M-Cruisers before opening the throttles fully and beating a retreat from the battle zone. The Eagles of the right wing, with a few more seconds' grace, took their final shots at the vulnerable M-Cruisers before turning round and heading back to base.

On the War Table, Chulling watched as the right line of the Bardomil formation swung round to try to cut off the fleeing Eagles from the safety of their carrier ships. The Harpoons and Flying Devils failed, but did attempt a half-hearted pursuit before their Flight Controllers pulled them back. The Bardomil had learned that flying into the hundreds of self-defence turrets that mushroomed up on a Star-Cruiser was a one-way ticket to the graveyard.

With the Bardomil breaking off the pursuit of the Eagles, Chulling had bought the Alliance some breathing space. The Flying Devils and Harpoons would have to return to their stations, whilst the M-Cruiser cordon would have to wait for their reinforcements to bolster their ranks for the next assault. Over forty M-Cruisers had been eliminated. And, although the Eagle raid had achieved very little in terms of damage, it had disrupted the Bardomil advance. Both the Alliance and Bardomil forces had halted to draw breath whilst Chulling worked out his next move. It wouldn't be long before the Bardomil would wish to continue their hostilities and Chulling needed a Plan B. His initial idea of conducting a 'turkey-shoot' was in ruins. This invasion force was going to need to be handled with finesse and guile rather than brute gunfire whilst standing behind the force-shielding.

In a straight pounding match, there was a very strong likelihood the Bardomil would win, so Chulling knew that he would have to use the advantage of home territory to weaken his opponent. He decided reluctantly that he was going to have to give ground and abandon his position on the frontier. Turning to the War Table, Chulling called up the three dimensional schematic of the Praxos system. Seven, barren, lifeless planetary bodies snapped into crystal clear view above the War Table. The first two outer planets, Sartek and Demlar, offered no strategic or tactical advantage. The third outer planet, Valnarim, however, was a large gas giant like Jupiter in the Terran system. And, with the realisation of Valnarim's potential, Chulling began to formulate his plan.

"Are the Eagles recovered yet?" Chulling asked the WATO.

"Nearly, sir," the WATO indicated that the last squadrons were circling their carrier ships ready to return to their hangers.

"Very well, once they're back, instruct all vessels to rendezvous at Valnarim," Chulling ordered, "Engineers status on Ticonderoga?"

"Ticonderoga has just completed critical damage repairs, sir," the Engineering Officer confirmed.

"Does she have Trion Drive capability?" Chulling questioned.

"That's an affirmative, sir," the Engineering Officer said proudly.

The Engineers aboard the Ticonderoga had performed near miraculous feats of repair to bring her main power back to a functional level.

"Good," Chulling responded, "get those Trion Drives warmed up and plot coordinates for Valnarim, standard dispersal protocol," Chulling instructed.

BENNING

The Trionic Web was a constantly fluctuating entity. The frequency at which Trions resonated in any fixed area was far from stable or static. Gravitational changes or radiation spikes could minutely alter the frequency of the Trions in that area. It had always been standard protocol for Alliance ships entering the Trionic Web to exit some one hundred thousand kilometres distant from each other to avoid disastrous collisions on emergence.

Aboard the Memphis, the energy hungry Trion Generators were drawing power from the proto-star reactors to create the Trion field around the vessel. The great loud whirring of the generators manufacturing the specifically-tuned Trion Field warned the crew that they were about to move almost twenty-five million kilometres in the time it took a person to blink.

"The New Thexxia and the Leonidas have entered the Trionic Web, sir," the Scanner Officer reported that the two Fleet Carriers had moved on to the next location.

On the War Table image, two blinding flashes indicated the departure of the two Carriers.

"Caractacus, Clemenceau, Valiant and Icarus are leaving, sir," the Scanner Officer continued as four more bright flashes showed the continuing Alliance retreat.

"Sir!" another Scanner Technician called out, "enemy approaching again!"

Chulling cursed softly under his breath as twelve M-cruisers broke out of the cordon that they had been holding. The Bardomil commander, Grattus Darrien, had seen the first of the Alliance vessels moving out into the Trionic Web and had flung his only fully operational M-Cruisers at the fleeing Star-Cruisers.

"They're opening fire!" the Scanner Technician warned.

On the War Table image, four trios of M-Cruisers fired at the Alliance position with one laser bolt striking the Memphis; which shuddered violently under the impact. The other three bolts struck the Ticonderoga.

"Ticonderoga's hit, sir," the Comms Technician called out, "main power lost and the proto-star containment chambers are failing, sir."

"Get those people out!" Chulling barked, "Navigation, get us between her and the enemy!" he ordered urgently.

With the Memphis immediately beginning to execute a painfully slow turn to try to protect the badly damaged Star-Cruiser, the Ship's Commander on the Ticonderoga ordered an immediate 'abandon ship'. The crew members on Ticonderoga dashed to their emergency stations as the Ship's Commander took over the Navigation Console in his Command

Cabin. With every last ounce of reserve power he pushed his doomed ship away from the rest of the Alliance formation and tried to build up some distance.

"Get them out!" Chulling urged the crew of the Ticonderoga to abandon the stricken warship.

But as Chulling willed the two thousand souls aboard the Ticonderoga into their Escape Capsules, the force-shielding around the Containment Vessels for the proto-star matter, finally failed. The proto-star matter, liberated from the confines of the ship, burst free, in a massive cataclysmic explosion that vapourised the Ticonderoga and everyone aboard her. The flash from the liberated proto-star matter was so brilliant that the entire War Room of the Memphis was dazzled. Even General Grattus Darrien, on his flagship, had to shield his eyes from the colossal explosion.

The remaining Star-Cruisers were buffeted by the blast, but had survived because of the Ticonderoga's Ship's Commander's heroism. With his last breaths he had managed to push the doomed vessel far enough away to save the remaining Star-Cruisers. When the blast wave had passed the Memphis, Chulling looked sadly at his War Table image and saw that a new star had been born on the very edge of the Praxos system.

In the years to come, this new celestial body would be called... Ticonderoga.

BENNING

Chapter 31

<u>The Terran System</u>

"Sir!" the alarmed Flight Surgeon announced "Spearhead One is down!"

"What!?" Marrhus Lokkrien shouted; the news that he dreaded the most finally manifesting to a horrifying, blood-chilling reality.

But, with that news, Lokkrien knew that he had to take charge of the situation and that billions of lives were now in his hands. He had to set his emotions aside and act quickly to avert disaster.

"Over-ride control commands on Spearhead One!" Lokkrien rapidly snapped out the orders, "full power to the force-shielding, everything we've got to all sectors," he barked, "every ounce of power we have...is Billy still alive?!"

"Sir," the Senior Engineer shouted, "we can't hold this configuration for long!"

"We won't have to, it's nearly over!...Flight Surgeon!?" Lokkrien called out his reply over the shuddering and clamour of the War Room.

"Spearhead One is still alive, sir!" the Fight Surgeon confirmed, "but, his vital signs are weak, we have to get him out of there!"

"Engineers can we teleport him out!?" Lokkrien shouted as the Aquarius shuddered once more under the impact.

"Negative, sir!" the Senior Engineer replied, "There's just too much radiation, and we can't get through the force-shielding on the vessel!"

Silently, Lokkrien cursed. He knew that he couldn't teleport Billy Caudwell to safety, and he had to leave the Black Rose in-situ to hold the protective umbrella in place. For the moment, Billy would just have to hang on in there and ride out this particular storm until he could be retrieved. The horrible churning sensation in the pit of his stomach did nothing to make the decision any easier for Lokkrien. They all just had to hunker down and hope and pray that they could weather the super-heated tempest that was being thrown at them.

"We're at full power to the force-shielding!" the Senior Engineer reported.

"Have you put Aquarius into the grid!?" Lokkrien challenged.

"Yes, sir!" the Senior Engineer responded, "we've thrown in everything, there's nothing in reserve!"

As soon as the Senior Engineer spoke, the buffeting on the umbrella intensified. Whereas Billy had carefully directed the power to the sectors of the force-shielding to deflect the super-heated material away, Lokkrien now had no such control. He could only push full power over the whole of the force-shielding. The violent jolts and tremors of the final waves of plasma striking the force-shielding would now be transferred to all of the vessels in the umbrella. The enormous Star-Destroyers were going to be particularly vulnerable to these hugely magnified shock waves, and Lokkrien quietly prayed that their colossal structures could stand up to the beating. With the plasma waves crashing into the fully powered force-shielding, the concussions began to batter the vessels as they gallantly held their positions in the face of such a fearful enemy.

Inside the War Room of the Aquarius, Lokkrien felt like he was in a tin can that was being pulverised by heavy hammers. Every concussion seemed to be echo around the great cavernous battle centre. The shuddering also seemed to intensify. Yet, the War Room staff all stayed doggedly at their posts. With grim professionalism, they held their stations, monitored their consoles, passed on their vital information and prayed that they would survive this terrifying maelstrom.

Looking round the War Room, for the first time, Lokkrien started to feel fear. For a moment, there was an air of unreality as he watched the Officers and Technicians trying to go about their duties. In those moments, everything seemed to slow down for Lokkrien. Small details suddenly sprang into focus. One female Technician, sitting at her console, was wearing a glittering necklace. An Officer was resting is hand on a colleagues shoulder trying to keep him calm and give him encouragement. Little details, that he normally wouldn't have noticed, now seemed important to Lokkrien.

However, the reality of the situation quickly imposed itself upon Lokkrien. Time, once again sped up as one of the front row consoles, no longer able to stand the buffeting and shaking, finally gave up and exploded in a great cascade of sparks and flame. The Officer seated at the stricken console caught the full impact of the explosion and was flung backwards from her seat onto the hard metal floor. Before she had even hit the floor, the fire suppressant gas burst upwards from beneath the console to stifle any flames or power surges as the safety protocol shut the malfunctioning station down. The Officer's supervisor dashed over to the fallen operator and quickly assessed her for injuries. Down on the Hospital Decks, the already overstretched Medical Technicians would be receiving distress calls from the War Room.

"Get her to the Hospital Deck!" Lokkrien called as the Officer's supervisor started to help the injured operator unsteadily to her feet.

No sooner had she risen to her feet; leaning on her supervisors shoulders than another Technician was at the console trying to repair it.

The injured operator, a nasty burn on her face, was led away by the supervisor despite the jostling.

"All vessels are starting to report structural damage, sir!" the senior Engineer reported, "We have to withdraw or we'll be shaken apart!"

"No!" Lokkrien barked, "We hold this position as long as we can, how long until this is over!?"

"Another two minutes, sir!" the Scanner Technician replied, "We're just about to hit the tail!"

The Sun, having been agitated by the Bardomil emitter, had thrown out one last intense burst of super-heated plasma before settling back down to its normal, more docile, state. This was what the vulnerable force-shielding umbrella would now have to survive.

"Can you hold us together for two more minutes!?" Lokkrien demanded.

"I don't know, sir!" the Senior Engineer shouted in response, "I just don't know!!"

"Well, we're just about to find out aren't we!?" Lokkrien added, "Brace yourselves everyone!"

Throughout the War Room, personnel sought what little safety and support that they could find. Most of the Officers and Technicians simply crouched beneath their consoles, like beasts hiding from a great storm.

The impact came a few moments later and was more intense than their original entry into the plasma stream. The massive concussions shook and rattled all of the Alliance craft, throwing personnel from their stations like rag dolls cast around by a petulant child. Lokkrien, flung off his feet by the impact, felt himself being swept across the War Room floor and landing heavily amongst the first bank of consoles. Around him, the War Room personnel were all undergoing a similar ordeal. Trying to rise to his feet, Lokkrien saw another console explode in a shower of dazzling sparks as a Technician was flung backwards into the row behind. A young woman screamed as she too was thrown into the air by an impact. Managing to get to his feet, Lokkrien lurched into the first row of consoles. Trying to impose any form of order and command on the situation, he knew, would be impossible. They would just have to try to survive as best they could. The only thing Lokkrien felt that he could usefully do was try to help those around him.

Stumbling amongst the consoles, Lokkrien caught a stumbling female Technician as she fell towards him. Catching her, Lokkrien felt the impact jarring most of the bones in his body. For a moment, the young woman stared in horror at him. Then, he realised that she was a Thexxian.

"Get under here!" he ordered, pushing the young woman under one of the consoles before moving on to see whom else he could help.

Lurching into the second row, another console exploded showering Lokkrien in sparks as he held up his arm to protect his face. A voice called out in terror as a body flew past.

Aboard the Black Rose, the unconscious Billy lay in the high-backed command chair, his head lolling backwards, whilst in front of him on the centre screen all five sectors were lit up and the power use bars were all deeply into the red zone with the word 'CRITICAL' flashing in yellow above the now-static bars.

Then, as quickly as the violent shaking had started, it stopped as the last of the super-charged plasma was cast harmlessly off into space.

On the Aquarius, Lokkrien was one of many who sat in the momentary peace and silence wondering what was going to happen next. Then, real life kicked in. Some of the injured War Room personnel started to groan and yell for help as comrades began to drag themselves, painfully and wearily, out of their hiding places and re-establish connections at their consoles. People were, shakily, rising to their feet once more and trying to restore some kind of normality. Fire extinguishers were activating adding a pall of harmless gas to the dust and debris of the shambles that was once the First Admiral's War Room.

Amidst the devastation of the War Room, Lokkrien took immediate command.

"Get the injured to the Hospital Decks! Call in the replacement crews!" he began amongst the debris and the groaning.

"Comms, I want back on the network, priority!" he shouted towards the Communications consoles.

"Engineers, get those damage assessments made fast!" he called out as he started to help an Engineering Officer to her feet.

"And, someone get a rescue boat out to the First Admiral now!" he yelled the loudest.

BENNING

Chapter 32

The Star-Cruiser Aquarius

Having been pulled from the Control Cabin of the Black Rose, Billy Caudwell was barely able to recognise the harsh antiseptic smell of the Hospital Deck that he had been brought to. Strangely, he felt that the radiation burns to his face and hands were giving him no pain or discomfort. The Medical Officers who hovered around his Med-Bed, however, knew that this was the sign of a serious injury. Even the protective force-shielding of the Personal Environment Suit, lying on the floor next to the Med-Bed, had been unable to defend Billy from the full harshness of the sun's fury. The deep, angry red welts on his face were interrupted by patches of pale waxy white flesh where the tissue had been completely killed off. The gathered Medical Officers had heartily concurred that it had been a miracle that his eyes had not been damaged.

Sitting up on his elbows in the Med-Bed that hovered about a metre from the ground, Billy was only just able to focus on the hive of activity that surrounded him. Medical Officers seemed to congregate like undertakers at a deathbed, whispering and arguing amongst themselves.

"Did it work?" Billy asked and found that his voice was no more than a shallow croak.

For a moment, the Medical Officers ceased their conference to look concernedly at their patient as a kindly-faced Medical Technician smiled and leaned in close to Billy.

"What was that, First Admiral?" she asked softly, pulling up the pale blue cover to his waist, and turning her head to place her ear close to his mouth.

"Did Earth survive?" Billy croaked the question he desperately needed answered.

"Yes, First Admiral," the Technician smiled, "now you must rest, sir," she added and carefully helped him to recline once more.

Lying on his back, Billy felt breathless and uncomfortable and tried to prop himself up on his elbows again.

"No, First Admiral" the Technician placed her olive Thexxian hands on his shoulders and gently pushed him back, "you must not agitate yourself."

"Can't breathe lying down," Billy croaked as he tried to resist her shove.

"He says he can't breathe, sir," the Technician called out to the Medical Officers, who quickly gathered around the Med-Bed.

"It might be scarring on his lungs or windpipe," one of the Junior Medical Officers commented as if Billy were on another planet.

"Keep his shoulders elevated," the Senior Medical Officer instructed.

A moment later, Billy felt his upper body being pushed upwards as the force-shielding on the Med-Bed's horizontal surface was adjusted to raise his head and shoulders up to a more comfortable position.

"Lokkrien," Billy croaked softly.

"He wants Admiral Lokkrien," the Senior Medical Officer said, "bring him in and commence the intensive phoronic radiation treatment."

The gaggle of Medical Officers quickly scattered to their duties as the kindly-faced Technician reappeared with what looked like a breakfast tray with two large hollow tubes at either side.

"We'll do your hands first, sir," the Technician smiled and clipped the breakfast tray contraption to the edges of the Med-Bed across Billy's stomach.

As Billy watched the breakfast tray contraption being attached, Lokkrien appeared at the foot of the Med-Bed.

"Welcome back to the land of the living sir; we thought we'd lost you for a moment there," Lokkrien tried to sound cheerful as he struggled to ignore the burns on Billy's face.

"You don't get rid of me that easily, Marrhus," Billy croaked as he tried to smile.

"We'll just put your hand in the treatment bay," the Medical Technician indicated to Billy's right hand.

"What's the situation then?" Billy asked, his throat starting to ease, as he nodded to the kindly Technician, who gently lifted his burned right hand and carefully slotted it into the hollow on the treatment device.

"Well, we, I mean you, saved the Earth from the solar flare," Lokkrien tried to sound positive, "but the Bardomil have pushed Admiral Chulling back to Valnarim in the Praxos system," he added the sting-in-the-tail as he stepped aside for the Technician.

"Just lifting your left hand now, sir," the Technician announced and began to slide the hand into the treatment bay.

"Is Chulling holding?" Billy asked.

"He's hanging on in there, sir," Lokkrien replied, "but, it's a tough fight, they've had to give ground and they've lost the Ticonderoga."

"What do you mean, 'lost' the Ticonderoga?" Billy queried unable to grasp the concept that a force-shielded ship could be destroyed.

"Her proto-star Containment Chamber was compromised," Lokkrien explained.

"Dear God," Billy mumbled as the enormity of the loss struck him.

"Switching on," the Technician announced and pressed a button on the left treatment bay.

A moment later, the breakfast tray contraption began to hum softly as Billy felt the gentle soothing waves of phoronic radiation stimulate his own healing processes. At first a gentle itch subsided into a sensation not unlike bathing his hands in tepid water.

"Then we have to get to Chulling with everything we can manage," Billy's voice began to clear.

"Well, what we have sir, is three of the five Star-Destroyers badly damaged and unable to move under their own power and the other two with major structural problems," Lokkrien replied.

"Can they initiate Trion Drives?" Billy asked.

"There we go, all finished on the hands," the Medical Technician said brightly and pulled the breakfast tray contraption away from Billy's hands.

Lifting his hands, Billy could still see the outline of the burns beneath the pink newly healing skin that the radiation had stimulated to grow over the injuries. The damaged nerve tissue would be starting to regenerate within a few minutes and Billy knew that he would have to get the Personal Environment Suit back on to ward off the intense pain that would entail.

"It'll be touch and go if they try to enter the Trionic Web," Lokkrien warned.

"Well, I'm not leaving Chulling to hang out to dry," Billy said determinedly, "round up every Eagle and pilot you can scrape together and cram them into the two functional Star-Destroyers," Billy ordered.

"Your face now, sir," the Technician held up a transparent mask in the shape of a human face attached to several spindly leads, "close your eyes now, sir," she added.

"It's still a terrible risk," Lokkrien warned once more, "if they're not up to scratch, the Trionic Web will tear them apart."

"Now keep very still, sir," the Medical Technician instructed as she gently placed the mask on Billy's face.

"What choice..." Billy began to answer when he was interrupted by the Medical Technician.

"I mean completely still, sir," the Technician said firmly immediately silencing Billy, "switching on," she intoned and the machine began to hum softly again.

Again, Billy felt the gentle itch on his skin rapidly transform to the tepid bathing sensation.

"I used to know a Drill Instructor like that at the Bardan Military Academy," Lokkrien smiled at Billy, "and he wasn't half as tough as this one."

"Oh, I'm so sorry, sir, I..." the flustered Technician began to apologise.

"Technician," Lokkrien smiled, "you're doing a fine job; just remind me to call for you should I ever need to tell the First Admiral to shut up, will you?" he joked.

Unable to move, Billy stifled a laugh as the waves of healing radiation swept over his face.

"There we go, sir," the Technician said shame-facedly as she removed the mask from Billy's face.

"How do I look?" Billy asked nervously.

"As pink as a boiled Terran lobster," Lokkrien answered honestly, "with blotches."

"Oh great," Billy said imagining his face in the same sad condition as his hands, "just what I needed."

"So, we still go with Titan and Colossus?" Lokkrien asked hoping that Billy had changed his mind.

"Yes, we don't have a choice," Billy said and swung his legs out over the edge of the Med-Bed with a pained groan, "and, make sure the civilians get back to Earth all right."

"First Admiral, I must protest!" the Senior Medical Officer stepped forward anxiously.

"Good," Billy sighed as he sat on the edge of the Med-Bed, "put it in writing and submit it to Admiral Lokkrien," he winced and pushed himself onto the floor.

Stumbling, Billy quickly regained his balance, and stood shakily on his own two feet as Lokkrien darted forward.

"Steady, old man," Lokkrien said catching Billy's shoulder as he stumbled again, "where exactly do you think you're going?" he added softly.

"If we're the Cavalry," Billy replied straightening up, "then I can't ride to the rescue on a Med-Bed can I?"

"The Cavalry tend to like their leaders living and breathing," Lokkrien countered.

"Oh, they will be," Billy answered, "give me that uniform," he indicated the Personal Environment Suit that lay on the ground.

Stooping down quickly, Lokkrien swept the pale blue uniform overall up in his right hand and passed it to Billy who draped it over his shoulder and began to hobble, stiff-legged and pained towards the doorway.

"First Admiral, I..." the Senior Medical Officer protested once more.

Stopping in his painful hobble, Billy held up his left hand to silence the Medical Officer.

BENNING

"It's all right, it'll be my responsibility," Billy assured the concerned Officer.

And, continued hobbling painfully away.

Chapter 33

The Star-Cruiser Aquarius

On another part of the Hospital Deck, Emma Wallace was feeling great. Lying on a strange bed-like apparatus, that levitated from the ground, in a darkened room, she felt her world spinning and a wonderful euphoric sensation of peace and warmth. Turning onto her side, she pulled up the strange blue cover and with a very broad, satisfied grin closed her eyes. Never, in her entire life, had she felt so good. Not even when she had gotten drunk that night with Tommy Warner had she felt so relaxed and comfortable.

The young Cerador Medical Technician stepped forward and lifted Emma's arm to check her wrist pulse.

"You look funny," Emma smiled blankly opening her eyes, and began to hum a childhood nursery rhyme.

The sharp featured Technician, with the hooked nose, nodded his head, satisfied that the relaxant drugs were now taking full effect.

"Here comes a chopper to chop off your head," Emma giggled loudly as the grey-opaque force-shielding of the doorway cleared to allow access to a familiar figure.

"Sir!" the Cerador Technician snapped to attention, causing Emma to roll over to see what the sudden commotion was about.

"At ease," Billy waved the Technician to relax as he approached the levitating Med-Bed.

"Hey, sweet cheeks!" Emma called out breezily to the figure that she recognised and reached her hand out to Billy.

"You quite happy down there?" Billy asked smiling softly; stopping himself from taking her hand in his own injured hand.

"Tee-riffic!" Emma announced and tried to focus on Billy's face, "you got something on your face, kiddo?" she asked with a puzzled look and then began to giggle again.

"Yep, it gets messy around here," Billy replied suddenly conscious of his damaged face.

"Well, you're gonna have to clean it up before dinner, or you won't get any pudding," Emma giggled as she scolded, wagging her finger.

"I'll get right on it," Billy smiled feeling waves of incredible sadness sweep over him.

"Yeah, can't have you at dinner looking like that," she smiled and closed her eyes again.

"Sir," the Technician interrupted, "it's time," he indicated the Memory Shredder in his hand.

One of the more unsavoury aspects of the Garmaurians was an ingenious mechanism that interrupted the synaptic flows from the area of the brain that converted short-term memories to long-term. If specifically targeted, the device could also erase the electrical activity in areas of the brain that held certain memories. It was primarily used by Garmaurian Intelligence to erase the memories of their agents in order for them to maintain their cover stories. If they had no memories of a previous life then they could not betray themselves to an enemy interrogator.

"Very well," Billy nodded to the Technician who stepped forward with a narrow, white strip that he placed upon Emma's forehead.

"Hey, sunshine, headbands and leg-warmers were last year," Emma mumbled.

"Step back would you, sir?" the Medical Technician asked, indicating that he was about to operate the device.

Taking a last look at the smiling and deliriously happy face, Billy took a single pace backwards.

"Switching on," the Technician said softly and pressed a button on a keypad.

Emma gasped as she arched her back and stared wide eyes at the ceiling. Then, a moment later, she slumped back down onto the Med-Bed. In her brain, the electrical charges had been interrupted for a split-second. And, in that split-second, the memories in her short-term memory were blocked from converting to long term memories. In a few minutes they would be forgotten, whilst the targeted areas of her long-term memory were also being electrically stripped.

"How much of her memory did you erase?" Billy asked quietly as the Technician stepped forward to check Emma's pulse again.

"Around four hours, sir," the Technician replied, happy that Emma's circulation had not been compromised, "but it varies from person to person."

"How do you mean?" Billy asked.

"It depends on the person, sir," the Technician answered carefully setting down Emma's arm. "sometimes a four hour erase can remove four hours or it can erase twenty-four hours, it just depends, sir, sometimes it can erase all the memories of a person or a series of related events."

Nodding slowly, Billy Caudwell had the feeling that Emma Wallace would awake back on Earth and have no memories of the past days. Deep down, he knew that it would probably be for the best. The part of his mind that was Teg Portan knew that unstable relationships and Supreme Military Command did not mix well.

"I'll leave you for a moment, if you'll excuse me, sir," the Technician made discretion the better part of valour and quietly left Billy alone with Emma.

Looking down at the sleeping figure, Billy gently drew the cover up to her neck. To Billy, she looked so lovely and yet so distant and unattainable. And, for just a fraction of a second, he thought about just giving up his quest to preserve his Alliance. But, as he listened to her gently breathing, he knew that the choice between the Universal Alliance and Emma Wallace was one that she could never win. Closing his eyes, he felt tears scalding on the newly stimulated flesh of his cheeks as they ran down to stain the blue Med-bed cover. Then, taking a deep breath, Billy sighed to stifle the sob that he felt building in his chest. In that moment, the bitter-sweet agony that almost choked him, surged into every corner of his mind and body. He wanted to cry out with that pain, but in his mind he knew that he had to walk away, as his face contorted for that brief second before he regained his composure again.

Opening his eyes once again, he smiled and gently cuffed his tears away with his sleeve.

"Go to sleep now," he said softly and took one last look at Emma before turning away.

Five steps later, he passed through the force-shielding of the door, out into the harsh light of the corridor. Dabbing his tender cheeks once more, Billy took several long deep breaths and then stamped his foot angrily as he gently exhaled. Shaking his head, to try to clear it, Billy set off, his jaw set firm as he marched purposefully down the corridor to the Teleport pad. Around him, people snapped to attention as he passed. However, Billy noticed none of them as he strode onwards, his eyes red and his throat thick with emotion.

Emma would be going home, but Billy was going to a fight.

Chapter 34

<u>The Praxos System</u>

The loss of the Star-Cruiser Ticonderoga hit the morale of Chulling's flotilla badly. Everyone aboard the Alliance vessels knew, and accepted, that death was a possible outcome for their service in the military. But, the comfortable sense of invincibility that had shrouded the Alliance crews with their force-shielding had now evaporated as they had witnessed the blinding and fiery demise of Ticonderoga. Ticonderoga was the first major warship to be lost in the Alliance and people were now faced with the reality of death in combat. It was hard for many to accept their new and very sudden vulnerability.

Turthus Chulling, having served in the military during the Thexxian Exodus found himself thrown back onto his old reserves of positive mental attitude, tenacity and showmanship. Chulling knew that crews who were demoralised would very quickly be defeated. He knew that he had to inspire his people to more and greater efforts whilst presenting a bullish and positive attitude of self confidence. It was a tough sell for Chulling. Many of the Officers, Technicians and crew members on the Ticonderoga had been friends, colleagues and comrades and their loss had hit him hard. But, with the flotilla extracted from the frontier, Chulling was planning a surprise for the Bardomil invaders who were rapidly approaching the new position, close to the planet of Valnarim.

With the pink and orange gas giant, Valnarim, anchoring the left wing of his position some half a million kilometres distant, Chulling was happy with his new position. The Eagles had been launched and were holding their pre-planned positions with a small contingent of five Star-Cruisers. The remaining Star-Cruisers and the two Fleet Carriers held their diamond formation in readiness for the Bardomil approach.

In the War Room of the Memphis, Chulling kept his own counsel as the Officers and Technicians went about their duties. Less than an hour previously, the War Room had been buzzing with excitement and confidence. Now, the mood of the War Room personnel was darker and more reserved. Losing the Ticonderoga had stunned many of them into a morose and anxious silence that Chulling knew he had to break. And, the only way to restore that shattered confidence was with victory. With his plans set and the ships in position, he hoped that much needed victory was only a few minutes away.

"Sir," the Scanner Officer said flatly, "enemy approaching," he continued with little enthusiasm.

"Very good," Chulling said determinedly, "let's have the force-shielding up at maximum and put everyone on standby."

Stepping over to the War Table, Chulling could see the dejection amongst his staff Officers. Long faces and downcast eyes were a signal to Chulling that his own Staff Officers were already half beaten.

"Right then, gentlemen," Chulling began bullishly, "it's time to start handing out some of what we've been taking."

"Sir!" the Scanner Officer announced, "enemy formation in range of video scanners."

"Very well, let's have a look at them, activate War Table!" Chulling demanded and the War Room was immediately plunged into darkness.

The brief few seconds of static cleared to show an image of the lead elements of the Bardomil strike force. Once again it was the classic formation with Flying Devils up front in a ragged cordon with more forming a protective perimeter around the M-Cruisers. Wryly, Chulling noted that the M-Cruiser complement was back up to full strength. The M-Cruisers in the invasion force convoy had been brought forward as had the Imperial Fighter Carriers. The Bardomil commander was trying to crush this Alliance flotilla as quickly as he could. Scanning down the lanes of the invasion convoy, Chulling noticed that several thousand supply and troop transports were missing, and theorised that they had been detached to occupy the two planets that the Alliance had to abandon. For a huge sacrifice in blood, the Bardomil had gained two large ice-bound lumps of rock. Not a very fair trade, Chulling considered, even if they were strategically important.

Tracking back through the War Table image, Chulling could see the Imperial Fighter Carriers clustered to the rear of the formation with the M-Cruisers making their way forward to challenge the Alliance Star-Cruisers once more. In the centre of the Bardomil formation, large numbers of Harpoons and Flying Devils were being launched under the soft warm glow of the pink and orange planet where Chulling had chosen to make his stand. With a shake of his head Chulling recognised that the Bardomil were still attempting to draw his Eagles out into a fighter-on-fighter contest with the more numerical Flying Devils and Harpoons.

"WATO, make ready," Chulling ordered, "get the pulsar-cannons warmed up."

"Sir!" the WATO replied.

On the War Table image, Chulling watched as the M-Cruisers started to move into their formations and the Bardomil fighters slotted into their positions in the feared and infamous Big Wing. The Bardomil commander was taking his time deploying his forces, Chulling considered and watched as the distance between the M-Cruisers and the Big Wing started to grow. This was not what Chulling wanted and urged the Big Wing to close the gap on the M-Cruisers. For his plan to succeed he needed the fighters much closer to the M-Cruisers and much further away from the Fighter Carriers.

Watching impatiently, Chulling could see more and more Harpoons and Flying Devils emerge from the Fighter Carrier bays to join up in the Big Wing.

"Come on, come on," Chulling urged the Bardomil fighters to move further forward.

"Enemy opening fire, sir," the Scanner Officer chimed as Chulling watched the M-Cruisers start to make up their trio formations and fire their first salvo at the Alliance position.

Almost immediately, the Memphis shuddered under the impact of the strengthened laser weapons from the M-Cruisers.

"Return fire, WATO, and tell the gunners to anticipate!!" Chulling ordered knowing that every shot was going to have to count in this battle.

Within seconds, the first salvoes from the Alliance high-yield pulsar-cannons were hurtling downrange to find the deadly trio formations. On the War Table image, Chulling was pleased to see that the gunners' aim had improved. Six of the trio formations burst like ripe melons in deep red, fiery plumes of destruction. Two more groups, just forming their trios, were also hit and the power feedback reached out like a deadly tendril to engulf all of the members in a cataclysmic explosion.

"Better WATO," Chulling praised and waited for the inevitable Bardomil response whilst the Alliance pulsar-cannons went through their fifteen second cooling procedures.

Keeping a steady eye on the positions relative to the Big Wing and the M-Cruiser formation, Chulling could see that the M-Cruisers had slowed their advance to allow the fighters to catch up. Without fighter support the M-Cruisers were vulnerable to Alliance Eagles and Grattus Darrien knew that if Chulling wanted to stop the pounding he would have to commit those fighters.

"Come on, that's the ticket," Chulling smiled wolfishly as the Big Wing crept closer to the M-Cruisers' position.

"Enemy firing again, sir," the Scanner Officer announced.

On the War Table, Chulling could see the tiny yellow laser streaks emerging from the front of the M-Cruiser trios. An instant later, Memphis and most of the other Alliance Star-Cruisers were shuddering from direct hits.

"Damage!?" Chulling yelled.

"We're holding up, sir!" an Engineering Officer called out.

"No major damage reported from the rest of the flotilla!" a Comms Technician added.

They're still too far away to really start to harm us, Chulling considered. If the M-Cruisers got close enough to the Alliance vessels they might be well able to overwhelm the force-shielding with the increased intensity of the laser weapons. It was an idea that Chulling chose not to dwell upon too closely. Short stabbing raids with the Eagles could keep the M-Cruisers away for a brief time. But Chulling knew that unless he did something to break up the M-Cruiser and Big Wing formation then his flotilla would be pounded to oblivion.

Still intently focussed on the War Table image, Chulling also knew that the time for that action was quickly approaching. The Big Wing was moving closer to the M-Cruiser formation whilst another Big Wing was forming around the fifty Imperial Fighter Carriers towards the rear of the strike force.

"WATO, make ready to launch the Star-Cruiser contingent," Chulling said calmly.

"Sir," the WATO responded, ready to implement the plan Chulling had outlined before the Eagles had been launched.

It was a bold plan, a risky plan, but, Turthus Chulling knew that you didn't win battles by playing safe. He had to take the risk or his flotilla was certainly doomed.

"Very well, release the Star-Cruisers," Chulling ordered.

High in the pink and orange atmosphere of the far side of the planet Valnarim, protected from the Bardomil scanners by the heavy gases and swirling radiation tides, five Alliance Star-Cruisers set off on their dangerous mission. The Clemenceau, Agamemnon, Light Brigade, Liberty and Sherman emerged from the atmosphere of the planet, on the Bardomil right flank, and began their attack runs on the Imperial Fighter Carriers. It was a desperate gamble by Chulling to try to damage the Bardomil strike force's fighter capacity by eliminating as many of their mother ships as he could.

On the War Table image, Chulling watched as the tight 'V' formation, led by the Liberty, swept towards the vulnerable Imperial Fighter Carriers.

"Comms," Chulling ordered in the War Room, "jam them!"

"Sir," the Communications Officer responded and hit the small blue button on his console.

From the nose of the Memphis, a huge burst of Cedrian radiation pulsed out into the emptiness of space and fried every Bardomil communications circuit in their strike force. The Bardomil communications personnel, who were screaming warnings into their equipment to the fighters around the Carriers, suddenly found all the channels were gone.

The Liberty formation quickly closed the range on the Bardomil Imperial Fighter Carriers, and, at extreme range, they began to fire on the vulnerable three-decked mother ships. With the Fighter Carriers in a close rectangular box formation, the first white-hot high-yield pulsar-bolts found their targets and began to carve great chunks of metal from the lumbering Carriers. Only the front turrets of the Star-Cruisers could effectively target the Carriers on the approach. But, once they were within the formation, all five of the twin-gunned turrets on each Star-Cruiser could wreak havoc amongst the big Bardomil Carriers.

On the War Table image, Chulling saw the first of the Bardomil Imperial Fighter Carriers start to fall slowly out of the formation as its huge stabilisers failed against the blast from the explosions. Falling with graceful, almost painful, slowness, Chulling watched with satisfaction as the doomed Carrier crashed into, and then through, the vessel beneath it in formation. That was the kind of collateral damage Chulling enjoyed seeing as two more Bardomil Carriers lost stability and fell from their positions in a crumpling and exploding mass of metal and flame.

The fighters massing around the Carriers in a second Big Wing quickly reacted to the intruders and began to turn their vessels to block the Alliance formations progress. As they were turning, the five forward turrets of the Star-Cruisers let fly with another deadly salvo at the stricken Carriers.

This time, three more Carriers sustained multiple hits from the savage hissing pulsar-bolts. The first Carrier exploded almost immediately throwing great chunks of devastation out into the cold empty darkness of space. The neighbouring Carrier was struck by the flying debris like a game-bird hit by shotgun pellets. The great chunks of metal ripped through the second Carrier, killing, maiming and destroying everything in their paths until they struck the huge electro-magnetic power generators that drove the vessel. Then, the second Fighter Carrier succumbed to its mortal wound and disappeared in a colossal explosion. With four carriers down in a matter of seconds and no communications, the Carrier commanders started doing what they had to do to save their vessels. Like large lumbering sheep, scattering before a quick and nimble fox, the Imperial Fighter Carriers began to break formation and run for safety.

Meanwhile, the five Star-Cruisers started to run into the Flying Devil and Harpoon fighters that were creating their own Big Wing formation, ready to be flung forward at the Alliance position. With no shortage of courage, the Bardomil Harpoon pilots and Flying Devil crews desperately threw their machines at the pathetically small looking intruder force. Hundreds of Flying Devils and thousands of Harpoons flew straight for the Star-Cruisers their laser weapons blazing. But, with cool professional calmness, the Star-Cruiser crews waited their moment and allowed the Bardomil fighters to overfly them.

Then, when the first of the Bardomil fighters was overflying, and strafing, the two rear Star-Cruisers, the Alliance Ship Commanders unleashed the full fury of their self-defence turrets. Built into every Alliance Star-Cruiser were close to a thousand twin-gunned, low-yield pulsar-cannon self-defence turrets. The Bardomil commander, General Darrien, had carefully avoided attacking the Star-Cruiser formations because of this close-quarter, self-defence capability. But, now, the Bardomil had to try to protect their vulnerable and valuable Fighter Carriers with the only weapon at their disposal.

Aboard the five Star-Cruisers, the WATOs unleashed the terrifying power of the self-defence turrets. The low-yield pulsar-cannons; targeted and controlled by the Tactical Computers, blasted five bolts per second at the swarms of Harpoons and Flying Devils that tried to strafe through the Alliance force-shielding. On the War Table image, Chulling watched as the tight 'V' formation cut its way through the great cloud of attacking fighters like a hot knife through butter. On the image, Chulling could see the fiery explosions of hundreds of fighters as the Star-Cruisers scythed a path of devastation and death through the serried ranks of the enemy.

To Chulling, each Star-Cruiser looked like a huge harvesting machine that relentlessly cut down the Bardomil fighters in great swathes. All round each Star-Cruiser, the desperate Bardomil fighters were vanishing in the red roaring death blooms that were the lot of the fighter pilot. In their formations, the Harpoons and Flying Devils attacked from all angles, trying to distract the relentless Alliance Star-Cruisers from the Imperial Fighter Carriers. And, in their hundreds they died as the Star-Cruisers belched out the deadly white-hot pulsar-bolts like sparks from a firework.

Aboard the Star-Cruisers, the Tactical Computers coldly, dispassionately and mercilessly calculated the threat potential of every Harpoon and Flying Devil; whether alone or in formation, hundreds of time per second. The Tactical Computers then passed the firing instructions to the self-defence turrets, which rapidly sent each target to a burning and screaming oblivion. The stolid courage of the Bardomil fighter crews could never hope to compete with the relentless computer-driven slaughter of the self-defence turrets.

With the Bardomil Imperial Fighter Carriers under attack and the second Big Wing being torn to ribbons, Chulling turned his attention to the M-Cruisers.

"Release the Eagles, WATO," Chulling ordered.

High in the pink and orange atmosphere on the near side of Valnarim, three thousand Alliance Eagles lay in wait for the attack order from the Memphis. In the War Room, Chulling, satisfied that the attack on the Fighter Carriers was progressing satisfactorily, let loose the Eagles on the M-Cruisers and first Big Wing. Sweeping round the face of the planet at full speed, the Eagles were amongst the right flank of the Bardomil Big Wing before any of the Bardomil could respond. The first volleys from the Eagles were deadly, the six low-yield pulsar-cannons blasting out five bolts per second hacked mercilessly through the astonished Bardomil fighter formations. Hundreds of Harpoons and Flying Devils were simply annihilated in those first moments of combat; their pilots dying before they realised what was happening.

On the War Table image, Chulling quickly discerned that the attack was going to plan. Having scythed their way along the edge of the Big Wing's heavy right flank, the Eagle formations split into three groups. The first group of fifteen hundred Eagles was to take on, and pin down, the Big Wing's right flank. The second group of five hundred was to sweep around the Bardomil rear and smash through the centre of the Big Wing to get at the M-Cruisers. The final group of one thousand Eagles was to attack the flank of the Bardomil left wing and drive them off. Once again, it was a bold and risky move by Chulling, who had committed the vast majority of his Eagles to this adventure. He knew that he dared not fail with this attack. If he did, then he would lose almost all of his Eagles and the Bardomil would pound his position into oblivion.

From the War Table image it appeared that the plan was succeeding. The first group of Eagles had burst into the formations of the Big Wing's right flank. With the initial contact inflicting savage losses on the Bardomil fighters, their advance was slowed by the stiffening resistance of the Bardomil. Within moments of making contact, the Eagles were caught up in the swirling, snarling scratching maelstrom of the fighter-on-fighter dogfight. Twisting and turning desperately, the Harpoons and Flying Devils locked horns with the Alliance Eagles in a fight to the death.

The second group, in the centre, found the Bardomil resistance bolstered by the extreme left of the enemy right flank.

The Bardomil squadron commanders realised that these Eagles would be after the M-Cruisers and threw in their lot with the centre. The Eagles, swarming in from the rear, once again inflicted grievous damage on the enemy in the first few seconds, but failed to punch through the protective perimeter to reach their primary targets. Once more the Eagles and Harpoons and Flying Devils started to fight it out.

The third group were far more successful than the other two. Having swept in from the rear, the Eagles had once more unleashed a deadly volley of rapid-fire pulsar-bolts that had swept hundreds of Harpoons and Flying Devils away in a savage torrent of red roaring destruction. And, caught entirely by surprise the left flank caved in completely within a few seconds. With orders to keep the left flank at bay, the Eagles gave chase to the Bardomil fugitives and began a savage running fight with the shattered enemy squadrons.

With the Eagles now fully engaged, Chulling turned back to the Star-Cruisers who were still carving a path of fiery death and destruction through the second Bardomil Big Wing to get to the Imperial Fighter Carriers. The Bardomil fighters, despite almost reckless courage, had no chance of stopping the juggernaut of the Star-Cruisers on their relentless progress. Formation after formation had thrown themselves at the five Star-Cruisers only to be savagely wiped out by the merciless fire from the Alliance vessels. The panicking Fighter Carrier crews had broken formation in the face of this almost certain death that was ploughing through the fighters to reach them. And, as they panicked, the great lumbering Fighter Carriers slowly began to scatter. Almost immediately, the clumsy and heavy vessels began to collide as they tried to escape the approaching death-dealers.

Many of the huge ships would ram into their neighbours, crushing and smashing through superstructures and critical systems. Huge explosions lit up the area as many of the fleeing ships met a fiery demise in the panic to escape. On the War Table image, Chulling saw three Fighter Carriers collide. The first Carrier attempting to make a left turn slammed heavily into a neighbour who was trying to turn to the right. The third Carrier, attempting to reverse away from the situation was slowly sandwiched between the first two in a great scream of shrieking and rending metal. Unable to stop themselves, owing to the sheer size of the vessels, when the second Carrier exploded the first and third vessels were engulfed in the massive fireball of destruction. The great chunks of wreckage strewn out by the force of the combined explosions, cut another Fighter Carrier in half; throwing debris, flames, and crew members out into the cold, airless darkness of space. The two halves of the doomed Carrier were then flung out of formation onto another Carrier, which exploded almost instantly.

BENNING

Amidst the panic and destruction, the Star-Cruisers finally reached the Fighter Carrier positions. Like a dog shaking off its irritating fleas, the Star-Cruisers continued to savage the swarms of attacking fighters through their self-defence turrets. But, having reached the Imperial Fighter Carrier positions, the Alliance formation started to break up. On the War Table image, Chulling watched as the carefully planned manoeuvre was executed. With the surviving Fighter Carriers trying desperately to escape, the Star-Cruisers broke formation and began their individual attack runs. The Liberty set her course to run straight through the centre of the Fighter Carriers' rectangular box formation from bottom corner to opposite top corner.

This was the longest and, theoretically, the most dangerous assignment. Clemenceau and Light Brigade veered off to the left of Liberty's run, whilst Agamemnon and Sherman swung off to the right.

Chulling knew that he was never going to reach all of the Bardomil Fighter Carriers with this raid, but severely weakening their fighter capability would help to even up the odds in this battle. And, as the Star-Cruisers fanned out for their attack runs, their turrets swung into position. The WATO aboard each Star-Cruiser had worked out the optimum course through the panicking Fighter Carriers to wreak the maximum destruction. For the Star-Cruisers it was going to be a one attack deal. With the high-yield pulsar-cannons set to rapid firing, Chulling knew that by the end of their attack runs the ten pulsar-cannons on each vessel would be totally ruined. Without the proper cooling protocols, the barrels would crack and the power transfer conduits from the proto-star reactors would start to melt. Chulling was effectively sacrificing five of his Star-Cruisers. But, he knew that he had to take that risk.

Starting their individual attack runs, the Star-Cruisers broke up the mass of Bardomil fighters that were still trying to pull them away from the Fighter Carriers. The great cloud of fighters broke up to pursue and harry their individual targets. On the War Table image it looked like insects swarming around a hedgehog with fiery spines that reached up and blasted its pursuers to oblivion. But with the Eagles now committed to smashing the M-Cruisers, Chulling had to split the War Table image to view, and, if necessary, to respond to the emerging situation in both battle zones.

Neatly dividing the War Table image, Chulling was able to watch the majestic progress of the Star-Cruisers through the Bardomil Fighter Carrier formation whilst also watching the dogfights that were occupying the Eagles. On the Star-Cruiser image, the five ships were slowly dispersing into the straggle of panicking Fighter Carriers. Focussing on the Liberty, Chulling could see her holding course whilst the self-defence turrets savaged the fighters that swarmed around her. Three of her turrets opened fire on a stricken Fighter Carrier.

All six of the high-yield pulsar-bolts smashed into the superstructure of the lumbering Carrier that was trying to execute a left turn away from its station. The six bolts slammed into the unprotected hull throwing debris out into space amidst explosions and flames. The doomed Fighter Carrier, shuddering like a wounded animal, lurched away from the monstrous impacts before slowly beginning its uncontrolled exit from the formation. Scattering debris and flame in its wake, the Carrier dropped its nose and began to slowly twist as it descended and the Liberty moved on to her next victim. Having fired six of her high-yield pulsar-cannons, Liberty turned her remaining guns onto the next Fighter Carrier. The four remaining guns unleashed their violent, fiery fury at a Fighter Carrier that was already damaged.

The first two bolts hammered into the Carrier, stripping away great chunks of metal, whilst the third passed straight through the top landing deck. The final bolt slammed through the superstructure and into the power plant. The colossal explosion shook even the well force-shielded Liberty as it prowled onwards looking for fresh targets.

On the second image, Chulling could see the Eagles locked in mortal combat with the Bardomil fighters around the M-Cruisers.

On the Bardomil right flank, the Eagles were gradually gaining the upper hand over the Harpoons and Flying Devils in a massive fighter-on-fighter scrimmage. The faster and more agile Eagles were starting to dominate the battle-space in a tough and costly contest. The presence of large numbers of Flying Devils on the Bardomil right was making it difficult for the Eagles to make headway in the twisting combat.

With the battle spreading over thousands of kilometres, Chulling could only make sense of it in Graphic Mode where different coloured dots and triangles dodged and weaved and vanished from the image as they fell to an enemy's guns. Casualties were high on the Bardomil right, for both sides, as they scrabbled in their own private battles.

In the centre, Chulling was pleased to see that the Eagles had broken through to the M-Cruisers. The Bardomil fighters had, however, followed in pursuit, which made it difficult for the Eagle pilots to concentrate on anything other than the Harpoons and Flying Devils as they zipped and sped between the slower and clumsier M-Cruisers. Taking their chance to strafe an M-Cruiser whenever possible, the Eagles were inflicting very minor damage on the real threat to Chulling's flotilla. Cursing himself for a moment, he wished he had committed all of his Eagles to the Big Wing fight. But, taking risks in battle was one thing. Stripping his two vulnerable Fleet Carriers of any form of fighter support and protection was another matter. And, once again, the Alliance Eagles seemed to be getting the better of the contest in the centre. Strafing runs on M-Cruisers were starting to increase as the number of Harpoons ad Flying Devils was gradually being cut down.

Still, only on the Bardomil left was there any real sign of a significant victory. Having shattered the much weaker left wing, the Eagles had given chase. This had developed into a running fight with Bardomil commanders unable to contact their Carriers for instructions or to request reinforcements. The Eagles were still herding the dwindling number of survivors away from the main battle. And, as the Bardomil formations fragmented and began to retreat, the withdrawal was gradually becoming a rout. With cohesion and formation lost, the Bardomil were fleeing for their lives.

Chulling watched intently for any break that would turn the tide fully in the Alliance's favour. It was frustrating for Chulling to watch the savage dogfights that had broken out amongst the fighter formations. Having cast his forces into the battle with the element of surprise, there was now very little he could do to influence the outcome. The pilots in their tiny, cramped cockpits would have to decide the issue themselves.

When the break that would settle the battle did come, it was not to be in the Alliance's favour.

Meanwhile, the Star-Cruiser Liberty was smashing pulsar-bolts into another Fighter Carrier, sending it to red, roaring fiery oblivion in another huge explosion. The pulsar-cannons barrels and power conduits were now dangerously overheated. The eight seconds of cooling allowed during rapid fire were simply not enough for the guns to survive for very long. But, at near point blank range accuracy was not a problem. In the rest of the Liberty's formation, the other Star-Cruisers were making slow, relentless and pitiless progress through the Fighter Carrier formation.

In their deliberate and calculated wake, the Star-Cruisers were leaving a trail of debris and destruction. Shattered and exploding Fighter Carriers littered what had been their impressive and deadly formation. The Flying Devils and Harpoons no longer threw themselves recklessly at the Star-Cruisers but rather watched, impotently, from a safe distance as the Alliance ships tore through the last of their Fighter Carrier targets. As Chulling had predicted, not all of the Fighter Carriers had been within reach of the Alliance's guns.

There would be some survivors, and it would simply be a question of numbers. Still watching the image, Chulling could see the routes of the five Star-Cruisers by the trail of explosions, fire and huge chunks of debris that littered their charge through the Bardomil heart. Already the Clemenceau was finishing her run and with one last salvo, she sent her farewell straight into the last two Fighter Carriers on her path. The first Carrier, already damaged, simply disappeared in a huge sheet of flame. The second, taking four pulsar-bolt hits lurched like a wounded animal. The Clemenceau, her guns almost white hot from the rapid-firing dropped into the Trionic Web with a blinding flash of light. The Sherman, Light Brigade and Agamemnon quickly followed, leaving only the Liberty to punctuate the devastating attack with one last salvo at a fleeing Fighter Carrier. Three of the bolts missed the target completely whilst the other seven slammed into the engine casing of the escaping vessel. The crew who were beginning to think that they were going to escape were vapourised in a huge cataclysmic explosion. With her job done, the Liberty bowed out gracefully into the Trionic Web.

Nodding with satisfaction, Chulling was able to view the vast majority of the Bardomil Fighter Carrier formation, which had been reduced to a mass of exploding and shattered hulks. Of fifty Imperial Fighter Carriers from six full Imperial Fleets, only five were capable of receiving or launching fighters. Of those five, only two were actually able to run under their own power. It was a stupendous victory for Chulling and the Alliance. The Fighter Carriers were no longer an effective force, plus a Big Wing had been savagely mauled. The Bardomil invasion, with little or no strike force protection, was, in realistic terms, over. The Bardomil General, however, still had one last card to play.

After a moment of quiet celebration, Chulling resumed his vigil on the fighter-on-fighter battle. The outcome, as Chulling saw it, was still in the balance; with a slight edge to the Alliance Eagles. The Bardomil left had collapsed entirely and was being chased into the distance. The Bardomil centre was holding on by its fingertips as the Eagles, Harpoons and Flying Devils slugged it out amongst the slow and cumbersome M-Cruisers. On the Bardomil right, the battle was fully joined. On the War Table image, the battle on the Bardomil right looked like a huge twisting tornado that raged and swirled in all directions as the combatants tore mercilessly at each other in the free for all. Losses were high on both sides. The speed, skill and dash of the Eagle pilots were well matched by the sheer professionalism, tenacity and courage of the Bardomil. Chulling may have hated the Bardomil as an enemy of his species, but he could not help but admire their fighting prowess.

But, as Turthus Chulling was watching the battle for the Bardomil right flank, Grattus Darrien was playing his last desperate gamble.

BENNING

With the communications network beginning to re-establish, General Darrien, aboard one of the few remaining Fighter Carriers, was gathering the survivors of the Big Wing that had been so savagely mauled by the Star-Cruisers. With just under one thousand Harpoons and two hundred Flying Devils at his disposal, Darrien scrutinised the situation. It immediately struck him that the important battle in the centre of his position was the crucial part of the fight.

The left flank had gone entirely, but their rout was drawing the Alliance Eagles further and further away from their own positions. Darrien knew that this could work to his advantage. Nearly one third of the Alliance Eagles were cut off from their bases and further support.

The Bardomil right was still making a fight of it, the huge swirling maelstrom raging and staggering over the thousands of kilometres of empty space close to the planet of Valnarim. The centre was the crucial battle ground, but the stubborn determination of the right flank was the foundation on which General Darrien had to build. With the cold determination born from the stinging humiliation of having lost almost all of his Fighter Carriers, the Bardomil commander launched his last hope to snatch victory from the looming jaws of a crushing defeat. Carefully, Darrien instructed his fighter controllers and squadron leaders of what was expected of them and sent them on their ways.

With the calmness of a seasoned professional warrior, General Darrien watched, what was to be his swan-song, set off towards the Alliance positions. Having lost almost all of the Fighter Carriers and the invasion, Darrien knew that his life would be forfeit. Better a blast from his own trusted sidearm than the agonies of an execution chamber, he considered. His suicide would save his wife, his children and their children from the Empress' wrath. But, it was now a point of personal honour for Darrien to see the total destruction of this Alliance force before he handed over command of what was left of the invasion force to his First Officer and ended his own life in traditional Bardomil fashion.

Calmly, General Darrien watched as the last remnants of the Big Wing sped off into the distance to join the fighter battle in front of the Alliance's position.

In the War Room of the Memphis, Chulling watched intently as the fighter battle raged on. For a moment, he considered that the Bardomil were about to break and run for safety.

"Sir!" the Scanner Officer called out, his voice close to panic, "we have more fighters approaching from the enemy Carriers!"

"Impossible!" Chulling yelled and, grabbing the Manipulator, focussed the War Table image on the new Bardomil formation that simply could not possibly exist.

Casting a professional eye over this new miraculous formation, Chulling could see that it was smaller than the traditional Big Wing; no more than a thousand Harpoons and a few hundred Flying Devils. But, Chulling could also see that this formation was heavily loaded to the left flank. For a second, Chulling was unable to comprehend what his opposite number was trying to do with this modified tactic.

Then, feeling as if he had just been struck by a hammer, Chulling understood the Bardomil commander's intentions. The gap between the Alliance centre and right wing was just too vast for Chulling to close in time. The collapsing Bardomil left flank had created a dangerous gap between the Alliance right and centre. The heavy blow on this new Bardomil formation's left was going to swarm into that gap and sweep away the Alliance centre.

With the Alliance centre gone, the deadly M-Cruisers could escape whilst the Bardomil Big Wing formation would do what it did best. With the loss of the Alliance centre, the heavy left flank would sweep round, reinforce the Bardomil right and cut off the Alliance left flank from their Carriers and Star-Cruisers. The Alliance left flank would then be hopelessly outnumbered, isolated and chopped to pieces. With the loss of those Eagles, Chulling knew he could never hold this Valnarim position. The surviving Eagles from his right flank, and his reserve, were just too few to hold off the remaining Bardomil fighters. The M-Cruisers would return and begin pounding his Star-Cruisers to space dust. It was a brilliantly engineered piece of improvised strategy. And, Chulling knew that he could do very little about it. Thinking quickly on his feet, he began to issue orders. His options were limited, but he would have to try to save as many Eagles as he could.

"WATO, disengage the Eagles on our right and send New Thexxia out to recover them!" he ordered.

The Eagles on the right flank would never make it back to their Carriers in time, but he could, at least, send the New Thexxia to recover them and spare them running the gauntlet of the Bardomil fighters on their return.

"And, start trying to disengage as many Eagles as we can without it becoming a complete massacre!" he added.

Pulling fighters out of a heavily engaged battle was a difficult task. Withdrawing the fighters left them vulnerable to the enemy. Bitter experience told Chulling that such a withdrawal was going to be very costly.

Cursing his opposite number softly, Chulling slammed his fist angrily onto the War Table's edge as he watched the image of this new Big Wing rapidly approaching the battle zone.

They were the harbingers of doom and disaster.

THE BURNING SUN

Chapter 35

Planet Earth

Elizabeth Caudwell took a deep breath and sighed loudly. In front of her, on the kitchen table, amidst the scatter of scrunched up paper, the old electric typewriter hummed quietly. Another chapter in her new work had just been completed. Being alone in the kitchen was a blessing to Elizabeth. This was where she could think, plan and write without the distractions of Billy or John. This was her little piece of Heaven amidst the mayhem of family life and the ongoing house move.

Standing up slowly, she moved over to the kitchen window and looked out over the weed strewn patch of pale green, drying grass that Billy had struggled valiantly to keep under control for the years that they had stayed in the house. With those memories of young Billy struggling with the old push mower flashing through her mind, Elizabeth switched on the kettle and found herself smiling and feeling nostalgic about the old house. There had been good days in the old house, and it had been the first real stable home the family had known since John had left the Police Force. The constant change of stations every two years had left Elizabeth feeling isolated and cast adrift in the world. But, now, the new house beckoned and Elizabeth felt that she could really start to put down roots. Her nomadic days were finally over, she considered. If only she could stop arguing with John, she chided herself. Turning to watch the kettle, Elizabeth heard the telephone trill in the living room.

Quickly, she dashed over to the stairs and lifted the cheap plastic receiver.

"Hello?" she tried to sound bright into the apparatus.

"Missus Caudwell?" a polite, male Scottish accent began the conversation.

"Yes, speaking," Elizabeth, mindful of the kettle, replied.

"Missus Elizabeth Caudwell?" the voice continued.

"Look, if you're trying to sell me something..." Elizabeth sighed and was about to replace the receiver.

"No, missus Caudwell; this is mister McLetchie at Gilfillan Academy calling with regard to your application for young William," the voice interrupted.

"Oh, mister McLetchie," Elizabeth responded, taken by surprise, "how nice to hear from you," she said and instinctively smoothed her hair.

BENNING

"We've received your application missus Caudwell, and we have been most impressed with young William's grades, especially in mathematics and sciences," McLetchie indicated.

"Well, yes, Billy, I mean, William takes after his father in that respect," Elizabeth had to concede.

"Yes, most excellent grades," McLetchie expanded, "he also seems to have a passion for History and Political Science. We like our students to have a much more rounded education here at Gilfillan."

"Oh yes, he has a lot of interests," Elizabeth lied not having the slightest idea what Billy did in his spare time these days.

"That's just the ticket," McLetchie replied as Elizabeth quietly prayed that he wouldn't ask what Billy's other 'interests' might be, "I wonder if you would be free to come up and visit us at Gilfillan on Saturday?"

"Erm, Saturday of this week, mister McLetchie?" Elizabeth asked.

"Yes, if that would be possible, we could meet yourself, young William and your husband, the Head of Science is particularly keen to meet William," McLetchie invited.

"Well, I'm sure we can manage," Elizabeth said optimistically hoping that she could convince Billy to curtail whatever it was that he did at weekends.

"Excellent, can you make it up to us by, shall we say, two o'clock?" McLetchie asked speculatively.

"I'm sure we can," Elizabeth replied equally speculatively.

"Splendid," McLetchie replied, "now if I may be so bold, are you the Elizabeth Caudwell who wrote that rather fine book?"

"Do you mean 'My Lost Little Angel'?" Elizabeth replied, blushing at the compliment.

"Yes," McLetchie replied.

"Guilty, I'm afraid," Elizabeth had to concede proudly.

"Then I really must congratulate you on a very fine piece of prose missus Caudwell," McLetchie praised, "My good lady has read your book three times," he added quietly.

"Well, I'm delighted that she has enjoyed it," Elizabeth replied.

"Oh, she did, and we shall look forward to seeing you and your family on Saturday," McLetchie began, "Oh, by the way, have you considered which University William would like to attend, missus Caudwell?"

"University?" the idea finally burst into Elizabeth Caudwell's consciousness, "erm, well, no mister McLetchie, he's only fifteen."

No one in either Elizabeth's or John's family had ever gone to University and the horizons that seemed to be opening up to Billy were a whole new country for Elizabeth Caudwell.

"Missus Caudwell, if I may say, students from Gilfillan usually matriculate after their fifth year of Secondary, when they're seventeen; so, I would urge you to get young William to consider what he wishes to achieve with his future," McLetchie sounded insistent without seeming to domineer.

"I'll certainly be discussing it with him this evening when he gets home from school," Elizabeth said with a degree of uncertainty.

For all she knew, Billy still wanted to be an Astronaut or a Rocket Engineer or something.

"Yes, please, missus Caudwell," McLetchie insisted, "we like to tailor our learning programmes to the needs and ambitions of our students," he added, "and time is of the utmost importance at young William's age."

"I shall make it my number one priority," Elizabeth said shakily, "thank you for calling mister McLetchie."

"Missus Caudwell, a pleasure to speak to you," McLetchie said and hung up.

Wow, Billy going to University, Elizabeth mused proudly, hanging up the receiver. Then the real world impinged on her daydream. With a start, she bolted towards the kitchen.

"Kettle!" she said urgently.

BENNING

Chapter 36

The Praxos System

An angry and deeply frustrated Turthus Chulling stood at the War Table, fists clenched, as he watched the piecemeal destruction of his Eagle fighters on the Alliance's left flank. Outnumbered nearly three to one, not even the superior speed and manoeuvrability of the wedge-shaped single-seat fighter could compensate for the sheer weight of numbers that they faced. On the War Table image, Chulling watched the isolated individual battles between the Alliance Eagles and the Bardomil Harpoons and Flying Devils grind to their inevitable fatal conclusions for the brave Alliance pilots. With their line of retreat cut off, with no hope of rescue and with no chance of surrender, the Eagles just had to fight on and try to take as many Bardomil with them as they could. The heroic futility of it all, and the waste of lives, angered Chulling, especially as he blamed himself for the disaster that was playing out before him.

From the moment Chulling had seen the new Big Wing formation appear, he had known that his gamble, heroic as it had been, had failed. The Fighter Controllers had tried, desperately, to extract as many Eagles as they could from the hideous swirling scrimmage of the dogfight, but it had been far too late. When the huge left flank of the Bardomil Big Wing had struck, the Alliance centre had simply caved in. The Eagles trying to contain the deadly M-Cruisers had been overwhelmed with the survivors being driven into the main fighter battle on the Bardomil right. And, with the Alliance centre gone, the Bardomil left flank had swept round to cut off the Alliance's line of retreat before pushing into the main fight. Meanwhile, the M-Cruisers, freed from the attentions of the Alliance fighters, were regrouping.

Now, the final 'dance of death' was taking place close to the planet of Valnarim. It had been a strategic victory for the Alliance. The Bardomil strike force had been fatally weakened and would never be able to support a full scale invasion. Tactically, it would be a defeat for the Alliance. Chulling's rag-tag flotilla would be pinned down by the First Admiral's orders and ground to dust by the M-Cruisers.

Forcing himself to watch the demise of the Eagles, a penance for his failure, Chulling gritted his teeth and suffered the mental agonies of a commander facing defeat. He knew that his mistakes had been costly and that it was those errors that were now losing Eagle pilots their lives out in the battle area.

"Sir," the Scanner Officer called out in the heavy oppressive atmosphere of the War Room, "enemy M-Cruisers are forming up for an attack."

Switching the War Table image to where the Alliance centre had once struggled and harried at the M-Cruisers, Chulling could see the Bardomil ships congregating.

"Well, here they come for the big finale," Chulling muttered to himself.

With the main fighter battle still raging, Chulling knew that there was nothing to stop the M-Cruisers launching their attack runs at the Alliance Star-Cruisers. There was no fighter cover to keep the Bardomil ships away from his weakening formation.

"Very well," Chulling shook off his feeling of despair and started to issue orders, "let's circle the wagons, WATO," he ordered.

Rather than abandon the Praxos system, Chulling planned to form his Star-Cruisers into a rectangular box formation for his last stand. In the box formation, each Star-Cruiser could protect the other with both force-shielding and weapons fire. And, whilst that formation stood its ground, the Bardomil couldn't move through the Praxos system to the neighbouring Terran system. The Bardomil commander dared not risk his supply lines by avoiding Chulling's flotilla, they had to be removed.

"And, order New Thexxia and Leonidas to get away from here," Chulling added.

The Alliance could ill afford to lose the Star-Cruisers of Chulling's formation, but any counter offensive that First Admiral Caudwell could deliver would need every Eagle and Fleet Carrier that he could scrape together. The two Fleet Carriers were just too valuable to be lost in a futile last stand.

"Yes, sir," the WATO acknowledged and slowly dragged his feet to his duties.

The infection of defeat had now taken hold of the entire flotilla and there was nothing that Chulling could do about it. Given the choice, he would have formed the Star-Cruisers into a huge 'V' formation and ran them straight at the Bardomil guns in one last blaze of glory. But, Chulling didn't have that luxury. He had been ordered to buy time with his ships and the lives of their crews. Every second that he could buy for First Admiral Caudwell's counter attack was precious. Every Bardomil ship that he could take out made Caudwell's task that tiny bit easier.

"M-Cruisers attacking, sir," the Scanner Officer warned.

"Continue move to box formation, and open fire when they're within range," Chulling ordered, as he turned once more to the War Table image.

The fighter battle close to Valnarim was still raging with the hopelessly outnumbered Eagles being gradually whittled down. It was a savage, uncompromising fight where the fighter craft tore at each other in brutal no-holds-barred combat. And, sweeping around the flank of the fighter scrimmage, the formation of M-Cruisers, in a ragged skirmish line, was there to push home one last devastating attack.

As Chulling watched the M-Cruisers began to form their trio combinations before opening fire. The Memphis, taking a direct hit on her force-shielding shuddered and lurched under the impact, rocking Chulling unsteadily on his feet. Other Star-Cruisers in the slow moving formation were also hit by the first salvo, creating damage and casualties.

A few seconds later the first Alliance pulsar-bolts streaked downrange towards the M-Cruisers in answer to the first Bardomil salvo. Three M-Cruiser trios disappeared in balls of red roaring flame as their formation advanced. But, as Chulling quietly celebrated, the Memphis was struck once more by a powerful laser blast.

"We've lost power distribution to the force-shielding and weapons!" an Engineering Technician announced.

"Get it sorted Engineers!" Chulling ordered, reeling from the last impact, "order Calypso and Thunderchild to cover us with their shielding while we get repaired."

Without force-shielding and weapons, the Memphis was a sitting duck in the middle of the Bardomil attack.

"Negative, sir!" a Comms Technician called out, "Calypso has lost her force-shielding generator; she's pulling out of the line."

"Tell her to keep her weapons firing," Chulling ordered switching the War Table image to that of the Alliance formation.

On the image, the lumbering Star-Cruisers seemed to be hobbling into place in a three-dimensional, roughly rectangular formation. Already, some of the vessels, having lost force-shielding, were slowly drifting into the centre of the formation where other ships could protect them. Streaks of light, the laser streams from the M-Cruisers, slammed against the Star-Cruisers at the front face of the box formation. But, whatever damage seemed to be inflicted on the shuddering and lurching Alliance ships, the pulsar-cannons still seemed capable of replying. The domed turrets on the top of the Star-Cruisers kept sending the white-hot pulsar-bolts against the advancing Bardomil.

As Chulling continued to watch, the Star-Cruiser Aurora, her middle three turrets a twisted, tangled mass of scorched metal also began to drop out of the firing line. With each withdrawal, Chulling knew that the formation would contract leaving those craft with functioning force-shielding no choice but to weaken their own defences to protect their sister ships. The Alliance formation was slowly shrinking under the Bardomil onslaught, and Chulling knew that all he could do was to try to hang on as long as possible.

Switching the War Table image back to the advancing M-Cruisers, Chulling watched as the trios began to form once more whilst Alliance pulsar-bolts streaked downrange towards them. But, suddenly, some of the expected M-Cruiser trios began to split up. Stunned for a split-second, Chulling watched the pulsar-bolts, which should have reduced these trios to exploding devastation, miss their targets entirely. Again, he saw the same pattern with another trio of M-Cruisers. The three craft would approach each other for an attack run, then, at the last possible moment, would veer away from each other. The Alliance gunner anticipating a weapon firing trio to form would let loose and then find that the pulsar-bolts would miss. With the Alliance pulsar-cannons then having to cool, the M-Cruisers would form trios with other craft and fire their weapons.

"They're learning how to draw our fire," Chulling mumbled, a wave of hopelessness sweeping over him as another Bardomil laser struck the Memphis.

With no force-shielding, a great gouge of metal was torn from one of the three Eagle Landing Bays that was facing the Bardomil attack. Debris and people were flung out into space as the Memphis lurched like a wounded animal under the impact. All around Chulling, alarms blared and air tight bulkheads were secured, trapping terrified crew members in the damaged areas. As the damaged and isolated areas de-pressurised, those crew members would also be hurled out to their deaths.

"Sir," one of the Fighter Controllers said softly, "we've just lost the last of our Eagles."

Despite the insistent blare of the alarms, the War Room seemed to fall into a deathly silence. Nearly two thousand Eagles, and their pilots, had been lost. Chulling closed his eyes and wanted to cry out with anger and pain, but knew he had to keep a professional bearing in front of his subordinates. Silently, Turthus Chulling cursed himself for his earlier complacency and then he cursed First Admiral William Caudwell for not getting to the Valnarim position in time. On the War Table image, the M-Cruisers were still randomly forming their weapon firing trios as they advanced on Chulling's position. With the M-Cruisers getting larger and larger on the projected visual, Chulling sat down resignedly on one of the seats attached to the side of the War Table.

It's all over, he sighed to himself as another stream of laser fire slammed into the Memphis, which sheared away the last of the high-yield pulsar-cannons turrets. Shaken and jolted by the impact, Chulling only just managed to remain in the seat. Switching to a wider view on the War Table image, Chulling saw the surviving Bardomil Harpoons and Flying Devils forming into another Big Wing. The new Bardomil formation reminded him of a Video Entertainment the First Admiral had once brought from Terra about a General called Custer, who had been surrounded by his enemies and killed alongside his entire command. Chulling knew that the M-Cruisers would grind away their force-shielding and then send the fighters in to destroy whatever remained. The Bardomil commander would have his vengeance for the loss of his Imperial Fighter Carriers. Sitting back on the seat, Chulling closed his eyes and hoped that the end for him would be swift.

"Admiral Chulling!" a familiar voice startled Chulling's eyes open, "I trust we have not missed all of the fun?" the voice of Billy Caudwell boomed out from the War Table image.

"Sir!" an astonished Chulling instinctively sprang to his feet as the head and shoulders image of a very pink and blotchy-faced First Admiral stared at him.

"Trionic Web!" a Scanner Technician had the presence of mind to yell, "Star-Destroyers! Eagles! There are thousands of them, sir!"

In a split second the mood of the War Room went from deathly resignation to unbridled joy and cheering.

"Sorry, we're a bit late," Billy said calmly as if he had just turned up for a birthday party, "withdraw your vessels for repair Admiral," he instructed, "get your people out of here."

"Yes, sir!" Chulling smiled ready to kiss Billy Caudwell with sheer relief.

"Good job, Chulling," Billy praised and switched his own War Table image to that of the battle situation.

In the War Room of the massive Star-Destroyer Colossus, Billy turned his attention to the battle situation. Around him, the Officers and Technicians from the Aquarius' War Room now scampered about their duties integrating their activities with the Colossus' War Room staff.

"Eagles are launching, sir," the familiar voice of Marrhus Lokkrien informed the First Admiral.

On the image, Billy could see a stupendous victory taking shape. Before leaving the Terran system with the Titan and the Colossus, Billy had summoned the Fleet Carriers, Leonidas and New Thexxia, to his position. On arrival, the two Fleet Carriers were loaded up with as many Eagles from the three badly damaged Star-Destroyers as they could possibly manage. It had taken precious time to load the Fleet Carriers and the two functioning

Star-Destroyers with additional Eagles. But, Billy knew that he would have to hit the Bardomil invading force with every fighter that he could gather. He knew that he would have the element of surprise and that he would have to deliver one massive strike to shatter the invasion force for good. With the fate of the Alliance at stake, Billy planned to deliver a crushing blow and send the Empress a clear message not to dare to challenge him ever again.

With the Eagles loaded up, Billy had brought the Colossus, Titan, New Thexxia and Leonidas to Valnarim. Ignoring current protocol, Billy had ordered the Navigation Officers to get as close to the battle area as they possibly dared. So, rather than appearing from the Trionic web at the safe distance of ten thousand kilometres from the battle area, the rescue flotilla had emerged, amidst the blinding flashes of collapsing Trion Fields, less than one hundred and fifty kilometres from the action.

Aboard the Bardomil flagship, Grattus Darrien had yelled with outrage and astonishment as the huge, two-kilometre wide, Star-Destroyers had emerged from the Trionic Web followed an instant later by the two Fleet Carriers. Whoever had navigated those ships had been a genius, Darrien cursed them. His final victorious tactical swan-song was now destined to be a final disaster as the new Alliance vessels had managed to appear in a flanking position between the surviving Imperial Fighter Carriers and the M-Cruiser and fighter formations. Worse still, the Alliance ships had begun to spew out thousands upon thousands of their single-seat Eagle craft from their Landing Bays. Isolated from his own fighter and M-Cruiser support, General Darrien now realised that it had been a huge mistake to bring forward the convoy protection Fleets to attack Chulling's position. His supply and troop transports were now completely unprotected from the horde of Alliance ships that had just appeared.

For a moment, Darrien stood in awe of the Alliance commander who would sacrifice the lives of so many of his own people to draw this invasion fleet into such a perfectly executed trap. General Darrien was, however, completely unaware that Billy had been fortunate rather than calculating in his strategy. But, having viewed the Bardomil dispositions, the part of his mind that was Teg Portan had spotted the Bardomil weakness and presented Billy with the ideal opportunity.

On the War Table image, Billy had explained his plan to his senior commanders. The Alliance position consisted of Colossus, New Thexxia, Leonidas and Titan in a skirmish line. With the manipulator, he highlighted the battle area and divided it into three sectors. One, the fighters and M-Cruisers that would be scampering back to the Imperial Fighter Carriers. Two, the surviving Imperial Fighter Carriers; and finally, three, the supply and troop transports that stretched back for hundreds of thousands of kilometres.

Colossus would send eight thousand of her expanded complement of nearly twenty-thousand Eagles to the first sector to protect the departure of Chulling's badly damaged flotilla and to finally dispatch the last of the M-Cruisers and fighters. New Thexxia would send one thousand of her expanded complement of four thousand Eagles to finally eliminate the last Bardomil Imperial Fighter Carriers. The rest, nearly forty thousand Eagles, were to attack the troop and supply transports with orders that none of them were to escape. Such a mammoth defeat would not only damage Bardomil prestige throughout the Empire, but it might encourage their long-time enemies, the Ganthorans, to cause trouble as well. The damage to Chulling's vessels and the Star-Destroyers would take quite some time to repair and Billy needed to take the heat off the Alliance's frontiers.

Splitting the War Table image into three parts, Billy settled down to watch the final end of the Bardomil invasion. To the left of the image, the Bardomil M-Cruisers and fighters had just realised the danger they now faced and were making full speed back to their Imperial Fighter Carrier positions. From the image, Billy knew that they would never make it. The Eagle contingent from Colossus was heading on an intercept course that would cut them off from the temporary safety of their Carriers. On the centre part of the image, the Eagles from the New Thexxia were forming into their squadrons to attack the last of the Imperial Fighter Carriers. To the right of the image, the huge Eagle formations were lining up on the flanks of the supply and troop transport convoy.

"WATO," Billy asked, "how long until our Eagles intercept their fighters?"

"Four minutes and fifty seconds, sir," the WATO responded.

"Thank you," Billy responded and turned to Lokkrien, "you, stay out of sight."

He indicated for Lokkrien to stand opposite him at the War Table, "Comms, I want to speak to the Bardomil Commander."

"Sir," a Communications Officer replied.

"Marrhus, I want to know everything about this person," Billy instructed nodding to the keypad on the table edge next to Lokkrien.

"Sir, we have established contact with the enemy," the Communications Officer announced as Lokkrien nodded his understanding and lifted the keypad.

On the War Table, the three-dimensional projected image of General Grattus Darrien loomed over Billy Caudwell.

"I am First Admiral Caudwell of the Universal Alliance Fleet, please identify yourself, sir," Billy began the conversation.

"I am General Grattus Darrien of the Bardomil Imperial Forces, what do you want?" the figure blustered angrily.

"I am requesting an immediate cease fire and the unconditional surrender of all your forces," Billy said calmly to the towering image above him.

The text below the image from Lokkrien's keypad sprang up 'Darrien, he's a good Officer, a good soldier'."

"What is your answer, General?" Billy asked calmly.

"Admiral Caudwell, you already know what my answer is," the image replied, "a Bardomil can never surrender."

"General," Billy continued, "the last of your combat capability is about to be wiped out and when that happens I will then turn my fighters loose on your undefended troop and supply convoy."

"Then you must do what you must do First Admiral," Darrien responded crisply.

"Make no mistake, General, your transports will not escape, the only question is will you see over seven million of your people slaughtered for nothing?" Billy pressed home the assault.

"I have already seen my beautiful Fleets annihilated," Darrien responded, "let them all find their own heroic deaths for the Empire, whether you kill them now or later it matters not, they will still be dead."

"Bardomil propaganda says we kill prisoners," Lokkrien's text appeared below the image.

"General Darrien, despite what your Empress tells you, the Alliance does not kill prisoners," Billy responded.

"I would like to believe you Admiral Caudwell," Darrien replied, "but your reputation and that of your Thexxian allies precedes you."

"General," Billy continued, "we are both professionals, we kill when we have to and when we are ordered to, that is the code we both live by. I have no reason to kill any more of your people; you are defeated and you cannot escape."

"Then we must die because it is our duty to do so," Darrien said matter-of-factly.

"General, enough blood has been shed today," Billy responded, "your people have fought with courage and honour and any further loss of life would be pointless."

"And, they have one last final debt of honour to pay to our Empress," Darrien answered.

"Give me strength," Billy muttered softly between gritted teeth, "you have done all that is expected of you as soldiers and more, you owe no debt to anyone except yourselves," he said aloud.

"Sir," the WATO interrupted, "Eagles are within range of the enemy M-Cruisers."

"Tell them to hold their fire," Billy ordered, "and to shadow their withdrawal."

"Why do you not attack?" a confused Darrien asked.

"Don't you get it yet, General?" Billy snapped angrily, slamming his fist onto the edge of the War Table, "we don't kill unless we have to, but if you are unwilling to surrender then that is exactly what we will have to do!"

"A very clever ruse, First Admiral," Darrien smiled, "and, once we are in your power, how long before your Thexxians butcher us all?"

"Admiral Chulling knows this one," the text from Lokkrien read below the image.

"Do you know our Admiral Chulling, General?" Billy sighed trying to control his anger.

"Yes, he is a gallant warrior, but he is also a Thexxian," Darrien replied, "however, I see no point in furthering this conversation..."

"Will you at least listen to his words, General?" Billy sighed in desperation.

For a moment Darrien paused to consider the offer.

"I will hear his words, First Admiral," Darrien consented.

As Billy made a beckoning gesture to the Communications Officer, the War Table image split into two equal portions. On the left, the three-dimensional image of Turthus Chulling appeared next to Grattus Darrien.

"Well, old friend of many battles, we finally meet," Chulling introduced himself.

"Admiral Chulling," Darrien acknowledged his adversary.

"Admiral Chulling, would you please inform General Darrien that we do not harm prisoners of war."

"The First Admiral speaks the truth..." Chulling began.

"I have no reason to believe that you would not simply kill us when we were unarmed..." Darrien interrupted.

"That's enough!" Billy barked and stepped away from the War Table, "stupid, pig-headed Bardomil idiot! Kill them all! Slaughter the whole lot of them!" Billy raged waving his hands with dismissive anger.

"Sir, I must protest!" Chulling interjected.

"No, Chulling, kill them all!" Billy ranted, pacing up and down the edge of the War Table.

THE BURNING SUN

"Sir, I will not be party to cold-blooded murder!" Chulling protested once more.

"You'll do as you're told, Chulling, you mutinous dog!" Billy threatened.

"No, sir," Chulling snapped, "I will not kill defenceless people!"

"You'll do what you're told or it'll be a court-martial!" Billy snarled.

"Then court-martial me, SIR!" Chulling bridled, angrily shouting out the last honorific.

"WAIT!" Darrien shouted holding his head in his hands with confusion.

In the War Room, the oppressive silence felt like a heavy stifling cloak as the air positively crackled with tension.

"Wait!" the confused Darrien called out once again, "why would you risk your career and your life for an enemy?" he asked Chulling.

"Because we Thexxians also have our honour, and our honour says we do not kill a defenceless enemy, especially those who have shown bravery in battle," Chulling said.

"But..." Darrien mumbled, still with his hands pressed to his temples, unable to comprehend the situation.

"It is not our way, General Darrien, just as I know it is not your way," Chulling answered, "you are not General Glabbrus or Methrien the Butcher."

For long seconds that felt like an eternity, Billy kept his mouth shut despite wishing to intervene. The Bardomil General was suffering his own particular hell of mental agony, and Billy knew that he would have to find his own answers.

"Do I have your word that my people will not be harmed, Admiral Chulling?" Darrien sighed.

"You have my word of honour," Chulling replied.

"And, what happens to us if we do surrender to you?" Darrien asked Billy.

"We have several abandoned Garmaurian cities, with the best facilities in the universe, where you would be held in internment," Billy replied calmly.

"What of our families?" Darrien asked.

"We will make it known that you all died heroically in battle," Billy assured, "the Empress will have no reason to harm your families."

"I must think on this," Darrien nodded slowly, contemplating the situation.

"Then you have ten minutes to consider," Billy said calmly, and the image of Darrien cut out.

When the image had disappeared, Billy swung into action.

"Chulling, that was brilliant," he praised the Second Admiral who had 'stood up' to his commander on behalf of a defeated enemy.

"Happy to help, sir," Chulling smiled and his image disappeared.

"Marrhus," Billy turned to Lokkrien, "get Briefing Room One ready in case he decides to surrender; I want him over here on our turf. I don't want him being the foolishly stupid, honourable Bardomil and killing himself; he's too valuable," Billy ordered.

"Sir," the Communications Officer interrupted, "General Darrien."

A moment later, the image of General Darrien appeared over the War Table again. Looking crestfallen and dismayed he sighed and then spoke.

"First Admiral," he began formally, "I have just issued the order for all of my people to capitulate to your forces."

"Very well, General, that is a wise and courageous choice that has saved many lives," Billy replied with equal formality, "I shall send a transport over to bring you here for the formal surrender in one hour. By our laws we can only accept the surrender from you personally," Billy lied as part of the strategy to prevent this brave soldier from killing himself.

"It shall be done," Darrien said sadly as the image cut out.

When the image had disappeared, the War Room of the Colossus burst into a loud cheer followed by great jubilation. Throughout the Alliance Fleet, the celebrations would continue for many hours.

"Congratulations, sir," Lokkrien emerged from the other side of the War Table and held out his hand.

"Why thank you, Second Admiral," Billy smiled shaking the offered hand as the War Room staff continued to cheer and celebrate.

"Chulling, you mutinous dog," Lokkrien smiled as he continued to shake Billy's hand, "I'm surprised Darrien didn't see through that one."

"Yes," Billy said slowly breaking the grip and scratching the back of his head.

"I did kind of over-egg that one, didn't I?" Billy smiled and then laughed softly.

Chapter 37

The Imperial Palace, Bardan

The Bardomil Empress, Lullina, sat with a face like a thunderstorm, perched on the edge of her onyx throne with her hands tightly clutching the uprights of the arms. It was the darkest part of the night on Bardan and the clear, orange glow of the solitary moon cast long shadows across the floor of the Imperial Throne Room. The black-uniformed Imperial Bodyguards stood nervously at their posts as their Empress muttered and scowled angrily to herself. Many of the black-clad guards had seen the Empress' monumental foul tempers, but none of them had ever seen her as angry as this.

The reports of setbacks from the Praxos frontier had been filtering back to the Imperial Palace throughout the day. As the news had become increasingly gloomy, the Empress' mood had similarly darkened. The sound of heavy military boots on the polished floors of the Throne Room announced the arrival of Bodyguard Captain Sudrus with the latest news from the frontier.

Stopping before the raised throne, Captain Sudrus bowed.

"Well?" the Empress asked with the icy anger that could mean instant execution for anyone who displeased her in even the slightest manner.

"If it please, Your Majesty," the otherwise favoured champion of the Empress spoke nervously.

"We take it that the news is bad?" she said with an air of calm anger.

"The news is bad, Your Majesty," Sudrus replied steeling himself for the ordeal that would follow.

"How bad?" the Empress snarled coldly.

"Everything is lost, Your Majesty," Sudrus anxiously delivered the gravest of news.

"Everything, Captain Sudrus?" the Empress probed.

"Yes, Your Majesty, everything," Sudrus confirmed.

"Our Imperial Fleets?" she questioned.

"Yes, Majesty," Sudrus replied.

"What of our Armies?" the Empress questioned again.

"Occupation garrisons have survived on the two uninhabited planets on the edge of the Praxos system, Majesty," Sudrus reported.

"The rest?" the Empress pressed.

"Destroyed by the enemy, Majesty," Sudrus reported and tried to stay as calm as he could.

"All of them?" the Empress continued.

"Yes, Majesty, they never got off their troop transports," he reported.

In the darkness of the Throne Room, Lullina took several deep breaths and then, with a loud animal bellow, flung herself down the steps of the Onyx Thorne barging past Sudrus to shout at the moon.

"TRAITORS!" she bellowed at the guard who had the misfortune to be standing close to the tall window.

"COWARDS!" she shrieked at another guardsman who almost passed out with fright as she stalked around the Throne Room.

"Bring me that traitor Batarrien!" she turned and, with a pointed finger of accusation, hissed the instruction to Sudrus.

"He's already dead, Majesty, took his own life," Sudrus replied.

"COWARD!.......TRAITOR!" she shrieked again, having been denied the pleasure of killing the handsome young Officer herself, "what about Tetherrien?" she rounded on the General who had presented the young Batarrien and his study.

"Also dead, Majesty," Sudrus answered.

Once more the Empress let out huge bellow and uttered a curse on the heads of the two dead Officers she would hold responsible for the disaster, conveniently forgetting that it was her orders that had sent the invasion force to its fate.

"Then, kill their families!" she ordered with icy coldness.

"Right away, Majesty," Sudrus replied.

But, Captain Sudrus knew that no innocents would die this night. Having discovered both Batarrien and Tetherrien dead, he had ordered their families away from Bardan. Captain Sudrus knew that by the time he was delivering the bad news to the Empress, the families would be on transports getting as far away from Bardan as they could. In the morning, when the Empress' mood had calmed, she would probably have forgotten all about issuing their death warrants.

"It was Caudwell, wasn't it?" the Empress pointed her finger of accusation at Sudrus once more.

"Intelligence reports that he was present at the battle," Sudrus could only speculate.

"Of course it was him," the Empress cursed, "it's always him, Sudrus, he has spies everywhere," she muttered conspiratorially to her Bodyguard Captain.

"As you say, Majesty." Sudrus knew it was best to simply agree with her when she was so angry.

"Find them, Sudrus, search them out, hunt them down, find them and kill them!" she ordered the deaths of First Admiral Caudwell's mythical agents on Bardan.

"As you wish, Majesty," Sudrus acknowledged yet another futile order to ignore.

"And, purge the Generals," she hissed, "They're all traitors; get rid of them!" she snapped.

"Of course, Majesty," Sudrus agreed once more.

"Oh yes, we'll get you Caudwell, and your precious, puny little planet" she snarled, "What of the Ganthorans?" the Empress snapped her mind into strategic mode.

"The frontiers are all quiet, Majesty," Sudrus informed having put the frontier garrisons on high alert, "the Horvath are making no moves either."

"Watch them, Sudrus," the Empress snarled, "watch them!"

"As your Majesty commands." Sudrus bowed and began to dismiss himself from the Imperial presence.

"Captain Sudrus?" the Empress called him back, "bring us Metgar the Threylan," she instructed before walking calmly back to the Onyx Throne.

Bowing once more, Sudrus marched as quickly as he decently dared back out of the Throne Room. It puzzled him why the Empress would want to speak to Metgar. One of the most disreputable characters in the galaxy, Metgar was from a vast nomadic species that lived either as mercenaries or planetary asset-strippers in the unclaimed territories. They had served in the Bardomil military many years before and had been treated as little more than cannon-fodder. You didn't have to pay the dead, the Empress had instructed her Generals on the use of the Threylans. And, the Threylans had never forgotten that cruelty. There was no love lost between the Threylans and the Bardomil; of course that was a common complaint amongst a lot of species within the Empire.

Quite what Empress Lullina wanted with the Threylans was not something Captain Sudrus wished to dwell upon as he headed back to his quarters.

But, whatever it was, Sudrus knew that it would mean no good for someone.

Chapter 38

Planet Earth

Micky Stewart lay on his comfortable bed, in his brightly decorated but messy bedroom, studying his favourite book of World War Two fighter aircraft. Model Spitfires, Hurricanes and Mustangs hung from near-invisible threads from his ceiling and caught the sharp sunlight that flooded through the large window. Pictures of scantily clad young women adorned his walls as he lay, on his stomach, lower legs raised. Flicking, left-handed, through the grainy black and white images of classic propeller-driven fighter aircraft from nearly half a century before, Micky quietly nursed his heavily bandaged right hand. His parents were out, leaving Micky with the run of the house, which gave him the peace and solitude that he enjoyed.

On his bedside table, the small black and white portable television played to itself as Micky languidly imagined himself some heroic fighter ace; a Knight of the Sky, vanquishing enemy fighters and saving the day once again. Oblivious to the television, Micky did not hear the ongoing commentary and speculation as to why the huge solar flare, that had so mysteriously appeared the day before, had managed to not overwhelm the Earth. Various experts had been paraded in front of the cameras with their pet theories. But, now that the supposed danger to all life on the planet had passed, much of humanity had returned to their state of blissful ignorance and apathy.

"...there is absolutely no reasonable explanation as to why our planet is still here," the scientist-of-the-moment's television voice expounded as Micky drew over the page to look at a picture of a silver-painted twin-engine American fighter.

"...by every known scientific law, this planet should now be floating in space as a burnt out shell. The magnetic fields around the earth could never have protected us from a solar flare of that magnitude and strength!" he continued on his astonished explanation.

Oblivious to the scientist's incredulity, Micky dreamily carried on with his fighter ace fantasy, as a blinding flash of bright white light filled his bedroom for a fraction of a second.

Startled, Micky looked up from his book to see the smiling figure of Billy Caudwell standing, arms folded across his chest, only two metres away from him.

"What the...!? How did...!?" an open-mouthed and astonished Micky sprang to his feet, his book spilling onto the floor, as he faced the intruder.

"Hey, Micky Mouse," Jedithram Prust; projecting the jeans and sweatshirt image of Billy, greeted his highly reluctant host, "a little birdie tells me you like slapping girls around?"

"What...!? How...!?" the incredulous Micky Stewart faced the entity that had just appeared in front of him in his own bedroom.

"Shut up and sit down!" the Billy figure interrupted his astonishment with a well placed fist planted squarely on Micky's nose.

Unable to comprehend what was happening, Micky received the full force of the blow, sending him tumbling backwards onto his bed.

Jed smiled savagely having enjoyed administering the wallop and the nose-bleeding and eye-watering results.

With his head ringing from the brutal impact, Micky felt the warm trickle of blood from his nose begin to run down over his mouth and chin as he tried to focus his streaming eyes on his assailant.

Jed, confident that First Admiral Caudwell was nearly two hundred kilometres away at that moment, lifted a discarded tee-shirt from the bedroom floor and threw it to Micky. Unable to focus on the flying object, the tee-shirt landed clumsily, draped over Micky's head. The real Billy, Jed knew, would be with his parents at Gilfillan Academy, deep in the Scottish Highlands, with lots of total strangers to act as impartial witnesses. And, it was with that knowledge that he had asked for permission to dispense a little bit of Thexxian payback to Micky. Permission had been granted with the 'don't-kill-or-cripple-him' proviso, which was not what Jed had wanted to hear. Jed's idea of payback was the use of the short, curved ceremonial blade of the Thexxian Scycarriam to open Micky's abdomen as a warm-up to the main event.

"There ya go Micky, make sure your mascara doesn't run," Jed smiled as Micky began to untangle himself from the tee-shirt.

Still smiling, Jed pulled up the armless plastic chair that stood in front of Micky's study desk before turning it, wrong way round, and setting it down in front of Micky. Sitting astride the chair, Jed leaned his arms on the back of the seat and watched as Micky tried to staunch the flow of blood from his ravaged nose with the tee-shirt. First Admiral Caudwell might have had reservations about attacking an injured opponent, but Jed did not.

"We're gonna have us a nice long chat, ain't we Micky?" Jed smiled viciously as he leaned forward and caught Micky with a quick, vicious open-handed slap to the left side of his head.

"A nice long chat," Jed said with a calm menace in his voice that indicated there would be a lot more of what had just been dished out coming Micky's way.

BENNING

Staunching the blood from his nose with a dirty tee-shirt, Micky cringed away from his attacker, shrieking with terror, feeling real dread for the first time in his life.

Chapter 39

Planet Earth

Emma Wallace sat bolt upright in bed, eyes wide, with a loud gasp.

Sweating and trembling, Emma felt her head dizzying and her mind spinning from the latest episode of a recurrent dream. In the still darkness of her bedroom, Emma checked the dull glowing digits of the radio/clock/alarm on her work desk. 1:58 the dull red digits seemed to mock her inability to shake off the dream in which she was aboard some weird alien spaceship being buffeted and thrown about like a rag-doll. Still panting heavily, Emma rose from her bed, her troubled mind trying to make sense of what she was dreaming. She couldn't believe how vivid the dream was as she slipped her bare feet into her pale green slippers. It was always the same dream, the same people and the same narrative.

Pulling on her dressing gown, Emma felt the same dry throat and thirst that she always had when her sleep was interrupted and began to walk slowly to the sanctuary of the bathroom. Scratching her head and yawning, Emma opened her bedroom door, having successfully navigated the minefield of her furniture in the darkness, and lumbered quietly towards the bathroom door. The Wallace household would all be asleep, and Emma had no intention of wakening them.

Reaching the bathroom, Emma pulled the cord, briefly flooding the landing with bright dazzling light before she closed the door. Squinting from the unaccustomed darkness, Emma leaned on the wash-hand basin and turned on the cold water tap. For a few moments the clear cold water sloshed heavily in the basin as she lifted her tooth mug and half-filled it. Raising the pink ceramic mug to her lips, Emma heard a familiar voice from the other side of the door.

"You all right in there, Princess?" the concerned voice of her father asked.

"Yeah, sorry dad," Emma apologised after taking a sip of the cool refreshing liquid and opening the door.

"Same bad dream?" a yawning and concerned Andrew Wallace asked scratching his thick curly blond hair.

"Yeah, I just can't shake it," Emma replied taking a longer sip of water.

"It'll be something to do with all that solar flare panic," Andrew Wallace speculated leaning against the doorframe in his white cotton tee-shirt and striped pyjama trousers, "those television people gave everyone a fright with that."

"Probably, but it's so real..." Emma began and felt strangely uneasy.

"I know, Princess; it'll just take a couple of days to pass. When I was a lad I had this dream about falling into a deep dark hole and that felt real too; it took me about a week to shake it off," Andrew tried to comfort his daughter.

"Yeah, but you'd be frightened of the dinosaurs that roamed the planet in those days," Emma joked weakly to try to reassure her father that she was okay.

"Hey, I'm not that old," Andrew Wallace protested with a smile, "it was the sabre-toothed cats we had to dodge."

Despite the joking and bravado, Andrew Wallace knew that something was troubling his daughter. Emma had never been prone to bad dreams before and he felt powerless and angry that he simply couldn't make things better for her as he had when she had been younger.

"It's just...it's just...it's just so real, I'm on this spaceship with my Biology class and it's being thrown around. I'm in this strange seat all strapped down and I can't move and I'm so frightened. I'm screaming, but no one can hear me and the ship is falling to pieces around me," Emma recounted the dream anxiously.

Quietly, Andrew Wallace listened to his daughter.

"The strangest thing is that then I'm lying in this strange room with funny looking people all around me and Billy Caudwell's there," Emma continued, "and I feel all tired and sleepy and he's leaning over me, but his face looks all pink and horrible like it's been all burned and he says 'go to sleep now' and then I wake up," she seemed to plead for understanding.

"You like this Billy, don't you? He's that red-haired lad that used to come over to help you with your maths? His mother's that writer isn't she?" Andrew questioned

"No! Don't be silly, dad!" Emma protested, "Billy's just a friend," she replied as a strange feeling of unease and guilt swept over her.

"Oh right," Andrew Wallace replied as he mentally rolled his eyes in confusion.

The word 'friend' had a far different meaning in his younger day than the current, more flexible, definition of 'friendship' amongst the younger generation. In Andrew's day you were either going out with someone or you weren't, there was none of this confusing half-way house that seemed to be called 'friends'.

"So, is he a friend-friend or a boyfriend-friend?" Andrew sought clarification.

"Ugh, no!" Emma protested and blushed profusely, "he's got red hair and he's so dull."

"Well, he looked like a nice enough lad..." Andrew continued.

"Anyways, he's going to some posh private school, up in the Highlands somewhere," Emma said with an overwhelming feeling of disappointment that she just could not understand.

"Well, that's that then," Andrew Wallace said with a knowing smile, "come on, give your old man a hug, then."

Emptying the remaining water into the basin, she set down the tooth mug and stepped over to her father. Slipping her arms around his waist she felt his strong, gentle and powerful embrace that made her feel safe and comfortable.

Andrew Wallace, holding his daughter in his arms, felt an overwhelming sadness. Emma was sixteen now; she was a young woman. She was no longer 'his little girl'. Deep down, Andrew Wallace knew that soon she would go her own way in life. He had always encouraged her to be independent, but a part of him wanted her to be five or six years old again, as cute as a little button, and to stay that way forever.

Breaking the embrace, Andrew Wallace smiled and gently swept away the strands of straggling hair from his daughter's face before kissing her softly on the forehead.

"Goodnight Princess, sleep tight," he said and turned to go back to bed.

"Night, dad," Emma replied putting out the bathroom light.

Walking slowly back to his own bedroom, in the new darkness, Andrew Wallace worried about Emma's future. She had some crazy notion of being a fashion designer, but she wasn't really all that academically bright. But, that was a worry for another day, he considered. Maybe she would flourish just before the Qualifying Exams, he prayed. Maybe it would all come out right in the end. At least she would have some kind of career to go to on that dreaded day when she would leave home.

Until then, he wasn't quite prepared to lose 'his little girl' to the adult world, not just yet.

Chapter 40

The Star-Cruiser Aquarius

Intelligence Technician, Junior Grade, Marilla Thapes lay on her bunk in the darkened cubicle she shared with a young female Scanner Technician named Desmus. The cubicle that passed for Quarters for Marilla and her room-mate measured exactly three metres by two metres and was dominated by a large two-tier bunk bed. However, owing to the vagaries of their shift patterns, the two Technicians very rarely met. When Marilla was off shift, Desmus was invariably on duty. Given the small size of their shared quarters, Marilla considered it to be a blessing.

Marilla Thapes was off-duty, yet she never seemed to stop working. There was always some aspect of her work that held her attention or required additional time for her to feel truly comfortable that she had dealt with it. This off-shift period was no different. For other Technicians, the off-shifts were times to catch up on sleep, contact loved ones or engage in some form of recreational activity. For Desmus, her off-shifts were divided between sleep and visiting the Social Interaction Areas where crewmembers could meet, eat, drink and interact rather than stare at the blank, sterile ceilings of their quarters. Marilla had no interest in the Social Interaction Areas as they tended to be very noisy and full of people she would prefer to avoid given the opportunity. At heart, Marilla was a quiet and reticent creature who did not like loud people and crowded rooms.

As was her usual custom, Marilla had brought several folios of work to her bunk, and lying on her stomach, she was busily devouring the latest data on supply convoys to the more remote Bardomil military garrisons on the Ganthoran frontier. Hacking her way through the interminable lists of supplies being delivered she scanned the data looking for the patterns, the out of the ordinary, that could be indicative of developing military action; and, hence trouble for the Universal Alliance. For a moment she paused and considered that there might be a Bardomil Intelligence Technician doing exactly what she was doing. Well, she thought, I hope that they're having better luck than me. The usual round of the mundane in Bardomil logistics was about as boring, clockwork-regular and tedious as it always had been. As she read it was becoming clear that there were no unusual patterns, no increases in certain supplies and no indication of a build up that would herald an offensive against the Ganthoran Empire.

It was with this mundane and yet comforting thought that Marilla prepared to turn in for a well deserved eight hours of sleep before her next shift. Extinguishing the small light built into the low headboard of her upper-tier bunk, Marilla had just rolled onto her side when the cubicle intercom buzzed the low droning note of an incoming message.

"Technician Thapes, Technician Thapes, report to Senior Intelligence Officer Sownus' Office immediately," the harsh tinny disembodied voice announced.

"Oh no," Marilla groaned, rolling onto her back.

"Technician Thapes, Technician Thapes, report to Senior Intelligence Officer Sownus' Office immediately," the voice repeated with added insistency.

"All right, I'm coming, I'm coming," Marilla sighed sliding out of the bunk and dropping to the floor, "keep your uniform on," she quietly scolded the intercom Technician.

"Technician Thapes, Technician Thapes, report to Senior Intelligence Officer Sownus' Office immediately," the harsh tinny disembodied voice announced for a third time.

"Yes, yes, give me a chance will you?" Marilla muttered fastening up her uniform overall.

"Technician Thapes, Technician Thapes, report to Senior Intelligence..." the intercom voice blared but was cut short by Marilla stepping onto the pressure pad behind the door as she left the cubicle.

Passing through the grey force-shielding that closed neatly behind her, Marilla began to trot purposefully towards the teleporter station at the end of her brightly lit accommodation corridor as she finished fastening her uniform. Being summoned by Senior Intelligence Officer Karap Sownus, when off-shift, either meant something major was happening or that she was in serious trouble. As she trotted along the busy corridor, the first pangs of anxiety began to gnaw at her mind.

At the teleporter station Marilla stepped onto the square yellow plate and entered the required six digit code on the key pad built onto the hand rail in front of her. Screwing her eyes tightly closed, Marilla always avoided the bright flash that accompanied the 'molecule scrambling' as she described the teleport process. After an internal count of three, Marilla opened her eyes and found that she was on the teleport plate in the Intelligence corridor. Taking a deep breath, Marilla wondered what was happening. The usually busy Intelligence corridor was totally deserted. No Officers or Technicians scampered to and fro carrying important data, interpretations or messages. There was nothing of the usual hustle and bustle of a busy Intelligence Department. Feeling slightly uneasy, Marilla Thapes set off along the oppressively quiet corridor moving rapidly towards the Office of Karap Sownus. With every passing step, Marilla felt more and more uneasy. Searching her memory, she found that she couldn't find anything that she could have done that was so wrong to merit a call to the Senior Intelligence Officers Office for a dressing down.

With her feet starting to feel heavier and heavier and her stomach knotting to the point of revolt, Marilla exhaled one last final heavy sigh of anxiety as she stepped onto the red plate outside Sownus' Office.

"Come in!" the voice of Karap Sownus sounded beyond the grey force-shielding of the door.

"You sent for..." Marilla began nervously as she stepped over the threshold of the doorway.

"Come with me, Technician Thapes," a stern faced Sownus indicated rising from behind his work desk and walking in a very brisk waddle towards the doorway.

This was not the quiet, friendly Karap Sownus that Marilla Tapes knew and had grown accustomed to. There was a coldness in his voice that sent her anxiety level into orbit.

"But, sir, what..." Marilla began as Sownus pushed past her to exit the office.

"The First Admiral has sent for you, so just keep your mouth shut and play it by ear," Sownus said flatly as he waddled quickly into the corridor heading to the teleporter.

"But, sir, I..." Marilla began to protest as she tried to keep up with the rapidly advancing Sownus.

Now, Marilla was genuinely frightened. She had never seen Officer Sownus like this. She had heard that when he was angry his manner turned icily cold and brought out a really nasty and sarcastic vicious streak in him. Still shaken at the response, Marilla tried her best to keep up with the Intelligence Officer whilst cudgelling her overheating brain to try to figure out what hideous transgression she had committed to deserve this kind of treatment. With her brain rebelling almost as much as her churning stomach she decided to keep her mouth shut as Sownus had instructed. With her head still swimming and her bowels dissolving, Marilla stepped onto the teleport plate as indicated by Sownus. With a stern-faced Sownus punching in the six-digit code, Marilla closed her eyes and counted to three once more. When she opened them again, she stepped down from the plate just in time for the bright, dazzling flash that heralded the arrival of Sownus.

Looking round, Marilla knew she was in the wide, spacious corridor outside the Observation Deck. However, no sooner had she identified her surroundings than Sownus spoke chillingly again.

"Follow me, Technician Thapes," he ordered brusquely and strode with his ungainly waddle to the Observation Deck door.

Like a chastised child, Marilla followed the few dozen yards to the large grey force-shielded doorway. The Observation Deck on the Aquarius had been one of Marilla's favourite off-shift destinations. Despite its huge size and capacity, Marilla found that she could be alone with her thoughts as she marvelled at the immenseness of space and her own insignificance amongst that vastness. Now, that same Observation Deck, so long a source of solitude and enjoyment, was taking on an aspect of dread and terror.

"You go first Technician Thapes," Sownus said darkly, "say nothing and speak only when spoken to, clear?"

"Yes, sir," Marilla stammered nervously, her mind afire with the terrors of what lay beyond as the force-shielding of the once-friendly Observation Deck door cleared allowing Marilla entrance.

Steeping warily through the entrance, Marilla was met with a sight that made her mind flinch with dread. A pathway was created for her flanked on both sides by all thirty-four Intelligence Officers and Technicians aboard the Aquarius, standing in the 'At Ease' position.

Their backs ramrod straight, heads up, eyes fixed straight ahead, feet slightly apart and hands behind their backs they stood like silent sentinels. Faces she knew from Duty Shifts stared coldly into the distance as she stepped gingerly into the Observation Deck. Beneath the bright lights, the familiar, friendly and comforting landmarks of the Deck now seemed menacing and oppressive. The foliage seemed denser and lurked menacingly over the walkway in front of her. At the end of the walkway, a stern-faced First Admiral Caudwell waited his hands behind his back.

"Go on," the stern voice of Sownus broke through her dread.

Stepping forward cautiously, Marilla, her mind crawling with visions of disciplinary punishments, stepped cautiously forward and began to advance along the avenue of stony-faced Intelligence personnel. Swallowing her terror down, Marilla shuffled forwards towards the looming figure of First Admiral Caudwell. Once more she interrogated her mind as to what she had done to deserve this and came up with no real explanation. But, the fear and dread she felt as she advanced through the 'walk of shame', as she imagined it, was very real to her and weighed on her like a huge, crushing burden. Looking around, the still silent figures held their discipline, avoiding her gaze and giving her no comfort or indication of what this was all about. For what seemed like an eternity she walked and stuttered as best she could towards the imposing figure of the First Admiral.

Stopping before First Admiral Caudwell, Marilla looked at the stern-faced young human, with the ice-cold grey-blue eyes, and prepared herself for the worst. Dishonourable discharge was the option that kept racing through her mind. But, she couldn't for the very life of her think why she was being disciplined. And, why, she thought, would she be disciplined in front of the other Intelligence staff?

"Intelligence Technician Marilla Thapes," a hard voiced Billy Caudwell intoned, "it is customary for subordinates to stand to attention when in the presence of a Senior Officer."

"Yes, sir, sorry sir," Marilla replied in a subdued voice pulling herself to the regulation attention position, fixing her gaze on the large plant that stood behind First Admiral Caudwell and waited for the axe to fall.

"Very well," Billy Caudwell began "Intelligence Technician, Senior Grade, Marilla Thapes, in recognition of your conduct in the recent detection and containment of the Bardomil emitter weapon, I award you the Duty Conduct Medal First Class."

"What?...Hey?..." Marilla gasped, feeling a slight pressure on her shoulders as something passed over her head.

Stunned, an open-mouthed Marilla looked down and saw a tear-drop shaped silver medal hanging from a blue and red ribbon around her neck.

"Turn around, Senior Technician Thapes," Billy Caudwell said to the confused and astonished Marilla whilst gently guiding her round to face the 'walk of shame'.

"Senior Grade?" Marilla mumbled in confusion still transfixed by the medal, which she held carefully in her trembling left hand as it hung around her neck.

The Duty Conduct Medal First Class was one of the highest awards in the Alliance military for exemplary conduct, dedication to duty and outstanding achievement. Very few such medals had been awarded, and this was the first to be awarded to an Intelligence Technician.

"Attention on Deck!" a clipped military voice called out.

In one smooth movement the 'walk of shame' snapped to the attention position.

"Present Arms!" the voice ordered.

Thirty-four left hands, including that of Karap Sownus, shot up to the salute position, fingers straight; forty-five degrees to the left eyebrow. For a moment, Marilla Thapes' head reeled with confusion. Only a few seconds before, she had expected to be drummed out of The Fleet.

"You did say Senior Grade, didn't you, sir?" a numbed and astonished Marilla Thapes turned and asked Billy Caudwell.

"I believe I did, Senior Technician," Billy Caudwell started to smile, "and, I'm not usually mistaken in such matters," he added, "it's well deserved Marilla, now go and acknowledge your comrades; I hear they've planned quite a party for you."

THE BURNING SUN

"Sir!" Marilla Thapes smiled broadly, the confirmation finally registering in her brain.

With her head held high, Marilla Thapes, stepped back through the saluting 'walk of shame' that had suddenly become a 'guard of honour'. Smiling broadly, she stepped confidently with swelling pride in her heart through the ranks of Intelligence personnel towards the saluting Senior Officer. The Observation Deck now seemed a friendlier and more inviting place than it had a few moments before. But, it all seemed to pass in a blur as Marilla marched proudly through her 'guard'.

"Congratulations, Senior Technician, Thapes," Karap Sownus said formally as she halted in front of him.

"Thank you, sir," Marilla beamed a smile that could light up several solar systems.

"Looks like I'd better keep an eye on you, or you'll be after my job?" Sownus smiled jokingly as he dropped his left hand from the salute and offered his right in congratulation.

"Recover!" the military voice echoed around the Observations Deck and thirty-four left hands returned to the Attention position.

"No, sir, I think you're quite safe there," Marilla smiled accepting the proffered hand, "for the moment," she smiled cheekily.

"Dismiss!" the military voice barked and a great cheer broke out as suddenly the beaming Marilla was swamped by her comrades.

Shouts of 'congratulations' and 'well done' punctuated the great press of bodies that pummeled her back and shoulders as she was swept away from a laughing Sownus. With the cheers and praise still ringing in her ears, a beaming Marilla let out a loud shriek of delight as she felt herself being lifted from the ground. Unbalanced, Marilla held onto her medal as she was hoisted shoulder high amongst the Intelligence Staff and carried away to whatever celebrations awaited.

As the cheering and celebration receded down the corridor, Billy Caudwell stood alone with his thoughts on the Observation Deck. This time, the Alliance and Earth had been lucky. There had been a Marilla Thapes with the intelligence to see the danger and the dedication to draw out the evidence and correctly identify the implications.

Next time, they might not be so lucky.

BENNING

Epilogue

<u>Planet Earth</u>

Trotting down the well worn sandstone steps at the school gate, Billy Caudwell spotted Emma Wallace sitting on the wooden bench beside the bus stop. It had been four days since he had last seen her aboard the Aquarius with the Memory Shredder. For a moment he shuddered at the thought of the device that had robbed her of those few hours she had spent on an alien craft. Still, he considered, it was a necessity to help protect the secret of the Alliance and his own ongoing role in that great adventure.

Since the battle at Valnarim, there had been no further activity from the Bardomil. Several rebellions within the Empire had required military forces to be diverted from the Alliance frontier. The Ganthorans were also building up forces on the Bardomil frontier as part of their ongoing game of sabre-rattling. The Alliance was being left in peace, just as Billy had hoped. However, with all five of the big Star-Destroyers still under repair, there would be no probability of the Alliance being able to eject the garrisons from the two uninhabited planets that they had occupied. The Bardomil, despite crippling losses, still kept a toe-hold on the Praxos system.

At a personal level, Billy's radiation burns were healing well. The Personal Environment Suit kept producing the low-level phoronic radiation that speeded up his body's natural healing processes, whilst the image generator kept Billy's appearance normal. The visit to Gilfillan Academy had been a huge success. The Head of Science, a tall, thin angular man who wore a black gown, had been so impressed with Billy's knowledge that he had offered John and Elizabeth Caudwell a place for their son there and then. That meant, that at the end of the term, Billy would be leaving his home town to be a 'boarder' at one of the most prestigious and expensive private schools in Scotland.

Stopping at the foot of the steps, Billy felt a strong reluctance to approach the seated Emma.

For a moment, he considered simply walking through the gate and hoping that she wouldn't spot him. But, the urge to know if she still remembered how they had been together, for those brief minutes, before Lokkrien had interrupted in the classroom, was just too much for Billy to bear.

Taking a deep breath, Billy forced down the sick queasy feeling that he felt in the pit of his stomach as he approached Emma.

"Hi Emma," he said as breezily as he could manage.

"Oh, hi Billy," a slightly startled Emma turned in the seat and flashed her most insincere smile at him.

In that instant, Billy knew that she had forgotten everything and his heart sank down through his stomach and into his shoes. The old Emma had returned and, to Billy, it felt as if she had never really been away. Aboard the Aquarius, he knew that he had lost her, now he was losing her all over again, and it felt as if someone had just ripped out his heart.

"Are you waiting for the bus?" he asked dropping into a routine of small-talk that he was developing for Diplomatic Functions aboard the Aquarius.

"No," she replied, "I'm waiting for Jim, my boyfriend," she smiled nervously, hoping that no one would see her with the un-cool red-headed boy.

But, as she mentally shuffled in anxiety, Emma was troubled by a strange sensation that she was missing something. The dream, that she just couldn't shake, and Billy with the burned and blotchy face impinged on her consciousness once more.

"Are you going somewhere nice?" Billy struggled to keep the conversation going.

Even speaking to her was torture for Billy. He wanted to rush forward, take her in his arms and kiss her. But, the sensible part of his mind told him that she would probably never respond as he hoped she would. Resignedly, Billy had to accept that the Emma who had kissed him in the stairwell had gone. But, like a puppy begging for one last treat, he tried to hold her attention for a few more precious seconds. Just speaking to her was painful, but it was the bitter-sweet, joyous pain that people never forgot for the rest of their lives.

"We might go down to the beach," Emma smiled nervously, still unsure of why she was still talking to the red-haired boy.

"Well, you've got a good day for it." Billy smiled weakly indicating the cloudless, blue sunny sky.

"Yes, we do," she replied, "funny thing about that solar thingy last week wasn't it?" she added.

"Yeah, somebody probably got a bit panicked, I suppose..." Billy began.

"Oh look, there's Jim!" Emma interrupted and stood up waving to the small, yellow, open-topped car that sped up to the bus stop and halted with a squeal of tires, brakes and throaty revving engine.

"Hey babe, what's happening?" the handsome, well-dressed driver of the vehicle announced his arrival to Emma.

"Sorry, Billy, I've got to go!" Emma chirped with relief and opened the passenger door of the vehicle.

Before clambering into the vehicle, she turned to Billy once more.

"Good luck with the new school!" she said brightly, with that edge of 'hopefully-I'll-never-see-you-again' tone in her voice, before climbing into the car and slamming the door behind her.

"Yeah, thanks," Billy smiled weakly as the car roared off in a cloud of road dust and petrol fumes.

"Who's the ginger wierdo?" the handsome Jim asked Emma as they sped away.

For a moment, Emma Wallace felt a sudden wave of anger and wanted to slap the driver full in the face. But, as quickly as the feeling appeared, it vanished once more.

"He's just some freaky guy in one of my classes," Emma said dismissively as they roared into the distance.

Alone at the bus stop, Billy watched as the small, yellow car sped away with the passenger's long blonde hair streaming out behind her in the wind. A few moments later, she was gone. Left with the silence of his own thoughts, Billy didn't hear the bustle of late afternoon traffic that rushed past him. Feeling desperately sad, Billy took a deep breath, closed his eyes and breathed a long sigh that pushed his feelings back down into his shoes once again. Then, opening his eyes he put one heavy foot in front of the other.

With eyes downcast, he began the long, weary and lonely walk home.

THE BURNING SUN

Author Biography

The author, William J.Benning was born in Dumfries (south west Scotland) in 1963. With his 50th birthday fast approaching, Benning has decided to grow old disgracefully. An intensely private individual, Benning recently returned to his home town seeking inspiration for his passion of creative writing. At age 18, Benning left home to take an Honours Degree in Psychology at Strathclyde University in Glasgow. He has some very fond memories, and many nights of vague recollection - which are, on the whole, probably best forgotten (!) - from his student days. After graduating, Benning had a career "false start" moving into the world of Pest Control Management. However, after several unhappy years, he switched tack and took further qualifications in Personnel Management, carving out a successful and enjoyable career in Human Resources as well as Learning & Development. Throughout his career, Benning has worked to support the activities of the British Red Cross. From his early days as a First Aid Volunteer, he enjoyed working for the organisation which gave him further skills and built his self-confidence. Progressing within British Red Cross, Benning became a First Aid Instructor (Trainer), Assessor and Lecturer plus becoming invoved in training other Trainers and Assessors. Having returned to Dumfries to further his writing career, Benning now lives alone, but has been adopted by four members of the Canine Community. With four dogs in his life - and a newly arrived litter of Tibetan Terrier pups - plus a newly published novel, life is never going to be dull for Benning. William likes his sci-fi, but is also keen on military history and speculative fiction. Among his fiction favourites are Harry Turtledove, the late George MacDonald Fraser, Bernard Cornwell and Clive Cussler. William collects Edinburgh Crystal and has a terrible weakness for malt whisky. He has published his novel First Admiral with Malachite Quills in 2012.

BENNING

Another excellent science fiction tale from Malachite Quills:

    The Seryysans and the Vyysarri have been at war for centuries and there is no end to the war in sight. The Vyysarri, nomadic savage warriors, are relentless in their efforts to wipe out the Seryysans once for all, while the Seryysans, civilized denizens, scramble to defend themselves by whatever means necessary.

    When Khai'Xander Khail, a retired war veteran and hero of the Seryysan People, discovers a government plot to raze the megalopolis Seryys City, to for a large deposit of a precious metal beneath its sprawling streets, he is ultimately forced into an adventure that takes him deep within Vyysarri Space.

    While there, he meets an aged Vyysarri with a message to deliver: an even deeper, darker secret that will shake Khai to his very core and threaten to unravel everything in which he believes.

The question: What is Operation: Bright Star?